Other Books by Marilyn Brown

Fiction

The Earthkeepers
(Earthkeeper Series:
Thorns of the Sun
Shadows of Angels
Royal House)
Light in the Room
Statehood
The Wine-Dark Sea of Grass
House on the Sound
Ghosts of the Oquirrhs
Serpent in Paradise
Christmas at the M&M
The Holly Christmas
The Macaroni Christmas Tree
The Merry Nutcracker

Poetry

Rainflowers
I Have Lost my Heart Again . . .
I Pray I Will Not Lose My Head. Amen.
The Grandmother Tree
Seven Ways of Looking at Watercress Farm

Nonfiction

Families Lost and Found (with Lee Nelson)
Provo, a Story of People in Motion (with John Moffitt)
I Cannot Tell a Life (with Florence Child Brown)
Images of America: Provo (with Valerie Holladay)

Musicals: Book, Lyrics, Music

Midsummer Night's Dream
The Merry Nutcracker

Fires of Jerusalem

MARILYN BROWN

FIRES

OF

JERUSALEM

Marilynbrownauthor.com
Marilynbrown@dishmail.net

Printed in the United States of America
ISBN: 978-1-4276-4977-5
Cover art: Douglas Grant Johnson
Map and chart: Simeen Brown

Parables

PO Box 58
Woodsboro, MD 21798
www.parablespub.com
parables@parablespub.com

In grateful memory of

Biblical scholar

and friend

Daniel Ludlow

(1924–2009)

What readers are saying about *Fires of Jerusalem*:

"Delivering some very gripping dramatic scenes, *Fires of Jerusalem* opens a window on a world most of us don't know very well, if at all. A stunning achievement." —**Marilyn Arnold,** Professor Emeritus, BYU, Author of the acclaimed memoir, *Bittersweet*

"Marilyn Brown is one of the stalwarts of our ethnocentric fiction, bringing zest, imagination, subtlety, and shimmering prose to a genre dominated by cliché. *Fires of Jerusalem* is a thoroughly researched, soul-expanding work which both tells a cracking yarn, and forces the reader to explore the meaning of Biblical passages we too often blithely glide by." —**Andrew R. Hall**, Associate Professor of History, Kyushu University, Japan

"I thoroughly enjoyed this novel. Marilyn Brown's retelling of the relatively unfamiliar Old Testament story of Jeremiah is fresh and exciting. This illuminating portrait of a complex, fascinating Biblical prophet provided the context necessary for me to make a personal connection with the ancient world."—**Angela Hallstrom**, Author of the award-winning novel, *Bound on Earth*

"Original and exciting . . . with emotion and insight. Parallels with our own time." —**Richard H. Cracroft**, Book Columnist, *BYU Magazine*

"Jeremiah's name is synonymous with a tirade, a long list of evils and social ills. Marilyn Brown captures this all in three words: *Jerusalem was broken.* From that opening sentence Marilyn goes on to give a six-decade portrait of Jeremiah from his first vision at fourteen years old to his hiding sacred artifacts in a hill to his flight from Jerusalem and hiding sacred records in a barrel. In between we see a portrait of Jeremiah as a sometimes reluctant prophet living among dangerous people, and among other prophets, Lehi, Ezekiel, Daniel, Jehu, Zephaniah, Nahum, his Aunt Huldah, the prophetess, and his father Hilkiah, who discovers the lost record of Moses. We see him descending into the valley of the shadow, into the miry pit. We wait for every writer's nightmare, to watch precious work burn page by page. But Jeremiah comes out of the pit, out of the shadow. And out of the fire come his words." —**Harlow Clark**, Literary Critic, Author of the introduction to Marilyn Brown's *Serpent in Paradise*

"I wasn't sure anyone could make an Old Testament prophet, especially one as dour and dishwater dull as Jeremiah, accessible to readers, let alone appealing. Marilyn Brown accomplishes just that in *Fires of Jerusalem*. The thing I like best about this engaging book is how well Brown has done her homework; for all her narrative expansion and psychological imagination, she's remarkably true to the Biblical text of Jeremiah. And I liked almost as much how thoroughly I was caught up in the drama, captivated by the action of the novel, from the first page." —**Steven Walker**, Professor of English*: Bible as Literature*

“This dynamic historical novel about the prophet Jeremiah made his life and turbulent times come alive for me. It will do the same for you.” —**Bill Pope**, Inventor of the Synthetic Diamond, CEO of U. S. Synthetic (1922–2010)

“I’m impressed.”—**Daniel Ludlow**, Biblical Scholar (1924–2009)

“Marilyn Brown’s novel about the Old Testament prophet, Jeremiah, filled many gaps in my understanding of this Biblical time. Well researched and believable.” —**Veda Hale**, Author of Maurine Whipple’s biography, *Swell Suffering*

“In Marilyn Brown’s *Fires of Jerusalem*, the prophet Jeremiah is a poet, a husband, father, grandfather, and friend. As we read Jeremiah’s story, we see how Biblical history may have been shaped. More than anything, Brown shows us that destiny—including the courses of entire governments—can turn on the relationships of a few significant people.” —**Jack Harrell**, Professor of English, BYU Idaho, Author of award-winning novel, *Vernal Promises*

“A well-written and compellingly inventive account of Jeremiah’s life and times.” —**Mary C. Walker**, Editor

“Powerful fiction can energize history. Adept at her craft, Marilyn Brown has woven a compelling tale around the times of the Old Testament prophet Jeremiah, an exposé of the royal families, political intrigue, high adventure, military threats and attacks, imprisonment and disasters. Through surprising and legendary twists and turns, *Fires of Jerusalem* still stays impressively faithful to the history of the Israelites and the destruction of Jerusalem.” —**Douglas Alder**, President Emeritus of Dixie College, Historian, Author of the novel, *Sons of Bear Lake.*

“I would not have guessed that the character of Jeremiah could be intriguing, but through the genius of Marilyn Brown’s imagination, this Old Testament prophet came alive for me. I intended to skim *Fires of Jerusalem*, but ended up reading every word in one sitting. It was so interesting, informative, such a good read—I didn’t want to quit. This well-researched book is a perfect example of the value of good historical fiction.” —**Darla Isaacson**, Editor, Author of *After My Son’s Suicide*

“With her captivating writing style and obvious Biblical scholarship, Marilyn Brown provides a compelling and unforgettable look on the life and times of Jeremiah in the setting of a historical novel. I loved it.” —**Sheila Olsen,** Public Speaker, Writer for Idaho Falls’ *Post Register* and the *Ensign*

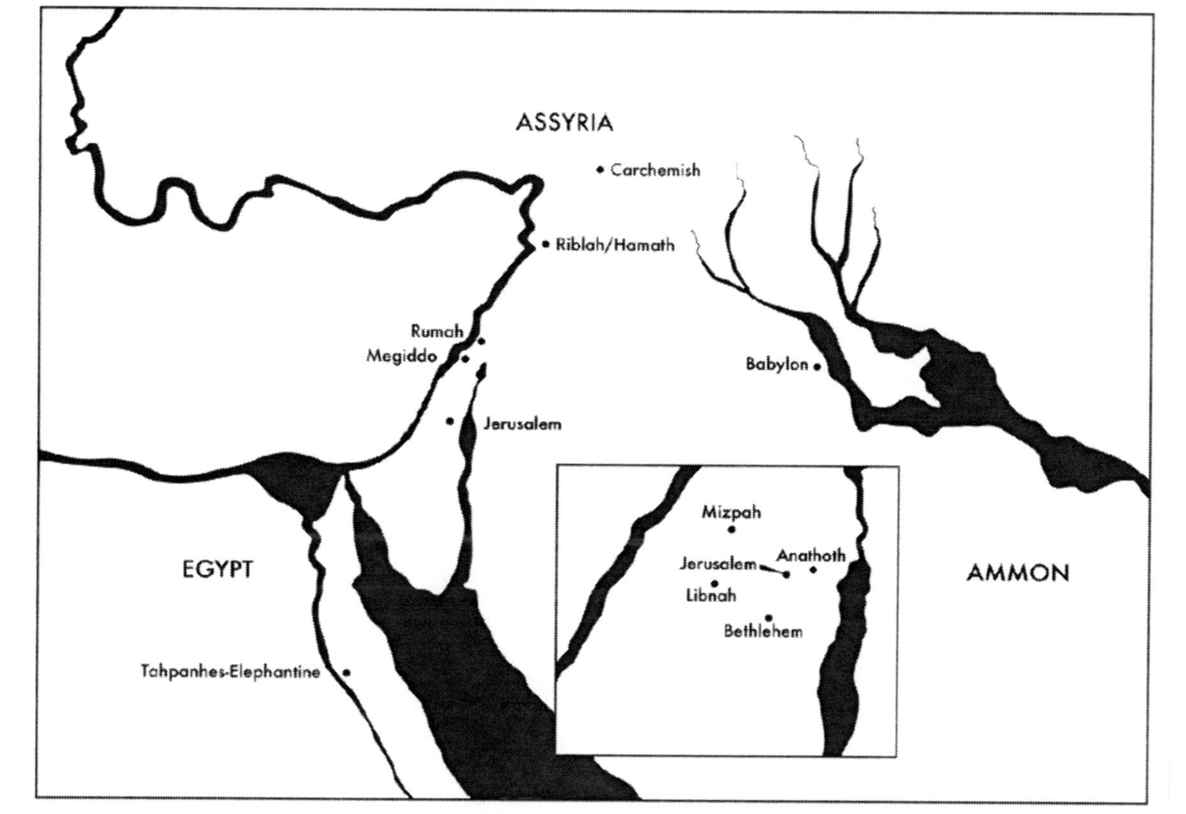
ASSYRIA
Carchemish
Riblah/Hamath
Rumah
Megiddo
Jerusalem
Babylon
EGYPT
Tahpanhes-Elephantine
Mizpah
Jerusalem
Anathoth
Libnah
Bethlehem
AMMON

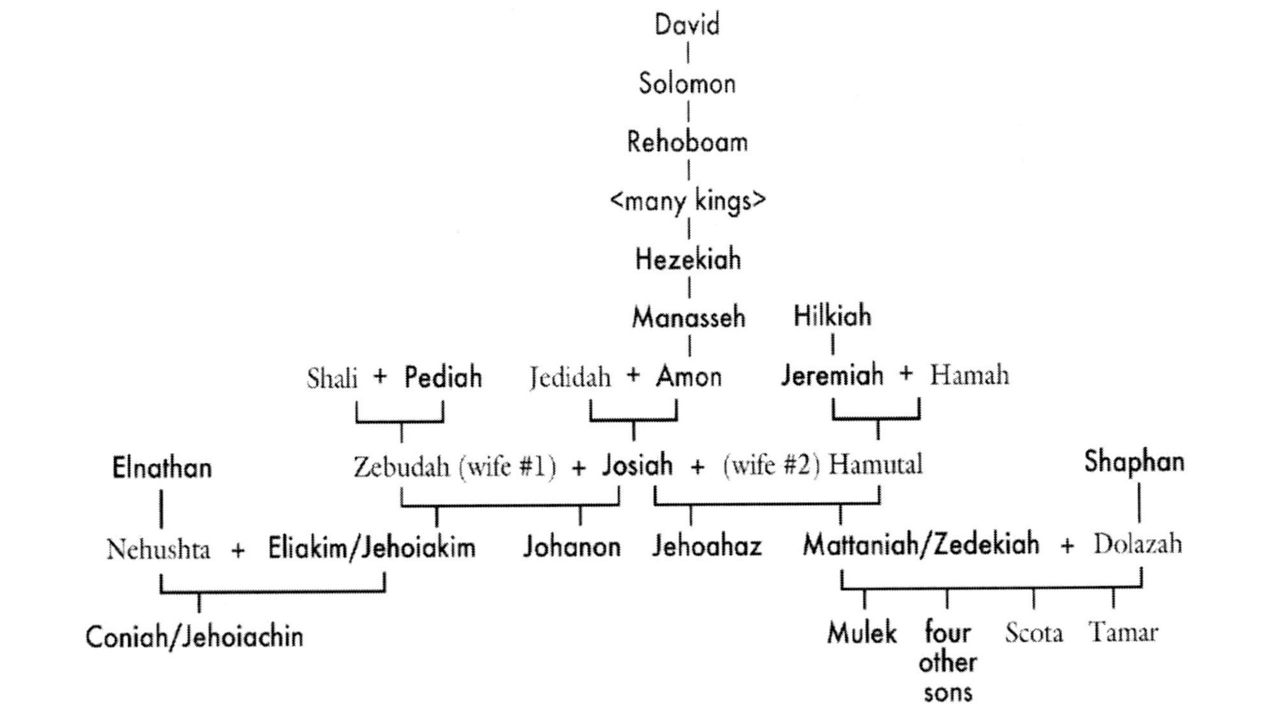
David
Solomon
Rehoboam
<many kings>
Hezekiah
Manasseh
Hilkiah
Shali + Pediah
Jedidah + Amon
Jeremiah + Hamah
Elnathan
Zebudah (wife #1) + Josiah + (wife #2) Hamutal
Shaphan
Nehushta + Eliakim/Jehoiakim
Johanon
Jehoahaz
Mattaniah/Zedekiah + Dolazah
Coniah/Jehoiachin
Mulek
four other sons
Scota
Tamar

Introduction

Through this well-researched and well-written historical novel, you will enter the life and times of the prophet Jeremiah (626 B.C. [?] to a few years after 586 B.C.).You won't likely emerge unchanged from the experience. In this unique novel, Marilyn Brown, author of numerous nonfiction histories and historical novels, has once again combined her storytelling genius with her deep spiritual gifts and love of the Word of God to render afresh the life of faithful but sometimes irritating Jeremiah in a way to make him real and his message pertinent for those of us who live some 2600 years later.

Jeremiah was a Hebrew prophet whose destiny was known to God even while Jeremiah was in his premortal state. In one of the few scriptures which describes the prebirth life of mortals, the Lord tells Jeremiah, *Before I formed thee in the belly I knew thee; and before thou camest forth out of the womb, I sanctified thee, and I ordained thee a prophet unto the nations* (Jeremiah 1:5 KJV). In a life-altering vision, Jehovah commanded this foreordained prophet to call the city of Jerusalem and the covenant kingdoms of Israel and Judah to repentance for their sinful, godless vanities, for their idolatry, and for their toleration of false, greedy, and deceiving priests. He prophesies that the apostate House of Israel, north and south, will suffer the Lord's wrath, the destruction of invading armies, and years of servitude and bondage.

Jeremiah, overwhelmed by the impossibility of successfully delivering this terrible warning to an oblivious people, was reluctant to answer the call. The Lord importuned, however, and Jeremiah went to work. He would spend forty years preaching repentance to a hardheaded people—and suffer continual persecution by priests, outlaws, militias, and kings. And he would spend years in hiding, in dungeons and in prisons, only, at last, to lament (not rejoice), in seeing his prophesies literally fulfilled in the destruction of his land, his people, and the Great Temple of Solomon.

Still, his message was, at last, hopeful and positive, for he had faith in the promises of God that, after the tumult and shouting, destruction, and captivities were past, the Lord would gather Israel once again, forgive them as they came repenting unto Him, ready to enter anew into covenant between Himself and the House of Israel.

Marilyn Brown, bless her imaginative soul, has taken some very understandable editorial freedoms with this book. Such freedoms, such fictions, are grounded in scripture, likelihood, and such history and anthropology as are available. Basing any suppositions or conjectures squarely in the culture and traditions of that era, Brown imagines for Jeremiah a wife, a child, and grandchildren, and she sketches logical destinies for them based on scriptural information. Jeremiah becomes grandfather-related (inconspicuously) to the royalty of Judah, including "grandson" Zedekiah.

While the scripture says nothing of Jeremiah's demise, and while tradition says he was stoned to death by Jews in Egypt, Brown follows yet other ancient legends in suggesting that he and his royal posterity may have fled Egypt by sea to ancient Ireland, taking some of the existing scriptures with them and planting the faith on northern shores. She also infuses into her account the scriptural description of a frenzied Jerusalem, frightened at the coming invasion of the Babylonians—the same frenzy that drove Lehi and his family from Jerusalem in 600 B.C. and launched the saga of the Book of Mormon.

Brown makes the connection, occasionally imagined by others, between Jeremiah and the Book of Mormon prophet Lehi, his fiancée and, later, wife Sariah (whose wedding Jeremiah attends), their sons Laman, Lemuel, and Nephi, and their unrighteous, wealthy, and greedy "cousin" Laban. In fact, Brown's integration into *Fires of Jerusalem* of major characters from the book of 1 Nephi in The Book of Mormon, as well as important passages from the Book of Jeremiah and the Lamentations of Jeremiah, along with her insightful integration of the history, culture, and anthropology of ancient Israel and Judah, make this a novel fraught with "ah-ha" kinds of interesting discoveries.

Jeremiah's witness and legacy live on in our era. He is traditionally credited with authoring the *Book of Jeremiah, 1 Kings, 2 Kings*, and the *Lamentations of Jeremiah,* with the remarkable assistance and under the editorship of Baruch ben Neriah, his faithful scribe, disciple, and a central character in this narrative. It is Baruch to whom we are indebted for the words of the prophet Jeremiah.

Indeed, Jeremiah's impact on our modern culture continues. His name is still a popular male name. The term *jeremiad* persists in our language, describing *a lamentation* or *mournful complaint* or *angry harangue.* There are novels (like this one) and plays (Stefan Zweig); symphonies (Leonard Bernstein's *Symphony No. 1, Jeremiah*; Bertold Hummel's *Symphony No. 3, Jeremiah*; TV movie, *Jeremiah* (1998), a film on Jeremiah's life, starring Patrick Dempsey.

I promise you an unforgettable entry into a world you may not have entered before. I promise you that Marilyn Brown's *Fires of Jersalem* will enhance your horizontal and vertical perspectives. It has mine.

Dr. Richard H. Cracroft
Professor of English, Emeritus
Brigham Young University
Provo, Utah

Chapter One

A Land of Darkness

Jerusalem was broken.

Rabble huddled in the temple courtyard eating from the gutters the uncooked remains of the priests' blood sacrifices. They scraped the blood from the stone trough and licked their fingers. Yet they cursed the God that gave them this meat—their thinning rags gathered about their thighs, their little ones crying, their sore mouths discolored and draining with pus and spittle.

Jeremiah and Baruch, anxious to finish their copy work in the temple archives, would never have attempted to track through the congestion if they hadn't been searching for Baruch's goat. Repulsed, they had always resisted the chaos of this desperate society. Crime was rampant.

"See-shi, See-shi," Baruch cried, while Jeremiah searched for the animal behind every rotted basket and in every child's arms.

The indigent in clumps of rags hooted and laughed at them, jutting their canes at the boys' feet to topple them. Children threw excrement, and the women giggled behind covered faces.

After they had traversed the entire square without success, Jeremiah approached the west gate that led down to the *Mishneh* district.

"Oh no." Baruch held back. "Not there."

"But she's not anywhere around here," Jeremiah asserted.

"No. Don't!"

"Come on, Baruch." Down the steps that led to the once elite, now tumultuous garment district, the darkness seemed to open up to them like a maw full of rotten teeth, the high buildings, charred and broken, standing in jagged rows. "It's not that bad. My aunt and uncle live here."

"And how long has it been since you visited them?"

Jeremiah hesitated. "A few years."

"It's worse now."

Jeremiah stopped for a moment. "Come, Baruch. God will protect us."

Baruch's face was white. "Jeremiah! No!"

"There are guards in the *Mishneh* district," Jeremiah said.

"Yes, guards who kill people."

"They kill lawbreakers to protect the rest of us," Jeremiah argued. At fourteen he had grown to be a lanky youth, the cords of his neck sleek and hard as rock. He had the same bright eyes as his father, the whites almost blue, like smooth stones under water. When he spoke, it was with a penetrating tone, bright with certainty.

"Maybe a few years ago they did," Baruch cried, shaking his dark curls, lifting his face, as though asking heaven for help.

Baruch was shorter than Jeremiah, with a round, beardless face and black eyes. He stayed his ground now, solid on his sun-browned feet. He clenched his fists while Jeremiah took another step into the yawning darkness below. Baruch stood at the top of the steps until Jeremiah had reached the befouled stones. "Oh God, help us," he prayed, then followed.

Here along the narrow street flanked by crowded dwellings, there were fewer people lying in the gutter, but their faces were darker, their limbs as wasted as bleached bones. It was not long before the boys came upon a narrow passageway that led into the high buildings on both sides of the stone walkway. Baruch reached for Jeremiah's sleeve, but missed. Jeremiah was resolute.

The walls leaned over the road like great strands of rock in a dark canyon devoid of any sliver of sunlight. The sky was folding into dusk. Next would come night. Unstoppable, Jeremiah plunged forward into the overcrowded quarter flanked by the rows of high apartments, their honeycomb windows like a hundred black eyes. Baruch fell silent.

The sky had already grown crimson. Jeremiah heard the clank of pots through the open windows, the thump of crude shutters and wooden doors. Above the clutter of sounds, he heard in the distance a faint bleat. He burst forward, pounding the street with his sandals, beckoning to the reluctant Baruch.

Baruch hung back, his face pinched with anger and fear. Because his father Neriah was a government official, he'd occasionally had the opportunity to visit these quarters. On those days, however, there would have been a convoy of other officials attending them.

Jeremiah stopped running to listen carefully. The soft bleat of the animal seemed to come from an alleyway near the stairwell to the building where his aunt and uncle lived. They'd inhabited the *Mishneh* section long before King Manasseh let the city crumble. Dashing ahead, Jeremiah and Baruch descended into such a dark corner that the walls seemed to close in on them. There, tied to the side of an old iron post, was Baruch's Seeshi, her little throat vibrating.

Catching sight of her master, she jerked at her tether; her plaintive cry echoed pitifully in the hollow cavern of walls. Behind the goat, perhaps twenty to thirty paces farther back in the darkness, sat a group of men in a circle on the ground, absorbed in a game.

With the goat's cry, one of the men turned to look at the animal. "Shut that bloody lummox up," he growled.

"Don't touch it," another roared. "It'll be my dinner. I'm winning!" They were tossing bones.

Jeremiah's breath stopped. The medallions on the mantles of the gamblers were the unmistakable regalia of the ignoble king.

"Your move." One of the men scrambled for his piece of bone.

Baruch stopped behind Jeremiah. "Don't you dare," he warned. "They'll kill you."

Seeshi, recognizing Baruch's voice, pulled at the rope until her little legs were taut. She struggled to breathe as the rope tightened about her neck.

Jeremiah calculated his advantage. They were only a few steps away from the goat; the men were another twenty paces.

"Wait here." Jeremiah raised his arm to stop Baruch. He pulled his knife from his tunic and lunged forward.

Baruch's breath quickened. "Forget it."

Without hesitating, Jeremiah darted toward the goat and took a determined swipe with the knife against the stiff hemp rope. With the harsh yank on her tether, the small animal shrieked. More men in the circle turned around to look.

"Hurry," Baruch cried.

Sawing with all of his might, Jeremiah cut strand after strand with his dull knife. While most of the gamesters stayed engrossed, those who had turned from the circle to look at the goat began to shout.

"What's going on?" One of the men scrambled to his feet. "What the . . ." He swore black words, and shouted, "Get away from there, you wretched scoundrels." He stumbled in the gravel as he tried to get his footing.

When the rope was almost cut, Jeremiah heard himself cry out. He, the goat, and Baruch all wailed. As the man lunged forward, the shutters in the compound began to open one by one. Heads came to the windows. Far above, on the third floor, Jeremiah saw Aunt Huldah leaning out the window, beating a heavy metal pot with a spoon.

"Hsst! Hsst!" she cried to the men below.

At the clamor, the entire quarter seemed to burst into an uproar. The approaching thug stopped for a split second, surprised by the noise. In that pause, Jeremiah's knife severed the rope, and Seeshi leaped away. Free, she vaulted into Baruch's arms.

The boys dashed to the stairwell and pounded the steps to the upstairs apartment where Aunt Huldah had already opened her door to let them in. They had no breath to utter a word while she shut the door quickly and slipped the bar into place. They stood panting in the middle of the room, their legs shaking.

"Jeremiah, Baruch! You could have been killed."

Gasping, the boys stood without moving, sweat running down their faces. Baruch clutched the goat to his tunic. The little animal's heartbeat visibly shook its body. Aunt Huldah, her eyes bright with fear, towered over them. She was a tall woman with a head of thick black curls tied behind her neck. She wore an imposing embroidered caftan of blue, the color of gemstones. The brightness set off her dark piercing eyes. "Do you know where you are?" she breathed.

Farther inside the room, Uncle Shallum was seated in a large chair, with pages of Egyptian papyri loosely gathered in his lap. He looked up at the visitors and nodded his graying head toward two leather chairs. Hanging on the wall over the chairs was a large, round, woven piece hung with colorful sheep's wool and bits of old wood. Jeremiah sat on one of the chairs.

Baruch, still clutching the little goat, was trembling. "Jeremiah saved Seeshi," he said. The goat had been his prize for writing the best copy at the archives.

Uncle Shallum scowled. "Your judgment . . . ," he began. But then, registering the abject fear in their faces, he hesitated. "I thought you boys would have known about this area, how much danger there is."

Aunt Huldah returned the pot to a black cauldron over a small fire in the hearth. As she worked, she changed the subject to dispel the tension. "You've both grown so tall I barely recognized you. Your father hasn't dared to bring you for a long time."

Facing them, she carried a small pot of water and two cups in her hands. "In this neighborhood . . . ," she began. She set the cups on a table beside Uncle Shallum. Slowly, she leaned forward to demand their attention. "The women weave the cloth for the temple robes, and . . . ," she murmured, glancing at her husband, who had knit his brows, "their wanton callers stalk close by."

She returned to the black cauldron over the fire. When she looked again at Uncle Shallum, he scowled and shook his head as though to quiet her.

Aunt Huldah asked Baruch if he wished to tie the goat to the table leg. The frightened animal still lay curled against the boy's tunic, her little heart visibly beating in her chest, her eyes dilated with fear. "She'll calm down in a few minutes," Baruch said.

Aunt Huldah busied herself with pouring hot water, honey, and herbs in the two thick clay vessels which she offered to her visitors. As she bent near to them, her face clouded by the hot steam from the cups, she said, "You must know by now that King Manasseh may be trying to do better since he returned from exile, but"—she paused as though finding the words in her mouth too bitter to speak—"there is no law here."

Jeremiah took the cup, closing his eyes against his aunt's dark gaze.

"Manasseh, for all his thirty or more years as king, has tolerated lawlessness," she continued. "Yes, he wanted to change things. Yes, they tortured him when he was in captivity in Assyria. That humbled him a little." A sadness crept into her tone. "But it was too late. Old habits are hard to break. He has long been set in his ways."

She gazed toward the window, at the city she loved. "And now, what will happen when his reckless son Amon becomes king?" Her eyes narrowed. She still held the teapot in her hands. "What we need . . ." and her voice dropped, "is the great king that Isaiah promised us, the king who will bring us peace."

Aunt Huldah had a clear voice with a musical tone. She hesitated before bending near them to whisper, "You are both sons of David. Could either of you be that promised king?"

The question startled Jeremiah—as though he heard a sudden gust of wind.

"We need a strong leader to save us all," she continued.

Though the room seemed stifling in the murky smoke from the hearth, the light that filtered through the woven window blind was bright. The sun must have been glaring directly over the ramparts of the temple and into their eyes. Her question unsettled him. *Could either of you be that promised king?*

In his work as a scribe, and as the dedicated son of a high priest, Jeremiah was well acquainted with all of the scripts in both Hebrew and Egyptian. He had often copied Isaiah and Joshua, all the histories of the kings, and the writings of Moses. He knew about the prophecy that a great king should come out of the House of David to bring peace. He and Baruch were both of the family of David. But day-by-day living had a way of obscuring all of these important factors. He knew that David's family was favored of God, but after his son Solomon died, his grandson Rehoboam was not strong enough to withstand the aggressive challenger, Jereboam, who seized power over the northern kingdom. So the country was split: Jeroboam ruled the north, and Rehoboam, the south.

Because a house divided against itself is weakened, the Assyrian enemies from the north easily conquered the northern people and sold them as slaves. Those of the ten tribes who escaped scattered abroad into many lands, while the southern section of Judah struggled to avoid the same fate. Those Judeans who were acquainted with the prophecies prayed urgently that someday the promised Lord would come to bring peace. But unanswered, their prayers became routine and worn.

While Aunt Huldah spoke in her low musical voice, Jeremiah glanced at Baruch, bent over the hot cup in his hands, blowing it cool. A forelock of curly black hair dangled in the steam. Both he and Baruch were descended from the daughters and sons of kings. Jeremiah had never thought the two of them looked much like royalty. Yet something in that instant touched him like a finger of light.

The boys promised they would not stay a moment more in this quarter. But they hoped Aunt Huldah and Uncle Shallum wouldn't mind accompanying them to the *Ha-Yehudim,* where it would be safer to get home. Baruch still held the goat nestled against his chest. Aunt Huldah smiled and gathered her shawl about her shoulders. Uncle Shallum rose from his chair to follow them.

At the thoroughfare, after saying good-bye to Aunt Huldah and Uncle Shallum, the cousins braced themselves for the rest of their journey. Quite a few of the oil lamps that usually lit the city had already burned out.

"Might be both of us are in trouble at home," Baruch said uneasily before turning down his street into the *El Wad* Section.

"I know I will be," Jeremiah answered, studying the empty road ahead.

And he discovered he was right. When he reached his home, the door was locked.

He barely tapped the surface with the handle of his knife. Through the open window, he saw the dark figure of his father, the bent shoulders moving back and forth across the house in the light of a small oil lamp. At the sound of the knife handle on the wood, the silhouette in the black cloak rushed forward. When the door opened, the light from the house flooded the stoop.

"Father!" For a moment, father and son stood looking at one another.

"My son." The man did not move from the threshold. With uneven breath, he cried out, "Jeremiah! What have you done?"

Awkwardly, the priest Hilkiah backed away, and Jeremiah entered the quiet room. No one else was present. His two younger brothers would have been asleep long ago, the two little girls curled in their woolen robes, hugging their soft toys. His mother Marika, who seemed to worry more about him as he grew older, had probably cried herself to sleep, staining her pillow with tears.

For another strained moment the dead stillness of the house seemed to ring like the echo of a colossal bell. "Father, I'm sorry. I was at Uncle Shallum's."

Hilkiah paused. He cleared his throat and tempered his anger. In his solemn voice he said, "There's no trust anymore in the streets of Jerusalem."

"Father . . ."

The man wiped his brow with a kerchief. He wiped the sweat from his eyes. "Do you know of the evils at nightfall?"

"Please forgive me, Father. Let me explain."

"Your mother and I . . ."

"I'm sorry, Father. We were with Uncle Shallum and Aunt Huldah." The words tumbled out of his mouth. "Baruch lost his prize goat, and the guards were gambling for it."

Though Hilkiah's anger was still visible, he was listening to Jeremiah's short speech. The news seemed to calm him. He stayed motionless, his hands still clutching the kerchief almost soggy with sweat. He drew up to his full height and adopted a benign look as though he were praying to keep control.

"Now your mother and I have decided," Hilkiah continued, pausing for effect, "since her cousin Latham has moved to Libnah, our family will take his offer to live on his vacant farm in Anathoth."

Jeremiah hesitated. He should have expected this. He had seen Latham's farm two miles northeast of town. He had visited his cousins there. Jeremiah's parents had talked about moving, but the prospect of relinquishing their cherished home in the city had always cut off the discussion.

His father's pronouncement swam in Jeremiah's head. "Father, is it because of me?"

"My son, you're just beginning to discover how perilous these times are. I must safeguard you to serve your mission for the Lord." The high priest did not often reach out to embrace his children, but in this moment the father stepped forward, opened his arms, and enclosed his son.

Jeremiah wanted to argue, but in his father's arms, he fell silent. He was still reeling with what his Aunt Huldah, the prophetess, had said in the rooms above the dark streets. The night's events swam before his eyes. "What mission, Father?"

Hilkiah held Jeremiah at arm's length and whispered, "We all have a mission, my son. It is written on the tablets of your heart. You will discover it and deliver your life to it someday."

Chapter Two

Anathoth

The move to Anathoth was not an easy one. Not because of the confusion when relatives and friends packed the borrowed carts with loads of furnishings: pots, pans, tools, bedding, cushions, clothes, and many other items. Not because of the lumbering two-mile journey, the weary animals, and the broken wheels on the road. It was because, once they were settled, Hilkiah seemed unable to let go of Jerusalem. Feeling it was his particular responsibility in the temple to watch over the Ark of the Covenant in the Holy of Holies, twice a week he took the donkey and cart into Jerusalem over the difficult country road.

His absence left Jeremiah in charge of the farm. But the responsibilities for the farm were trifling compared with the copy work Jeremiah and his younger brothers were expected to accomplish at the archives.

The priest Shelemaiah who at last had become manager at Anathoth, had waited many years to inherit his position from his father Hananiah. Suddenly, with the prominent priest Hilkiah's arrival, Shelemaiah seemed threatened. As he walked down the rows of tables grumbling and spitting into a red handkerchief, he rapped the new boys' fingers with glee.

Though Jeremiah harbored resentment at these alterations in their family's lives, he could not argue with the situation, as he had been indirectly responsible for it. Swallowing his rancor, he suffered his humiliations in the archives, patiently waiting to get outdoors, where he had the more pleasant responsibility for the crops and the sheep, and could train his younger brothers to help. The boys loved the open spaces, the distant hills, and the sight of the sun burning like a hot coin and slipping behind the walls of Jerusalem. Like Jeremiah, every one of them balked at sitting under the archive master's gaze at the copy table.

On every assignment Shelemaiah demanded absolute perfection. Each boy was constrained to copy the legal documents on the papyrus twice without mistakes; the first was to be read, and the second to be rolled tightly, sealed with wax and attached as a "safety copy" telling what the main document said in case of loss or damage. As student apprentices, the boys worked, without pay, to satisfy the growing interest in the sale of these papyrus documents in both Hebrew and the Egyptian Demotic text. Some of what they wrote would be engraved in metal.

The work was tedious, but Jeremiah applied himself diligently, exceeding the production of any of the other boys—even Shelemaiah's son Irijah. Though the lanky troublemaker giggled and mocked Jeremiah's every error, Jeremiah showed him up by producing more copy. Jeremiah delighted in this rivalry until he realized he was making a relentless enemy.

Finally, after dodging Shelemaiah's coughing and wheezing, and feeling the sting of his stick and of Irijah's laughter, Jeremiah began leaving the archives every day in haste.

One day as he swept into the hallway anxious to hang up his stylus and papyri, Shelemaiah planted himself in the way. Over the rippling sound of his stiff cloak and the wheeze in his windpipe, Shelemaiah's voice rang with an edge of sarcasm. "You seem eager to get away."

Jeremiah paused. The son, Irijah, standing nearby, was trying to hold his laughter but could not stop it from escaping through his tight grin. Jeremiah wanted to run into the yard. But he stayed firm and counted in his head until his silence turned the hecklers away.

For two long years Jeremiah was patient, not revealing these abuses to his father. But for the last three months he began begging his father to let him go with him in the donkey cart to the archives in Jerusalem. He wanted a wider berth. And lately, he had also begun to receive letters from his cousin Baruch, saying, *My father will let me go to the Street Festival for Passover only if you will come with me.*

Jeremiah would soon be sixteen. He explained to his father that he wanted to participate in the Passover celebration, and with the money he had earned from the sale of his sheep, he would like to purchase a gift for his mother.

Hilkiah, though his shoulders were slightly stooped under the burlap robe, was still a commanding presence. His eyes gleamed as he listened to Jeremiah's plea.

Jeremiah heard that vendors at Passover displayed gifts and treasures unavailable for purchase at any other time of year. There would be hundreds of booths in the streets, where vendors would sell hot breads and pottery, magnificent documents in both Hebrew and Egyptian, and precious inscribed silver amulets. Jeremiah explained that he was curious to see if some of these documents might be the product of the work he and Baruch did for the archives. Besides, he had not seen his cousin for many months.

Hilkiah cleared his throat. "Tell me what you want to purchase, and I will get it for you on my way back from the temple."

But this was not what Jeremiah wanted to hear. For weeks he brooded, until, just a few days before the celebration, his mother finally entered the discussion. As he hung his shepherd's staff at the entrance to the farmhouse, he stopped in the front hallway before moving into the open central courtyard. His mother seemed to be waiting for him.

The entry was crowded with the children's toys, large hoes, rakes, and other implements for use in the outdoor garden. When he caught his mother's eyes through the clutter, he saw a flicker of light in her face. She had pulled her headcloth back from her brow, revealing a slight smile.

"I have received a message from Baruch's mother," she said. "She wants you to come to the city. You are almost of age, Jeremiah. Your father doesn't want you to grow up."

Not much was said in the household for a few days. There was a soft silence between mother and father. Many evenings, when the music of their quiet voices droned long into the night, Jeremiah supposed they were discussing him.

One day his father stood by the window, narrowly gazing at Marika as she nodded and said it was all right, he could go. She placed her hand on his arm. "You're becoming a man, my son."

Chapter Three

Passover

The festival was all Jeremiah had hoped it would be. When he saw Baruch he took both of his cousin's hands and shook them with glee. Baruch responded with a warm smile, bouncing his black curls.

Musicians in the streets strummed small harps and sang popular melodies as they walked along the festive stalls. In the narrow passageways, crowds jostled one another, bearing great burlap sacks filled with cuts of meat, pumpkins, squash, giant blood-red onions, and radishes as large as carrots. Other stalls were crowded with knotted, woven carpets, heavy with fringe, and colored with modern dyes. Shawls and robes hung in rows near tables of pounded silver pots engraved with the images of Asherah. Hundreds of the incense burners Manasseh tried to discourage lined the walkways. Statues of the Egyptian goddess Hathor, the Assyrian Asherah, and other pagan gods still lined the shelves.

Jeremiah was drawn to the sheepskin and parchment manuscripts hanging on lines to dry in the sun. Those men who copied documents for a living sat below the awnings of the balconies in the street and created perfect letters with the expensive camel hair brushes dipped in the charcoal inks they had crushed in their pen pots. He was also fascinated by the *ostracon*, the shards of pottery bearing poems, and the brass and gold plates produced by the metalworkers and gold merchants. He liked the look of the small amulets of silver engraved with impressive sayings. Jeremiah was awed by the perfection of the copy work. He wondered if he could match the skills of these artisans. He believed that Baruch would come close enough, for his writing often had the hallmark of genius. The two young scribes stood at those stalls for what seemed like hours, watching the cutting and chiseling.

In the presence of such treasures, Jeremiah gazed with longing at the small leather-bound books of poetry in a stall close by. At last he untied the bag of coins at his belt and purchased a small book of psalms for his mother. Along with the book, he purchased a tiny engraved signet she could use to press into the sealing wax when she wrote a letter. It read *Love God.* He tucked the seal inside the cover pocket of the small volume and placed the treasures in his tunic, feeling the smooth leather of the book against his skin. She would love these gifts. She would let him use the seal and read the songs.

It grew late in the afternoon, but Baruch had not yet spent any of his money. Jeremiah had promised his father they would meet him at the archives of the temple before it got dark; he encouraged his cousin to make up his mind. "So what did you like best, Baruch?" he asked him.

Baruch had loved the pots carved with the figure of Asherah.

"But it is pagan," Jeremiah protested.

"There was one pot with the head of a goat," Baruch said uneasily. Goats had always been his favorite pets. But those pots had been displayed on the first stretch of their journey. Now they were ten minutes away from that particular vendor.

"Do you want to go back?"

Baruch thought he did.

"Let's hurry, then," Jeremiah said.

By now the streets were packed with drunken stragglers. The sacred religious festival of Passover had become a profanity. King Manasseh let it happen over a period of thirty or more years. At one time the religious ceremonies were completely eliminated from the holiday until Manasseh spent those months in Assyria tied up and tortured by the Assyrian soldiers who had strung wires through his cheeks and hung him from the ceiling. He came back to Jerusalem repentant. However, restoring some of the rites to Passover had not seemed to change the behavior of the masses, and the revelry continued.

Down both sides of the street people had begun to reel drunkenly about from their wine, now searching for places they could sit down in order to devour their flatbreads and slobber over their large skewers of lamb. Small eating establishments had placed boxes outside their doors to be used as tables, where men and women could pull benches forward to lounge and feast. Laughing and pouring wine from leather bottles, they scooped the cabbage and onions into the bread on their plates and cut off huge mouthfuls without wiping away the grease that dripped from their chins.

To avoid the crowds, Jeremiah and Baruch ducked down a quiet street which they believed would lead them to their destination more quickly. As soon as they turned the corner into a dark passageway, they realized they had made a wrong turn.

Only two doors away, a donkey stood in their pathway, braying pitifully. Three men in hooded cloaks were beating it and howling with drunken laughter. Seated on the poor animal was a young girl tied to the animal's back by a long shawl around her waist. She was swaying awkwardly, waving one of her arms over her head, leaning one way and then another. The small white-knuckled fist of her other hand gripped the mane of the donkey. She was half crying, half laughing.

Jeremiah bolted forward. "She needs help, Baruch."

"She's just drunk!" Baruch lunged to stop him, but missed grabbing Jeremiah's sleeve.

Jeremiah thought he recognized the girl. Without question, he knew the men with her: Kamut and his son Pazael. Both muscular men with shaggy black hair, they had joined the king's guard service several months earlier, after winning a chariot competition in the arena.

Now Kamut and Pazael strode with purpose toward a door to one of the crowded buildings. Kamut barked an order to the unruly servant. Wearing a soldier's headdress and waving two swords, the man screamed vile epithets to the donkey at the top of his lungs.

Closing in on the scene, Jeremiah saw the servant glance toward him, and he backed into the crevice between the two buildings. He looked back to see his cousin race after him. As Baruch charged from behind, his full body and face came into view.

"Here!" Jeremiah cried out. Baruch ducked into the space between the walls, but not before the servant had seen him. Jeremiah hoped this blackguard, and the others with him, were too drunk to pay attention. Praying silently, he peered out from between the buildings to watch the servant tie the donkey to a hitching post and untie the girl. Jeremiah could see the shape of her eyes, the white cheeks, the tiny chin. She was someone he had definitely seen before!

The three drunks, cursing, grunting, and spitting, dragged the laughing girl off the donkey as though she were a rag doll. The servant hoisted her across his shoulders and lurched toward the entrance of the building where the boys were hiding.

Still jammed into the dark space between the two buildings, Jeremiah asked Baruch to stand under the high, narrow window so that he could climb on his shoulders to peer inside.

"Let's go, Jeremiah," Baruch begged, standing unsteadily under Jeremiah's weight.

Jeremiah remembered his mother's warning to return early. She had reminded him several times that on Passover morning Uncle Latham and his family were coming to visit the farm at Anathoth. Jeremiah would see his cousin Hamah, Uncle Latham's daughter. Thoughts of Hamah brought him instant recognition. He was sure now that he recognized the girl on the donkey. It was Hamah's friend, Yoanna. His heart beat fast.

"They saw me," Baruch lamented. "Do you think they will remember me?" His breathing became ragged. "I think we should find the guard."

"Baruch," Jeremiah said. "Those *are* the guard."

The street began to fill with people. Jeremiah took a quick look into the window, but a piece of gauze over the opening was so filthy he could see nothing but a lamp burning and men standing in a circle over something he could not discern.

He climbed down from Baruch's shoulders, his heart sinking with helplessness. Seconds later he heard the scream, the most terror-stricken, bloodcurdling shriek he had ever heard in his life. It was a rippling sound, similar to the cry of the sacrificial goat if its joints cracked open before its throat was cut. The groups of people in the street looked at one another in surprise. Others, cawing and shouting obscenities, pushed their way across the threshold.

"I'm going in to rescue her," Jeremiah cried.

When Jeremiah began moving forward into the crowd, Baruch pulled at his sleeve. "You'll be killed!"

Jeremiah's throat felt dry. Echoes of past wary voices whirled in his head. He had sometimes been reckless. Reluctantly forcing himself to move more slowly, he tried to listen as Baruch paced back and forth.

At the entrance of the main building, three figures emerged into the street, carrying a roll of carpet toward the advancing mob. The men slipped into the murky space between the buildings where only moments ago Jeremiah and Baruch had stood in the shadows to peer through the window.

"Kamut and Pazael," Baruch whispered.

"Quiet. Wait."

Soon the three men came out of the darkness, their black shadows moving along the front of the building as they followed another party of revelers back through the door. They were no longer carrying the roll of carpet.

Jeremiah felt a cold shock of anger. He reached for his knife and curled his fingers over it. Something was terribly wrong.

When the parties of men and women slipped inside the building, the two boys waited until the street cleared. Finally they crept up to the cavern between the buildings. Back in the recess of the wretched darkness Jeremiah groped slowly until his feet contacted the fringed edge of the rug. Leaning down, he pulled on the carpet until the end of it trailed out of the shadows into the faint light of the moon. He lifted the edge of the fringe. The fair, sand-colored hair was matted with blood.

Chapter Four

The Hidden Documents

After he left Baruch to walk the two miles to Anathoth, Jeremiah reviewed what had happened over and over again. It was dark when he reached his house, and his family had finished their meal. They remained reclining in the main room in the far end of the open courtyard. He was not surprised they'd waited for him to join them. Jeremiah vowed he would not yet say anything about what he'd seen. He would talk to his father when they were alone.

Every breath of his father's life, every exertion of his limbs had been reserved for the glory of the God who brought Israel back from Egypt. Hilkiah lived to preserve the records that must remind his children and their children of God and of His commandments. Without the records, the children of God would forget. Without reading them, the children of God would lose their faith.

Hilkiah did not reach for the scrolls he usually read. There was something serious he was anxious to talk about. "I want you to remember today. It has been a day that will change our lives forever."

As his mother cleared the mat, and the family gathered themselves into comfortable positions, they began to listen. Hilkiah told how he'd left the house as he usually did after their earnest prayers. All of them lived with the knowledge that every time he took the donkey cart to the city there was no guarantee for his safe return.

"This morning was like every other morning, driving the cart to the temple," Hilkiah told them. It was an ordinary morning, except that it was the day before *Pesach,* and he noticed most of the priests had stayed home to prepare for the holiday. Built in front of the temple porch, which faced east toward the Mount of Olives, between the outdoor altar and the cleansing basin, the dais had already been raised for the ceremony that would honor the high guard tomorrow. Inside, all three rooms of the temple were empty: the large front room, where the crowds usually gathered, the next room where the altar of incense and the *menorah* sat next to the shew-bread table, and finally, the room behind the veil in the Holy of Holies where some of the few remaining precious artifacts were stored. Though long ago the Assyrian King Sennacharib had taken as tribute the first version of the Ark of the Covenant to melt down the gold, there were still in hiding some gold, the pillow of Jacob, and other precious writings. Even the three-story archive/office building that wrapped around three sides of the temple was unusually quiet. The halls rang with Hilkiah's footsteps as he checked on the artifacts. All of the construction workers, who had been tearing up floors for Manasseh's remodeling jobs, were absent.

"Didn't you write today?" the smallest daughter asked her father.

Hilkiah smiled at her. "There are so many orders for scrolls, I am always copying pages for several hours."

Jeremiah visualized his father bending over the manuscripts so diligently at the high table in the upstairs temple archives. Not until someone interrupted him would he get up to exercise his cramped limbs.

"After I took the lamp to check the main floor hall, I noticed something odd," said Hilkiah. "I saw a gaping hole in the hallway, as though one of the floors had fallen in after the men had left work yesterday. When I peered through the dark hole in the middle of the rubble, I saw an ancient stone stairway leading to a hidden lower level. I wondered where this passageway might go. This stairway had possibly been buried for centuries."

Testing the steps, Hilkiah found them to be solid. With first one foot and then the other, he crept forward. Holding his lamp high, he slowly made his way down the narrow stairwell, carefully pressing the palms of his free hand against the dusty spider webs on the walls. When he reached the bottom of the stairs, he saw a door standing ajar. Though his lamp sputtered in the darkness, he was able to see by directing the feeble light against the opening of the doorway. Inside the storage space on the dark floor, he saw what used to be grain containers—oddly carved barrels now ravaged by corrosion. Curious, he set his lamp on the stone floor and made his way into the small room. Leaning down, he pushed at one of the murky crates with his foot. Behind it was a chest covered with old straw. He opened the chest. Hidden in a deep corner near the bottom, was a dusty, rotting scroll. Although he could barely make out the faded marks, he knew he had come upon ancient writings.

"I read only a few words before I put the papyrus down. Ancient letters! Could they have been from Moses? If only the king could see this! At that moment I was convinced I had found something valuable. Something that could change people's lives. I knew I must show these writings to the king.

"Being very careful, I lifted the scrolls from the chest and carried them in a fold of my robe up the stairs.

"I was the only one in the archives, so I laid pieces of the parchment out under the afternoon light from the high windows. Carefully I spread pieces out one by one on the open tables and studied the characters to see if I could read them. When I examined the figures, the numbers, the way the small cuneiform markings marched across the pages, I clearly saw they were exactly what the scholars had found in the ancient writings of Moses. Under the afternoon light, I pored over all of the manuscripts and knew they were letters Moses wrote before his death. It was a fifth book to the commandments, a powerful testimony that God still speaks to us.

"I hurried home. I have been jubilant. I waited until this special time to tell the story when my family would be present.

"These are the records that will help drive the truth home to all who read them. We will have something to change the heart of the king!"

After Hilkiah's story, a hush settled in the room. Jeremiah was still on edge from witnessing the horror that had occurred in the city. He would not interfere with his father's hope of reaching the iniquitous king, yet he was obligated to tell his father what he and Baruch had seen.

Continuing with subdued words, Hilkiah lowered his eyes. "After I read the documents, I walked out behind the temple into the garden for a few moments and bent over the vine leaves." He paused. "I sat on a stone and leaned over the ground. With the end of a stick I wrote cuneiform figures in the sand. In those quiet moments, writing prayers I might have said to God, He whispered to me that I must take this record to the king."

Because Hilkiah's relatives were cousins-in-law with the descendants of King David, they were related to Manasseh, the king. Yet none of them had ever dared to approach the man. The hush continued in the room. At Hilkiah's elbow was a bowl of parched corn. He pushed the bowl away and leaned over the mat. The children kept their eyes on him. Marika cleared away the bowl.

Jeremiah watched, suppressing the darkness of his terrible secret. Like his father, he could not touch the food in his dish. He stayed in his corner, observing his brothers and sisters weave their restless fingers.

Marika broke the silence. "Manasseh has been king for forty years. Perhaps he will not last forever, and then his son Amon may listen to the good news of this discovery."

Hilkiah, who knew Prince Amon was not the leader everyone hoped for, stared into the fire.

"And remember our pretty cousin Jedidah," Marika continued. The room rang with the hum of the coals dying in the pit. "When Prince Amon turned fourteen he saw Jedidah and wanted her for his wife. We thought her quiet nature would help him." She was standing over the kettle at the fire. "Amon is next in line to be king. If he fails us, at least Jedidah is a good mother. Perhaps their little son Josiah will be the great promised king." She walked to the cistern and dipped water to wash the utensils.

Hilkiah said, "The promised king? That is the hope, I know. But the government is so corrupt, it would be a miracle if any man could bring about change. It will be years before the baby Josiah could be king. And even then something powerful—perhaps it will be these ancient words—must come forth to help our people return to a reverence for the law."

The words tumbled out of Jeremiah's mouth: "They probably won't read it anyway." His voice was like the noise of a small bird chirping in a nearby tree. "The people won't read the new scrolls."

At his son's challenging statement, Hilkiah steadied himself. "I'm aware collectors purchase records to be fashionable. I know they don't heed them." He lowered his eyes. "But even if I must risk danger, I feel it's my duty to alert the king and the people of Jerusalem."

Jeremiah resolved not to wait much longer before telling his father what he had witnessed that day.

Chapter Five

Jeremiah's Mission

The opportunity to approach Hilkiah didn't come until the children were tucked into bed. Marika reminded the children that their Uncle Latham and his family would be coming in the morning. When she began to sing her quiet lullabies, Jeremiah drew near his father and sat on the floor at his feet.

As Jeremiah forced the terrible story out of his mouth, Hilkiah grew as white as chalk. He held his palms over his face and didn't speak for a long time. Finally, he said, in a firm voice, "You see why I must go and show these records to the king."

Jeremiah pulled back. Instead of convincing his father it was too dangerous to cast the sacred documents before the unworthy king—as pearls before swine—he had only intensified the man's determination. Brooding, he couldn't sleep. Images of butchery and death came into his mind: how the girl's hair had been twisted and clotted with blood, how the men in their black robes and hoods carried the carpet roll out of the doorway and down the steps. "She's unclean," he'd heard one of them say. They had surely made it so.

On the way home from the *Pesach*, Jeremiah repeated over and over again the girl's name: Yoanna. He'd seen Yoanna only once before when she played in the Anathoth farmhouse with his cousin Hamah. The two girls would have laughed together and shared secrets here as they wove stems of goldenrod gathered from the fields outside these garden walls. Hamah might have slept here in this room with her little friend Yoanna. Jeremiah wondered how he would tell Hamah his terrible news. Hamah would cry with grief. How could this tragedy be? Both Hamah and Yoanna were so small—their bones like the tiny bones of birds. How could Yoanna have been so violated, the blood raging from her onto the stone floor?

He did not sleep that night. Just before the fullness of dawn, he sensed an unusual quiet. In the deep silence he seemed to hear a still small voice. It came with an intense rush of air, almost like the breath of a hot fire. He lifted his head from the linen cloth under his cheek. A presence seemed to shimmer through the faint light in the east. It wavered like vapor through the arch of the garden wall. The voice came from deep inside his heart. *It is your duty to stop such wrong. You must say something.*

The faded light from the courtyard seemed to spiral from a strange glow in the outside garden. He slipped from under the sheepskin and walked to the open window. The moon had spread silver in the olive trees. The juniper looked blue. The almond trees swept their golden branches over the wall. He stood by the window for a moment before he walked outside.

There was no audible voice in the vast hollow of the stars. Yet he heard, echoing in his blood, the voice of majesty: *You must say something.*

Jeremiah hesitated, watching the moon.

Before I formed you in the womb I knew you; and before you were born I consecrated you; I appointed you a prophet to the nations.

The face of the moon seemed dark to him, as though painted with a frown that looked upon the world. Jeremiah stiffened. *Sovereign Lord, I don't know how to speak. I am just a child,* he said. He was fifteen, growing into a man, feeling a child's fear.

Do not say "I am a child," for you shall go to all to whom I send you, and you shall speak whatever I command you. Do not be afraid of them: for I am with you to deliver you.

He trembled. He felt the night air on his lips, and he drew back from the chill.

Now I have put my words in your mouth. Today I appoint you over nations and over kingdoms to pluck up, and to pull down, to destroy, and to overthrow, to build, and to plant.

Jeremiah stood back. Raising his eyes skyward, he shuddered.

Jeremiah, what do you see?

At first the almond trees stood erect in his view. They were straight and tall. But there was more to see. When he looked beyond the trees, he saw the formation of the stars, the north cauldron spilling, simmering. The pot was about to boil over. His father had said it many times. "Our people are not living the commandments of God. Something's going to happen. The pot is about to boil over. I can feel it."

Out of the north disaster shall break out on all the inhabitants of the land.

Out of the north. The Assyrians—the same army that had tortured Manasseh. They had let the king go, but now it seemed they wanted more. Jerusalem was deluded to think obeisance to the royalty of Egypt—Assyria's enemy—protected the inhabitants of Jerusalem from Assyrian predators. They weren't safe, after all. Yes, the city had been saved in King Hezekiah's day. But Hezekiah had been a righteous king. When he prayed for help, the Lord helped him. The Lord inspired him to build the underground aqueduct to protect the water supply. When Hezekiah urged the people to gather, fast, and pray, they had been humble enough to obey. In the morning when they surveyed the countryside, they found two hundred thousand Assyrians dead. It was believed the Assyrians were killed by drinking the poisonous water outside the city. This miracle had been retold for half a century. The people knew God saved them. But they'd forgotten God.

Tonight Jeremiah had received a message; he'd be required to issue a warning.

Stand up and tell them everything that I command you. . . . They will fight against you; but they will not prevail against you; for I am with you . . . to deliver you.

Jeremiah waited for many moments, watching the moon sail in the sky. He huddled in the cold, spreading his hands over the upper parts of his arms to warm them. He waited, because he did not want to interrupt this moment with the Lord.

He stood from his kneeling position and hesitated, wondering if there was anything more. All was quiet; the summons was complete. He'd been called. Someday, perhaps soon, he'd be required to face the corruption of the people and speak out against them and their deeds. He trembled and recoiled at the knowledge. He turned back to his room and fell to his knees.

Chapter Six

Hamah

As the day of Passover dawned, the travelers from Libnah arrived. Cousin Latham walked ahead of the caravan, stirring the dust with his heavy sandals, the silk of his *tse'ifim* billowing around his thick fingers crusted with jewels. Jeremiah's little sisters ran to meet them. The cousins hooted and threw coconuts from the cart. They laughed while their mother, Abigail, held them back by the hoods on their capes.

Behind the little cousins were the white faces of the young girls. Jeremiah looked for Hamah. There were unspeakable words he must tell her. He waited until she stepped down from the *mekhonit*. Her face was covered with silk to protect her cheeks from the sun. Wisps of dark curls around her brow escaped the silk. Her large dark eyes lit up when she saw him and she dropped her veil.

He could not find a time to speak to her alone while the family performed the rituals of Passover. As the women prepared the symbolic meal, Jeremiah's older cousin Beriah, who worked for the king in the palace, spoke in general terms of the execution of a robber who had stolen the butcher's knives. He said that just recently he heard of a terrible murder, though he could not name names. There were no suspects. His beautiful wife Bethany, dressed in a flowing white robe sewn with embroidered white roses, lowered her head when he spoke. Everyone lamented the city's atrocities King Manasseh had never seemed able to stop.

Just before supper, Jeremiah led Hamah away from the others, whispering that he had something he must tell her. He beckoned her to the garden. The thick walls enclosed them as they walked through the hedges of eucalyptus to the stones by the pond, where they could be alone.

"The recent murder . . . ," he said softly. "It was . . . it was Yoanna." He hadn't wanted to tell her, but felt he must. It burst out of him. He'd thought if he breathed it quickly and quietly it wouldn't hurt as much as hard words formed like cold iron. But the name Yoanna sliced through the air like a knife.

"Yoanna?" Hamah was also small, like Yoanna, with bones as delicate and slender as reeds. When she began to sob against his sleeve, he watched her thin hands and the fine, light furrows of down on her arms. "Yoanna? Are you sure you saw her?"

"Yes," he said.

Her tears fell on his hands, the drops so large they pooled there. He found he did not want to move to shake them off or wipe them away. He couldn't see her face when she was seated so close to him on the rock in the garden. But he could feel her body shaking.

His mother began to call more insistently for the *shelamim*, her voice coming from the courtyard kitchen where the priests and the cousins from Libnah had gathered to end the fast. Earlier they had killed and bled the lamb. When he heard his mother's cry, he placed tentative fingers on Hamah's wrist. "It's time to go," he said.

"Will they find who did this?"

"They're looking for the culprits," Jeremiah said. "The judges are asking questions." He heard a spoon strike metal. "It's time to go."

When Hamah raised her face to him, he could see how cruel the news had been to her. Her eyes looked swollen, as though the tears that stood in them had poisoned her. He knew she identified with Yoanna, wondering when her own turn would come, when the terror of undisciplined men would find her. They could crush her, wring her tiny neck until she could no longer cry out, and her heart would stop.

"Why?" she managed to say. She put her slender fingers against his arm and raised herself slowly. She smoothed her skirts with her flat palms, standing as tall as she could, as though to keep from crying at supper. Jeremiah followed her, wondering what had happened inside his heart. Her touch on his arm stayed with him. He let his eyes rest on her lithe walk under the raiment. It was perhaps the way she stepped with one foot in front of the other, as though the tears had blinded her. He felt something he had not felt before for this second cousin from Libnah. Then in his mind he envisioned the face of the dead girl lying in the carpet on the street, and his heart twisted in pain.

When he and Hamah came to the courtyard, he saw his father standing with the other Levite priests who had traveled from Libnah and Anathoth. The lamb the townspeople had brought to them as a gift was still roasting as the women and children sat back against the walls of the courtyard, ready to serve the feast. Hilkiah bid his cousin Beriah, the palace manager, to pray, and when Beriah lowered his head, he petitioned God the Father to help them remember that, in gratitude for their release from Egypt, they would stay obedient to His laws. When the men opened their eyes and the women began to serve the meat, Hilkiah brought a piece of new papyrus out of the folds of his robe and began to read from it.

"Aha! Your precious discovery," Cousin Latham said. There was a murmur among the priests, who drew closer to Hilkiah to examine the copy he had made of some passages of the ancient text.

Beriah moved quickly to his side. "Ah yes, Aaron's syntax," he said.

"Why hasn't it been available all these years?" Cousin Latham asked.

Without answering their questions, Hilkiah unrolled the papyrus, and the priests murmured with curiosity and alarm. When Hilkiah began to read, there was a hush over the crowd. Even the children seemed to understand the importance of this first reading of the buried treasure.

We cried to the Lord, the God of our ancestors; the Lord heard our voice, and saw our affliction, our toil, and our oppression.

The lamb still sizzled over the fire, as the women waited with raised utensils.

The Lord brought us out of Egypt with a mighty hand, an outstretched arm, with a terrifying display of power, and with signs and wonders. And he brought us into this place and gave us this land, a land flowing with milk and honey.

Though Jeremiah's eyes were fastened upon his father, he felt the gaze of Hamah on his face, and he dared to look to her. Tears were slipping down her cheeks.

Then you . . . shall celebrate with all the bounty that the Lord God has given to you and to your house.

He let his eyes rest on her for a moment. He was not sure what she was saying to him, but he felt his heart race as though he were being told something providential, something he had already known, as though he were receiving a message, one that might have included Hamah's thoughts—that they should surely *rejoice in every good thing*. But why was there so much sorrow, tragedy, and devastation?

Struggling with his perplexities, Jeremiah barely heard Hilkiah's sonorous tone.

This very day the Lord your God is commanding you to walk in His ways, to keep His statutes, His commandments, and His ordinances, and to obey Him as He has spoken.

"This is a miracle," Beriah said.

"It is much the same as the other records," Latham affirmed. "Very beautiful—beautiful beyond measure." Tentatively he questioned Hilkiah, "So this is the record you want to present to the king?"

The women lowered their utensils. The hush in the courtyard seemed charged.

"It is. It is," Hilkiah said. He raised his hand. "Yes, I know. The king doesn't read much and has forgotten what he learned as a child." He paused, and his large hand began to shake. "But I have a plan."

With the meat still sizzling, two or three of the women began to replace the lids on the heavy iron kettles.

"There seems to be a growing prestige in buying relics—scrolls, metal plates, and silver amulets engraved with the words of God. But do the buyers pay attention to what God is saying?" Hilkiah paused. "Does anyone realize how sacred these words are? They must be read again and again."

"Yes, but your plan?" Latham interrupted. He sat back in the large carved wooden chair, his massive thighs spread apart, his thick, heavily jeweled fingers locked in his lap.

Jeremiah sat frozen, hearing the wind in the olive leaves, the sizzle of the meat. He watched his father.

"Perhaps," Hilkiah continued, glancing at his cousin Beriah, the manager of the palace, "I can ask Beriah to drop a word or two in court about this new discovery?" But when his eyes caught a tentative expression on Beriah's face, his voice wavered. "Or perhaps Bethany might write a new hymn, sing it to the king, and then . . ."

No one moved for a moment, until slowly, Beriah shook his head. As one of the workers at the palace, Beriah, out of all who were there, knew the intensity of Manasseh's power. "The king's temper. I am leery." Beriah kept his eyes down. "Perhaps Prince Amon? He reads, collects relics." There was quiet. "Must it be Manasseh?"

"Yes." Hilkiah's eyebrows met. "It must be the king."

Everyone in the courtyard was so quiet Jeremiah could hear the children playing ball in the lane.

"I am thinking," Hilkiah continued. "Perhaps if I take Jeremiah with me to Jerusalem?" He looked at him. "Manasseh might listen." He paused. "Soon Jeremiah will be sixteen." His gaze was penetrating. "You would go with me, wouldn't you, Jeremiah?"

"Yes, Father." He swallowed his fear.

"We will talk about it," his father said. "You and I will talk about it soon, Jeremiah. Will you ready yourself with prayer and fasting?" Jeremiah nodded. Of course he would obey his father, even if the last thing on earth he wanted to do was to seek an audience with the king. He felt Hamah draw very close to the sleeve of his robe.

"Jeremiah?" she said, her mouth still quivering. "If you go with your father," she said, silent for a heartbeat, "can you tell the king about Yoanna?"

Tell the dishonorable king? Manasseh had inherited an insidious witchcraft from his grandparents Ahab and Jezebel. The long tradition of false gods had left a trail of laxity in the courts so that not a judge was left who dared to prosecute any officials who had power—especially for the murder of a small girl. Only three generations back, Manasseh's great-grandfather Uzziah sacrificed his own sons to the god Molech. In his early, unscrupulous reign Manasseh had burned some of his male children at the altars, saying he wanted no contest between his own sons for the throne. Amon alone, his oldest, was allowed to live. Some in Judah still believed in the practice of child sacrifice. There were even sacrifices made in the temple. The Hinnom Valley was filled with the bones of murder.

In his quiet room that night Jeremiah prayed with concentration. "If there is another way—please, bless us that we will be spared from facing the king."

Chapter Seven

Other Matters

During the nights of the *Omer*, the seven-week period between Passover and *Shavuot,* Jeremiah found it difficult to sleep. Often he lay awake pondering how to get in touch with Baruch again. Now the Lord had told him to speak out. How could they speak out about what they had seen?

Shortly after *Pesach,* the judges had beheaded a robber in the square. Yet there was no action taken to apprehend the heinous murderers of a girl who had been thrown like an apple core into the dung. Even now her body was likely wrapped in the rug and lying in Hinnom Valley. Many of his other thoughts had been of Hamah, and her tears.

During the *s'firah,* or the thirty-three days of daily gifts of grain to the priests, Jeremiah worked in the garden. While he guarded the sheep, he tried not to think of Hamah's eyes, the light hair on her arm. He chased certain speculations out of his mind—things he knew were not right to imagine—holding her, touching her cheek with his lips. He wanted to ask his father if Hamah's family would be coming for the *Lag Ba'Omer.* But he knew he would betray his feelings before the words left his mouth.

At an appropriate moment during *Omer,* he hinted to his father that he'd received an unusual spiritual message. Trying to stay calm, without revealing the details of the almond tree, the large moon, and the voice he had surely heard, he told his father that he knew the Lord wanted him to speak out against evil. But he was afraid.

Hilkiah, the priest who must have had similar experiences hearing the Lord's voice, nodded his head and said calmly, "I know there are no safe ways to speak against this government. I know you will do what the Lord asks you. The best thing we can do is to present the new material to the king."

After their talk, Hilkiah increased momentum to transcribe and organize the documents. He dared to ask Shelemaiah, the boys' taskmaster, if they could send for the expert scribe Baruch. Shelemaiah resisted, but finally agreed. Baruch, with his exceptional talent, would do the most professional job of any of the scribes.

At his post with the sheep, Jeremiah waited anxiously for Baruch, hoping they could discuss their shared burden. They hadn't seen each other since that night of horror. Finally, as the sun crossed the high point in the sky, Jeremiah saw the small figure in the linen cloak approaching the sheep. The dark curls matted on his head were longer now, bobbing against his brow. When their eyes met, both of them seemed to understand how much pain they'd suffered. Baruch put up his hand to stop him.

"The first thing I need to tell you," Baruch said, "is that I've just left the archives, and your father wants to see you."

Jeremiah put down his staff and brushed his hands together to rub off the dirt. "Yes, I'll come," he answered Baruch's request. "Will you walk back with me?"

As they passed down the slope of the meadow through the sage and stunted grasses to the archives, Jeremiah said, "Baruch, I can't stop thinking about it. Can you?"

Baruch stayed hidden behind his curls.

"I've told my father," Jeremiah said. "But he just wants to take the lost writings. I think he's afraid. Shouldn't we come forth and inform your father? He works in the offices there."

Baruch looked up at Jeremiah from behind the dark hair over his brows. "Uh, no," he stammered. "Please. These men . . ."

Good friends from childhood, Jeremiah and Baruch had a history of shared memories: rolling the copies, applying sealing wax to the scrolls. They had talked about many things. Jeremiah had been to Baruch's home, a large stone house near the Water Gate where King Hezekiah had built the underground tunnel so that the water supply had been denied to the Assyrian army. As children, Jeremiah and Baruch often sat above the waters, breaking the grasses near the wall with their fingers, and talking together about what they were going to do with their lives. Jeremiah's father Hilkiah had loved Cousin Baruch like another son.

"Kamut and Pazael. Shouldn't we . . . ," Jeremiah continued.

Baruch backed away with a look of terror on his face. Jeremiah felt him out on a different tack. "Could we search Hinnom? Would you be able to recognize the color of the rug?"

Baruch shook his head and lowered his eyes as they walked along the road to the archives.

"We are the only ones who know. Shouldn't we stop them? Shouldn't we get justice for Yoanna's life?"

At this question Baruch found his tongue. His eyes spoke his fear. "Jeremiah, you may do what you like, but do not mention my name, I beg you. Anyway, she was not clean." The words were muffled.

Ah, yes, Jeremiah thought, the perpetrators and even the judges would blame the girl, saying that she had invited it, that it was her fault. They would have said, loud enough for everyone to hear, that the girl had smiled or laughed, and become flirtatious. Yoanna had been only fourteen years old. Jeremiah could not hold the questions back. "Shouldn't we tell the judges? Isn't it our duty to tell them that we know who murdered the girl in the rolled carpet?"

When the young men reached the archives, they hesitated before the huge door. Two thick slabs of Lebanese cedar had been brought to replicate the doors of the Temple of Solomon. Although the building itself was deteriorating—its floor tiles scratched and broken, its door frames slivered and sun bleached—the formidable doors were still standing in good condition.

"Your father wants to speak to you right away," Baruch said.

"Baruch, to spurn justice is a blot on our city. The Lord wants someone to speak." He could not do it alone.

"If we tell them, we will die." Baruch looked at Jeremiah with panic in his eyes. "I know it, Jeremiah. We will die."

This was likely true. Since corruption had become common, every year there were probably a hundred girls like Yoanna who lost their lives in dark places—in brothels, in the beds of men who used them up and discarded them or made sacrifices of them and threw the bodies into the Valley of Hinnom. No one stopped them. "Baruch," he began, "They executed a man for stealing the butcher's knives." He paused. "What have they done to punish men for stealing a life?"

Baruch cast his eyes toward the street, crowded now with a merchant's caravan. "He was not just a man," he said. "He was an officer in the king's army."

Baruch did not follow Jeremiah into the archives. He excused himself to begin the long walk back to Jerusalem. Feeling drained and alone, Jeremiah walked down the passageway to another set of doors carved from olivewood. What would his father say? His usual topic these days was their mission to take the discovered writings to the king.

Hilkiah sat at a table in the scribes' room translating the scrolls and pages into the three texts Judea had commonly used since the influence of the Egyptian capture six hundred years ago: Hebrew, Egyptian Demotic, and Egyptian Hieretic. The papyrus was donated by a wealthy businessman whose ancestors invested money in the ships that fetched the wood for Solomon's temple from the faraway islands of the sea. The room was cool; the huge cedar beams overhead were hung with scarlet and purple flags.

Jeremiah stood a distance away from Hilkiah's table, hesitant to interrupt his father's work. He felt the cold tile floor through his leather sandals. He wanted to ask his father to talk to Baruch and convince him to come out as a witness to the authorities.

Hilkiah raised his eyes and smiled, tapping the stylus on the tabletop. He moved the papyrus aside, laid the stylus within the scroll, and nodded to his eldest son. "Jeremiah," he said.

"Father, you . . ."

Hilkiah held up his hand for quiet. The high priest always chose his words carefully, and this seemed to be a time when his words must resound with unusual weight. "Do you wonder why I have called you?"

"Yes, Father." Jeremiah's hands grew clammy. "You want to take the writings to the king."

His father smiled. "That is not all, son," he said. "Come, sit by me."

Jeremiah would never forget this moment—the moment he took his place beside his father, though he had to steady himself to stay on the high stool.

"You are almost sixteen years old. Do you believe in God, my son?"

"Yes."

Hilkiah smiled and quietly placed his hand over Jeremiah's curled fingers. "You are no longer a young person, but a man."

Jeremiah waited.

"For now, there is something special, isn't there? Isn't there something you might want to ask me?"

Jeremiah felt a flush in his cheeks. He could not answer.

"I watched you at Passover," said Hilkiah. "Soon I'll take a trip to Latham's to discuss a land purchase in Anathoth and to invite his family to our place for the coming celebration."

Jeremiah felt his throat tighten. "Go to Cousin Latham's?"

"You are very interested in seeing Hamah, aren't you, Jeremiah?"

A sharp feeling struck Jeremiah's heart, as though something sacred had been revealed out of context. His father had seen something on the evening of the *shelamim.*

"We are pleased," Hilkiah said. "Marriage is a sacrament, Jeremiah, the most precious sacrament of our lives."

Jeremiah had not expected this. Even before he could analyze every nuance of his own heart, God had told his father everything, and his father was responding. "We will arrange for Hamah if you desire it. You must be willing to sanctify yourself."

Jeremiah nodded. The room seemed to tip. He hoped he wasn't going to topple off the stool.

"Marriage is the most sacred institution of God. It binds two beings in spirit as well as flesh. Marriage demands focus: prayer, chastity, cleanliness, purity, gentleness, patience. All of the virtues of life are honed in the union of man and woman. From the days of our ancestor Adam, through Noah, through Abraham and Moses, it is obedience to law, both spiritual and civil, that protects the future generations of men. My son, there is nothing better you can do in your life than choose a righteous woman, love her, follow the laws of God, and bear righteous children for the future well-being of the world."

Jeremiah saw his mother at the cooking fire with different eyes that evening—as his father's wife. She looked beautiful in her light yellow *glima,* only wisps of her hair visible through the edges of the *kulna* clasped at the back of her neck. The appeal of her face did not lie in the lines of her cheeks, or the beginning of crow's-feet around her eyes. It was in her smile. While she was intent on her tasks in the kitchen, she held her mouth in a grim line. But when Jeremiah came into the room, she smiled at him. Her eyes glowed. Her face lifted, as though the essence of her very life was enhanced in the presence of her children.

"Can you fetch the milk bucket from the cellar, Jeremiah? We're almost ready to begin," she said.

"Bless us, dear God our Father, with peace. And to bring peace to those whose hearts are buried with the treasures of this world." When he was finished with the prayer, Hilkiah put the cloth in his lap and passed the meat and rice around the circle. "Soon it will be *Lag Ba'Omer*. Jeremiah and I will travel to Cousin Latham in Libnah."

Standing to serve the leeks, Marika smiled. It was obvious that she had talked to Hilkiah. "Good," she said.

Hilkiah nodded. "We'll leave in the morning."

Jeremiah always believed that on this memorable night, he never slept at all. But he must have dozed, for an unfamiliar "Tick, tick," woke him from an anxious dream. It was still dark, though a hem of light in the east crowned the almond trees.

Jeremiah thought he heard stones cracking against one another beneath his window. Rolling from his pallet, he moved quickly to the opening and focused his eyes in the half-light.

"Jeremiah."

In the dark beyond the garden wall Jeremiah could see a head rise above the gate.

"Baruch?"

"Please, it's locked."

Jeremiah hurried for the door and sped over the ground in his bare feet. "What happened?"

Baruch's face looked like paste in the shadows of the olive trees. "They came to kill me."

Jeremiah froze, then swung the gate open to the disheveled Baruch.

"You know my room is isolated in the east wing," Baruch gasped for breath. He had run almost two miles from Jerusalem. "I woke when I heard the dog whine. I saw two black figures climb the garden wall . . . slipped down the hall and out the front door . . . ran here as fast as I could."

"Do you know who they were?"

"I'm not sure," Baruch stammered, "but I think that father and son . . . I think I recognized their voices."

A bobbing light appeared in the passageway. It was Hilkiah, carrying a lantern. "What is going on?" he said, peering from behind the light.

Jeremiah shaded his eyes from the glare. "Baruch believes the murderers remembered him from that night of the *Pesach*. They came for him."

"Perhaps it was robbers," Hilkiah suggested.

Baruch was shaking. "I'm pretty sure it was them," he said.

"Can you tell us what happened?" urged Hilkiah.

Baruch stared ahead, frozen with fear.

"The more we know, the better we can help," said the priest, bringing the lantern closer to Baruch's face. In the light, Baruch's black curls took on an unnatural sheen. Sweat poured down his thick brows and cheeks and through the fuzz of his adolescent beard. His eyes glistened.

"Kamut," Baruch finally said.

"Kamut?" Hilkiah repeated. "One of the chief guards?"

"And his son Pazael." He paused. "They know me. Their servant saw me that night in the street."

Hilkiah cast his eyes to the floor as he often did when he was thinking. "We can't keep him here," he said. "We can take him with us."

Jeremiah started. "On our journey?"

"Yes. Hook up the mules. We'll take him to Libnah. We'll leave now."

"Tonight? Now?"

"There's little time," Hilkiah said, rocking the oil lamp as he walked down the hall. The beams cast eerie patches of shadows on the walls.

By running the animals, they were able to cover over twenty miles by noon. During the long ride, Jeremiah had time to think, to worry that the guards might follow them. Kamut was one of Manasseh's most prominent henchmen. "Kamut, the king's man," he'd heard his father say.

Jeremiah had not yet been to Libnah to Cousin Latham's olive orchards and vineyards. The dawn revealed endless walls, then whitewashed gates shimmering in the sun. The vines surrounding the handsome white-block house were divided by hemp in such straight rows that the field looked like striped silk. Jeremiah could not take his eyes from the land. The property glowed like an emerald. In the dry hills beyond the vineyards, orchards of olive trees stood, their leaves dancing.

Latham's sons, working in the vineyards since early dawn, must have seen the dust on the road, because they had already fetched their father. Latham was at the gate when they arrived, waving both of his heavy arms, his voluminous sleeves whipping in the wind.

"What brings you, my cousin?" When Cousin Latham smiled, his big white teeth looked like small marble stones in the cavern of his mouth.

Knowing Kamut's men might be able to track them, Hilkiah explained their mission quickly and thoroughly. "We don't know if the judges will indict Kamut or if Manasseh will ever know. If the past forty years is any indication, justice in Jerusalem is simply an illusion."

Latham nodded. He joined his hands at the front of his robe and walked slowly toward the house. While Latham and his father talked, Jeremiah cast furtive glances through the courtyard and the hallways. He didn't see any sign of Hamah. However, he could not help but feel she was watching him from somewhere.

As they moved into the cool shade of the rooms, one of Hamah's brothers appeared. Latham beckoned to him. "Take Baruch and Jeremiah to a room in the courtyard. Baruch may stay at our place until he is no longer in trouble," Latham directed.

The brother, Chilian, motioned them toward the back.

In the large inside garden, Jeremiah ducked his head to avoid a cluster of low vines. When he looked up to a second-story apartment covered with gleaming white and gold tile, he saw Hamah smiling at him through a grate. She did not call out to him, or wave. She held the bars of the grate and fixed her gaze upon him as though bestowing a blessing.

Stoically, Jeremiah nodded toward her to acknowledge he had seen her, trying to maintain his dignity while all the time his heart hammered in his ribs.

"Are you coming?" The sound of Chilian's voice startled him. He followed toward the back of a garden flanked by whitewashed storage compartments and rooms on the wall surrounding the quarters. At the eastern end, almost as far as they could go, Chilian unlocked the door to a room with windows high above the outside wall. Shimmering on the floor was a surprising profusion of light.

Chilian said, “It isn’t much, but it’s one of our best for the workers.”

“It’s very nice. I’ll be happy here,” said Baruch. Along one side was a narrow cot, and in the corner was an olive-wood table and stool. “I can write here. I can work here on your father’s document.”

On the way back to the front of the house, Jeremiah saw that Hamah had left her place behind the grated window. When he came into the front rooms, his father and Latham were seated on a long settee upholstered in a shimmering gold cloth. Latham beckoned him forward with his fingers—all five of them weighted with heavy gemstones set in gold rings. “Come here, Jeremiah. I’ve just learned something about you, and I’m very pleased.”

His father said, “Rejoice, Jeremiah. The arrangements have been made.”

Chapter Eight

Marriage

The slaves at Libnah built an arch in the courtyard and laced it with strands of verbena. The fourteen-year-old bride and sixteen-year-old groom would stand under the archway before the priest, Hilkiah, who would give them bread to break and later the richest juice of the grape to drink together through entwined arms.

When Jeremiah saw Hamah dressed in the white robes, he caught his breath. He remembered years ago watching her run along the sand, laughing at the river, her hair flowing behind her in the sun. She had always been lovely. He was filled with a joy he'd never known before.

Long after the wedding celebration was over and most of the family and guests had taken up their tents and slipped away, Jeremiah and Hamah waited to be together for the ten-day waiting period. Family and servants watched with unflagging diligence, assuring themselves that Jeremiah and Hamah could make the most important element of the union work—their friendship. If the verdict was yes, the two would be allowed into their own chambers in a ceremony of fresh linen and sheepskin. Finally, together on the pallet in their room off the courtyard, they would begin their lives.

Except for the menacing dreams that sometimes plagued him, this was the happiest time Jeremiah had ever known: the scent of the olive leaves with the hot sun shining on the branches, the light that shimmered through the trees when he helped the crew gather Latham's harvest into great vats, the weariness of the muscles in his arms and legs after a good day's work. At night there were the delicious suppers prepared by Hamah's mother, Abigail: the lamb dishes, the curry, the sweet basil. Finally there was his precious quiet time with Hamah.

Only on occasion did Jeremiah's dreams resound with the terrible cry of Yoanna's murder. Another dream that terrified him took place on his father's journey to the palace to take Moses's discovered records to the unpredictable king. In that reoccurring dream, people mocked them with vile language and threw stones. The guards took their knives from their belts and crushed the blades against his father's throat. Jeremiah would wake up in a cold sweat.

Jeremiah did not mention these dreams to his father. In the missives he sent to his parents in Anathoth he never brought up the proposed journey to the king. Yet he knew Hilkiah was working diligently on the transcription, doing his best to keep his activities from the jealous priest Shelemaiah.

Away from the demanding work going on in Anathoth, Libnah was like heaven. Miracles happened every day: the evenings in the room with Hamah, the sweet sleeps, and the mornings with unbelievable light trailing through the transom, the sun playing in the lace of the trellis where the leaves shimmered and whispered while he waited for Hamah to waken, her hair lying in dark ribbons on his arm. As she slept, her breath as light as morning, he watched the landscape of her body rise with the life of their child.

Jeremiah and Hamah rejoiced at the birth of "Little Hamah." They called her Hamutal. The tiny hands came perfectly formed, with fingers almost transparent.

"I planted you like a choice vine from the very best seed," Jeremiah whispered in the tiny ear while Hamah watched, totally content. "This is God's child," he said to Hamah.

He held the little head in his hands and lowered his face to her cheeks, breathing in the scent of her new life. When the tiny mouth opened like the mouth of a bird to Hamah's breast, he heard its sound as though it were the most precious of all human music. The light skin seemed so thin, the delicate limbs so fragile, he feared for her vulnerability. In those moments he sometimes suffered the dark flash of Yoanna's death. He saw how easily a blackhearted predator could crush this frail child, but he never let the horrible thought stay. No. It would never be. Jeremiah leaned over the child, praying for her, aching to protect her, understanding the cries of parents everywhere who lost their children in the streets.

Hamutal grew like a little flower. Jeremiah took pleasure during the days, working in the orchards and spending joyful hours with the family and his friend Baruch, who worked tirelessly in his back room copying the precious documents.

Chapter Nine

The King Is Dead

A few years flew by peacefully until a letter from Jeremiah's father in Anathoth sent a ripple through Libnah. King Manasseh had passed away. The words, *the king is dead,* rang like the clang of metal all through Latham's courtyard. Hilkiah's letter asked Baruch and Jeremiah to come to the funeral. But it included another request.

Amon likes to collect old documents, Hilkiah wrote. *This is our time. We will go to the funeral and try to talk to King Amon about the writings. Your mother's cousin Jedidah is now the queen.*

And bring Baruch with you. The king's guards have forgotten that Baruch witnessed any indiscretion. I need Baruch with his perfect hand to help us copy.

Baruch, enjoying his stay at Libnah, still felt nervous about appearing publicly in the city. But Hilkiah's entreaty persuaded him to go back to Jerusalem with Jeremiah. He would be careful to keep his head down, so few would see him.

The moment they entered Jerusalem and tied the mule with the cart at the north gate, Jeremiah sensed how much the city had altered. King Amon had changed many policies. The rabble that previously occupied temple square was now situated outside of the temple walls. Left on their own, they starved, stagnating in the squalor of the surrounding streets. There were no children running and playing. The entire city seemed quiet, as though waiting to die.

"The funeral speeches will praise King Manasseh, but they will seem hollow," Hilkiah said. As they walked through the gates of the courtyard, they could see the stone sarcophagus below the temple porch. Crowds of officers, magistrates, and their attractive wives gathered on the temple square.

Jeremiah added under his breath, *And you will find the new king Amon to be hollow.*

From a distance he recognized Uncle Shallum in conversation with the priest Shelemaiah and his father Hananiah. As Jeremiah struggled through the crowd on the flagstone courtyard, he recognized many of the authorities in attendance. On the raised dais near the pillars that graced the temple entry, sat the famous captain of the militia, the medal-laden Laban, whose feathered, silver headdress sparkled in the sun. Laban was well known as the most honored military man in Manasseh's kingdom. He held his head high, celebrating his importance. Jeremiah recognized him, but not the others who surrounded him.

"Who are the people around Laban?" Jeremiah asked his father.

"The little woman in black is Manasseh's widow." Holding to the side of the coffin, the tiny widow dabbed at her tears with the edge of her head cloth. "Next to her is Amon's cousin from the north, Chief Pedaiah. King Amon appointed him Chief Magistrate. It is rumored that he is the one who is really in charge."

The tall Chief Magistrate, Pedaiah, stood two heads above the little widow. Jeremiah wasn't sure he'd ever seen such a large man, his arms and chest thick, his beard black and coarse, yet his head as bald and slick as a wet stone. On the man's left was a woman of striking, dark beauty. She wore a gold filigree vestment and lumps of turquoise set in claws of silver. Her cascade of thick black curls was loosely tied at the nape of her neck. She clutched the hand of a very pretty little girl who looked lost and unhappy.

"Who is that woman with the sad little girl?"

"Shali, the wife of the large man, the chief magistrate Pedaiah. And that is their little daughter Zebudah."

While the woman named Shali seemed to comfort the widow, the massive Chief Pedaiah scanned the crowd below with a glassy gaze, as though he expected trouble. Over his muscular frame, he wore a robe laced with gold as rich looking as the king's.

"They look foreign," Jeremiah said.

"King Amon's cousin, Chief Pedaiah, is from Rumah, close to the northern border," Hilkiah continued. "His wife Shali's ancestors are from Assyria. The court believes we can have peace with Assyria if this little daughter with Assyrian blood marries Amon's son Josiah, the future king."

The pouting child stood with her head forward like her father's, her shiny black curls hanging in her eyes. An arranged marriage. Jeremiah wondered if this might be why Amon had planned an elaborate funeral that resembled a party more than a religious ceremony. The excessive pots of flowers, the music, Captain Laban's meticulous guard on duty must all have been assembled for the benefit of Chief Pedaiah, whose little daughter was already engaged to the four-year-old Prince Josiah. Jeremiah studied the little girl's doleful black eyes. So this was the little child who would beget the royal line?

When the extravagant ceremonies were over, and the crowds stayed lingering in the courtyard, Jeremiah and Baruch wanted to leave. But Hilkiah had come to speak to the king. The problem was that Amon, surrounded by his guards, was thronged with people. At the moment, he was engrossed in a conversation with Captain Laban and a young couple.

"The king is busy," Baruch murmured, anxious to go.

But Hilkiah hadn't finished his introductions. "That young couple talking to Amon is the prominent gold merchant Lehi and one of your mother's young cousins, Sariah. They're engaged to be married," Hilkiah pointed out. "I have known Lehi's family for many years. They market gold and brass plates."

Queen Jedidah smiled as they walked toward her. "Hilkiah!" she exclaimed. "Did Marika come?"

"Not this time." Hilkiah smiled his regret, nodding graciously. He glanced at her little son standing at attention. "Josiah is a fine boy. It looks as though you've been a successful mother." He paused and glanced Amon's way. "And Amon a successful father as well."

"Yes," she murmured. Her eyes traveled toward her husband, but her smile faded. She left the subject quickly. "I haven't seen Marika since you moved to Anathoth." She peered around to look at the boys. "And how Jeremiah has grown!"

Jeremiah's mother had many cousins, but Jedidah had perhaps been the loveliest of them all. Above her full lips was a perfect nose and a pure white brow graced by a small cowlick that curled upward under the lace of her *glima*. Her rounded cheeks were a soft rose color. The family acknowledged she had a perfect temperament; she had never joined in any mischief making. She had been desired by many men, including Prince Amon.

Amon, the new king, glanced in their direction. He stepped away from Captain Laban and Lehi, pushing his way through the crowd toward them as they stood with his wife Jedidah.

King Amon was not very tall. The dark hair on his neck was thick and curly. He wore huge gems on his fingers and beaten gold rings in his ears. He tilted his head and looked askance when he spoke. "So, Hilkiah! They tell me you have uncovered some old writings in the temple archives."

Aha, Jeremiah thought. It seemed Amon had already heard the news. Perhaps the busybody Shelemaiah had been the one to spread it.

"I was fortunate to find more words of Moses," Hilkiah said. "Very precious. They are being transcribed and copied."

"When you are finished copying those documents you must come and show them to me. I enjoy collecting old writings." Amon smiled. "I have just left a conversation with Captain Laban who also collects genealogies and old writings. His cousin Lehi mentioned that if Laban had any extra documents, he would like them for a wedding present." When he smiled, the narrow slits of his eyes retreated into his sunburned cheeks. "But Laban did not seem eager to part with any of his relics."

"You might be interested in what these particular documents say," offered Hilkiah.

"Finish them. Bring them in. They should amuse me."

Hilkiah answered in a guarded way, "Well, if you are interested."

"Of course, of course."

"I'll bring them soon," said Hilkiah.

Hilkiah was sullen all the way back to Libnah. "I sense he is not interested in reading the messages of the document. It seems all he wants is . . . to be amused."

Yes, that was what mattered to so many: the quest to be amused. Jeremiah prayed they would not pursue Hilkiah's scheme. "I don't think he cares, Father. We probably shouldn't bother him."

Hilkiah must have heard Jeremiah's words. But he was also listening to another's petition. He lowered his tone and spoke slowly, almost through his teeth. "On the contrary. We must not wait. The Lord wants this text to reach the king."

As the cart rumbled toward home, Jeremiah felt the weight of Hilkiah's anxiety hang about them like a heavy cloud. "Before the king forgets, there must be another journey soon," Hilkiah kept repeating. "Soon. Very soon."

Anxious to see Hamah, Jeremiah puzzled over how he would explain to her that he had to turn around and go back to Anathoth again.

He decided to talk about it as soon as he stepped inside the door. "I've already been gone for a long time," he said. "Will you be all right?"

Hamah was quiet when she heard this news, but for only a few moments. After some hesitation, her eyes brightened. She had a solution. "This time I'll go with you. I haven't seen your family in Anathoth for a long time."

Jeremiah pulled back from her. Dazzled by the light in her face, he was hesitant to speak. Yet her proposal unnerved him. "We'll see what happens when the time comes."

But it seemed Hamah had already decided. "The time has come," she laughed. "Please."

Without hesitation, she took Jeremiah by the hand and half-dragging, half-dancing, pulled him to her mother in the garden. Abigail, sitting in her special chair attached to wheels, was playing a peg game with three-year-old Hamutal. At her feet was a servant girl rubbing the mistress's weak legs. The grandmother was intensely involved moving a wooden game piece across the board. Tied to its wire was a bright piece of yellow cloth, like a flag. The child laughed, and from time to time, Abigail leaned her cheek into the curly dark hair, planting kisses.

The sun was particularly bright in the late summer sky. Jeremiah always remembered the way it slanted into the garden that day.

Abigail drew her little granddaughter to her side, looked up at her daughter and son-in-law, and said, "This time will be good for the two of you. I can take care of Hamutal while you are doing the Lord's work."

Chapter Ten

The Green of Her Robe

The task of preparing for their journey together became a time of anticipation and excitement. Jeremiah enjoyed helping Hamah pack. They laughed together when she asked so many questions. And they laughed at his answers. How many of her sandals should she take? "One for each foot." Should she take the red cloak or the green one? "Take the green one," he smiled. "You don't want to call too much attention to yourself."

Finally, with the load packed into the larger cart with two mules, they moved slowly northeast until they were only a few miles from Anathoth. Passing the city of Jerusalem on their right, Jeremiah gazed at the walls of the temple and remembered everything the Lord had told him in the garden that long-ago evening. His heart ached because the city was so beautiful, yet the new king Amon's weak reign seemed to have plunged it into further confusion and disarray.

Approaching the north gate, he thought he could hear a hum of subversive voices. The city seemed to buzz with the murmurs of a *seething pot . . . and weeping . . . of the children of Israel for they have perverted their way, and they have forgotten the Lord their God.*

Again he heard the words from the Lord that had surprised him that special night: *Out of the north evil shall break forth upon all the inhabitants of the land. . . . I will utter my judgments against them for all their wickedness in forsaking; they have burned incense to other gods, and worshipped the works of their own hands.*

Near the end of the tiring journey, with less than a mile to his parents' house, Jeremiah heard a loud crack. Looking back, he saw that the right wheel was wobbling at a sharp angle. Then he heard bolts pulling apart. The wheel looked as though it would buckle. It began to crunch with such a grinding sound that Jeremiah was forced to stop before the cart was torn to pieces. "We are stuck," he said. The wheel had broken in two.

Hamah sighed and clutched her hands together.

The road ahead looked empty and desolate. “I don’t think we ought to leave our cart,” Jeremiah said.

Hamah, resilient as she often was, stood up to look down the road. “Oh, Jeremiah! We are not that far away! You protect the cart. I can run to the house and get help!” Laughing, her eyes bright with excitement, she looked like a lively bird poised to fly. “You protect our goods. I’ll run to fetch your brothers. It’s close, and I haven’t seen your family for so long.” Before Jeremiah could protest, she leaped from the cart and began running toward the farm.

“My brothers will have some tools,” he called after her. “Tell them to bring tools.”

Eager with joy and anticipation, Hamah ran, the green of her robe bright as she flew into the wind. Because of childbirth and nursing, she had not been back to Anathoth for almost three years. It held wonderful memories for her—of her early childhood on the farm, of many family gatherings. It was the home of her favorite cousins as well as of the man she loved.

As he examined the broken wheel, Jeremiah heard the sound of hooves in the distance. Looking back, he saw a small contingency of men drawing a huge wagon covered with cloth. He recognized the breastplates of Manasseh’s guard on one or two of the men on horseback.

He stood beside the wheel as the party of men approached. He recognized Pazael, dressed in military vestment, on one of the front mounts. Kamut’s son Pazael had been present with his father the night Yoanna was killed. Jeremiah was glad that Hamah had left before these men arrived. He turned his back to them and knelt by the wheel, pretending to repair one of the broken bolts. The guard walking near the wagon came to him and asked if they could help. Jeremiah said he was within a mile of his house, and if he couldn’t fix the wheel, he could drag the cart to his yard.

When the party passed, he looked toward the house hoping Hamah had made it safely. He pictured seeing her again in the distance, the shimmer of her dark hair blowing in the wind.

Anxious to move, he kicked the wood of the wheel until the two pieces fell apart. He prodded the mules. Without the weight of its human travelers, the wagon could be dragged slowly behind the animals toward Anathoth. He expected to see Hamah at any moment after he turned the corner.

When he reached the stoop, his mother rejoiced to see him. "We had a message that Hamah was coming. Didn't she come?"

Jeremiah pulled back from his mother's embrace. "Hamah? Hasn't she been to the house?"

Marika looked surprised. "No." She paused. "I have been alone in the house with the girls."

When Jeremiah did not say anything, he saw a questioning look of astonishment cross her face.

"No, Hamah has not come."

"Oh, God of Abraham." Jeremiah lowered his head. This moment loomed in his mind with a clarity that frightened him every time it crept into his consciousness. "Oh, dear God, what has happened to my Hamah?" He asked the question, though in his heart he knew. He walked around the yard. He called. There was no response.

Barely moving, his eyes white circles of pain, Jeremiah stood by his father, Hilkiah, while the archivists gathered the guards of Anathoth to search. Jeremiah would search. But he knew. As the officers of the king arrived from their post in Anathoth, they looked like gilded birds, their legs clanking with silver. They carried swords and spears as though outfitted for battle. Some of the faces he saw were from the group that had passed him on the road. He recognized several of Pazael's cousins.

Jeremiah cast an oblique look in their direction. He rode with them on horseback through the streets crying out her name. "Hamah! Hamah!" He heard nothing from Pazael or his cousins, or from the other guards—a silence that weighed in Jeremiah's heart like a stone. He wished he had let them steal the goods in the cart rather than that which was most precious to him.

For days, for weeks there was nothing. Jeremiah guessed what had happened to her. But who would help him? In all the moments of his anguish, there was no one he could trust in Jerusalem. It seemed there were only lies to cover the rapes, the kidnappings, and the murders. There was wickedness and heartbreak, and the judges had let it all go. He carried a weight in his heart that cried out to his God and berated the terror of the entire world.

Jeremiah never forgot that instant when he saw Hamah turn out of sight at the bend in the road. That was the memory that came to haunt him more than any other. The movement of the cloth was what he remembered most. It billowed in the breeze like a sail at sea, full and beautiful above the stream of her rippling hair.

Chapter Eleven

Hinnom Valley

The letter they received from Latham was short and desolate. Uncle Latham begged Jeremiah to come back to Libnah to be with his small daughter. And further, he added a rumor that had been floating on the fringes of their lives for several years—that, adding to the burdensome tribute Jerusalem had been paying to Egypt, they would likely be paying more heavy taxes to the insatiable Assyrians soon. Nothing had stopped their aggressive schemes.

There are rumors of widespread violence. You don't want to be in Jerusalem, Jeremiah. Your daughter has but one parent now. When you finish taking the records to the king, please come home.

But Hilkiah had his own agenda. He begged his son to stay in Anathoth. "Do not leave, Jeremiah," he entreated. "Amon will read God's words soon."

Reluctantly, Jeremiah promised his father he would stay, even though his heart was not in the work. Often he bent over the transcriptions, feeling unable to write.

But even the torment of tragedy didn't last forever. He found, after a time, that it was the work itself, the documents that began to heal him. As he read God's words, the once-hidden writings began to unveil revelations to him. The repetition brought a familiar voice from the depths of his sorrow to his ears, a voice he had not heard since that dawn in the garden years ago. He knew who it was. Soon he found himself leaning over the old documents, dropping his head, squeezing his eyes shut so the tears would not blur the ink. And he began to write his own words that came to him—his anger and frustration flowing across the page. He had avoided his calling. Long before, God had wanted him to speak, and still he had not spoken.

O Lord, behold my affliction. . . . Look and see if there is any sorrow like my sorrow which was brought upon me. . . . The Lord has trodden as in a wine press the virgin daughter of Judah.

Sometimes he could not see the marks of his stylus. All he could do was cry out to God with his heavy heart. When his eyes were too cloudy, he asked Baruch to write the words for him. Slowly he gathered courage. His heart changed. Simmering with anger, his timidity vaporized like dew. He began to understand his father's yearnings to challenge the kingdom. He believed that someday he might send these words of the Lord to the king.

Jerusalem has become a filthy thing. . . . The enemy has stretched out his hands over all her precious things.

"These are strong words," Baruch said to him. But Jeremiah continued to ask Baruch to write them nevertheless.

When Hilkiah saw them, he lowered his head and looked aside.

A lion has gone up from his thicket, a destroyer of nations has set out; he has gone forth from his place to make your land a waste, and your cities will be ruins without inhabitant.

Hilkiah hesitated. "I'm not sure . . . You want to show this to the king?"

"He must know the people are behaving sinfully. They don't know what God requires."

"I think they know." Hilkiah kept his eyes lowered. He spoke with emotion. "I believe they have just chosen to turn away. They have chosen it."

The words were sharp. *When I fed them to the full, they committed adultery, and trooped to the houses of harlots. . . . The people of Israel and Judah have betrayed me completely.*

Hilkiah choked on these words. "The king himself is guilty."

Jeremiah raised his hands and pressed them against his temples while Hilkiah continued in his gentle voice. "They spend their desires rashly. Instead of working to achieve ecstasy in God's way, they focus on relieving their needs, consuming them upon one another, turning to the same gender, or to children, or even animals. They are delighted to laugh at God's laws."

"Is it possible that not even Moses's words will convince them of the truth?"

Hilkiah paused, his eyes downcast. "Words persuade only if the heart listens."

Though there was still work left to be done, Hilkiah decided that they must show the document to the king, even in its half-completed form. He brought the mules and cart out at four-thirty in the morning while Jeremiah and Baruch prepared the animals and packed the provisions. They wrapped the document in linen and placed it on the floor of the cart. As the light from the east began to gild the sky, they watched carefully to see that Shelemaiah was not anywhere about. No one appeared until just as they were about to pull away. Suddenly a flame on the morning candle in Shelemaiah's window began to flicker and burn. When they glanced back, they could see the taskmaster standing in the road. He was coughing into his red kerchief, looking puzzled and irritated, tugging at his night-cap and mouthing words no one would hear.

There was not much conversation on the road to the city. As the mules slowly dragged the three of them across the desert, they had plenty of time to question the wisdom of their undertaking. As they approached southwestward toward their destination, they remarked on the astonishing beauty of the temple that loomed above the rosy walls.

"A beautiful city—to turn so evil they need such a grim warning," Hilkiah said.

As they neared the walls, they could see small groups of people milling about the marketplace at the gate. Standing a little apart from the vendors who were hawking food and pottery, small groups were listening to the words of different speakers poised on stone benches, or wooden platforms, waving their arms, pointing with warning gestures.

"It's important to know which men are true prophets," Hilkiah said as the cart drew close to the gate. "Some, like Shelemaiah's father, Hananiah, only say what pleases the crowds."

As they passed the guards of the marketplace, Baruch pulled his hood over his mouth. Even though it had been almost six years since the two of them witnessed Yoanna's murder on the eve of the *Pesach*, he was still wary.

Two men were engaged in a lively dialogue. The small man, whose voice rang out over the heads of the onlookers, wore a rough woven cloth over his wiry brown hair. The other was a young man with a lean, rugged look on his face. He seemed to be fielding questions to the smaller man. The crowd seemed spellbound by what they were hearing.

When the two men turned, Jeremiah caught a glimpse of their faces. At once he recognized his father's acquaintance, the well-dressed merchant Lehi, who reproduced writings in precious metal. The gold in his cloak glittered in the sun.

Though Baruch seemed anxious to move on, Hilkiah stopped the cart for a moment and nodded toward the noted merchant. "Ah, it's Lehi," he said. "My friend whose family engraves metal. He might rejoice to know I have found this manuscript. Perhaps someday it will be carved in brass or gold."

"He can read it when the king publishes it," Baruch said. "We shouldn't tarry."

"But if we were to enlist the support of Lehi? He has a great deal of influence with the king."

Jeremiah clutched the side of the cart. "Father, we might be too late already. The king is busy. Perhaps he has forgotten he asked to see the writings. Or he has changed his mind."

Hilkiah paused and leveled a firm look at his son. "I know. I know that, Jeremiah. But the king's guards are not here. I am curious. When Lehi marries your mother's cousin Sariah he will be related to us."

At that moment the gold merchant, Lehi, turned to glance at Hilkiah. His eyes flashed with recognition, and he stepped down from the platform. As Lehi walked toward them, Jeremiah scrutinized his face. He wore a tight thick mustache and beard. A thread in the striped silk that wrapped his brow glittered with the same gold thread of his cloak. He smiled as he walked forward. When he drew close, he raised his hand in greeting.

"Hilkiah, my father's good friend. It's been almost a year since I saw you. I'm glad to see you."

Hilkiah hesitated.

"You came just in time to help Ezekiel convince these people . . ."

"Go ahead, Father, if you must," said Jeremiah. "Tell him about the writings."

They stopped the cart near the vendors at the wall. The tables were loaded with dried gourds and large yellow squashes.

As Hilkiah, Baruch, and Jeremiah climbed out of the cart, one of the vendors beckoned to them and offered up a few handfuls of berries. Others stepped forward with colorful produce for sale: bright red radishes, roots of field lilies, chives, and cabbages.

The young merchant Lehi smiled. His rugged face was sun darkened; his lips parted on gleaming white teeth. "A man of God has come among us," he shouted to those gathered at the gate. He pressed Hilkiah's hand. "My good man, help Ezekiel to convince these people to obey the law—that obedience is the only way to safety."

"I too desire to return to God's word," agreed Hilkiah.

"There are so many words God has given us," said Lehi. "What we need now is to read them and follow them. We have forgotten so much."

Lehi turned to the man who stood behind him. "Isn't it true, Ezekiel? Not even twenty years passed before the children of Israel forgot that it was God who saved them."

Ezekiel gave a slight nod.

"This is my friend, the prophet Ezekiel," Lehi continued. "He has convinced me we must feed the flocks of Israel."

Jeremiah thought the prophet Ezekiel had a startled, haunted look, his face half hidden under a blue cloth bound by a leather tie.

Hilkiah acknowledged the wiry man whose eyes seemed like two small fires. "Yes, I believe I have heard of you, Ezekiel. I am grateful to meet you."

"Hilkiah from Anathoth?" Ezekiel's voice was as piercing as his eyes.

"Yes, Hilkiah from Anathoth," Lehi repeated. "His son, Jeremiah, and his scribe, Baruch. Do you know them?"

"Yes," Ezekiel said. "I have heard of a deed done to the family of Hilkiah." For a moment Ezekiel lowered his eyes to the ground, and the sun seemed to darken, shaded by clouds over the walls of the city. The small man paused as he gazed at Hilkiah. "Are you . . . ," he began. "Are you missing a daughter?"

Jeremiah's heart leaped.

"Yes," Hilkiah said. "A daughter-in-law. How did you know?"

"There was talk," Ezekiel said. "I overheard a rumor that they took the daughter-in-law of Hilkiah to the Valley of Hinnom."

The refuse yard of Jerusalem! Jeremiah froze. How many times had he wondered, yearned, for some final knowledge? Thousands of times. He turned to his father. Hilkiah's face was as white as a stone.

"I must go," Jeremiah said.

"We will go with you. We'll take you in the cart." Hilkiah did not look at Jeremiah. "King Amon . . . the transcript . . . ," he began. "That is something we can do later."

On their way south to the Hinnom Valley none of them spoke. Along the west wall of the city different groups of slaves were moving stones over the rough ground, erecting scaffoldings to repair the walls King Manasseh had allowed to deteriorate. Some of the workers, shading their eyes from the sinking sun, stopped to look at the travelers.

As the hot sun slipped into the western hills, they reached the valley and stopped at the top of the incline. Climbing out of the cart onto the dusty rim, they peered into the deep ravine. A sudden rush of wings surprised them—a flock of angry birds screeching and scolding as they flapped their wings and batted the air overhead. Below, steep trails led into the dark gully. Jeremiah leveled a stern look into his father's eyes. "Please, Father," he said. "Let me go alone. Baruch, stay with my father."

With the trees and brush clawing at his feet, Jeremiah lowered himself slowly down the steep incline to the gully. The stench overwhelmed his nostrils and rose with a force that robbed him of breath. He choked, feeling dizzy and weak from the poison in the air. Below him was a vast sea of mud and protruding bones, tangled in a reeking mass resembling an odorous soup. He prayed for God to sustain him as he searched for the information he sought. He hoped to discover Hamah—even in this desolation. He must have faith to move forward.

The grasp of the rancid waste seized his sandals. He removed his shoes and carried them tucked in his cloak. The vile mud sucked at his heels.

The valley was so dark and protected from the sun that the terraces above him, crowded with green trees and lush growth, seemed to lean into the center like gathering spirits mocking him. The trees seemed alive, as though to say: "We grow from the dead—from human flesh."

"God, please help me," Jeremiah said. "God of Abraham, who led our people out of Egypt, please I beg of you. If there is some way you might show me where she is, please show me. You called me to speak for you when I was a boy, and though I have not yet obeyed that call, I am writing the words you give to me." He lowered his head into his arm. "Oh, God, my heart is heavy. If you will show me what I seek, I promise that someday, when the time is right, your words will get to the people."

Raising his eyes in the glut of decay gnawed by vultures, he spotted movement. In a slight wind against one beam of direct sunlight, he saw the edge of something green. As he drew closer, he saw that it was the cloak—the beautiful wool carded and spun by her mother. He pulled at it. The corner of the garment would not come loose. He leaned over into the sludge of bones and wept.

Chapter Twelve

Murder

Jeremiah returned to Libnah.

His mother wrote to him that his father was ill. Hilkiah continued to feel the pressure of the city's wickedness and of his failure to reach the king. In her letter, his mother also wrote that the family would be coming to Libnah for Passover.

Jeremiah walked with Hamutal around Latham's compound, holding fast to her little hand. They threw leftover food to the dogs, and he pointed out how the sun shimmered in the olive leaves and shone through the twigs of old birds' nests. He told her that her grandparents were coming for a visit.

At the celebration on the night before Passover, Bethany sang for them. She had written melodies to some poetry she loved. "There is in our city a prophet by the name of Nahum," she told them. "He writes beautiful poetry, and I have put some of the verses to music."

When she began to sing, the pure sounds of her lute hung like birdsong above the courtyard. *The Lord is good, a stronghold in the day of trouble,* she sang. *He knows those who take refuge in him.*

Jeremiah leaned over and closed his eyes. He could have listened to her voice for hours. Like the pure tone of reed pipes, her voice was unwavering. *The Lord is slow to anger, and of great might, and the Lord will by no means clear the guilty. His way is in whirlwind and storm, and the clouds are the dust of His feet.*

The Lord will by no means clear the guilty. Jeremiah leaned over Hamutal, who sat curled in his lap. He breathed in the freshness of her hair. If he had the gift to write such beautiful poetry as this, he would sing God's praises and warn the people in glorious songs.

For while they be folded together as thorns, and while they are drunken as drunkards, they shall be devoured as stubble fully dry.

Hilkiah turned his chair from his place at the table. "That was beautiful, my child," he said, "and strikes fear into our very hearts. For all of us are wondering what will happen now with Amon as king."

Bethany's husband, Beriah, the manager of the palace, took his wife's hand. "Now that Amon is king, we should pray for him."

"Yes," said Hilkiah. "We must have faith. Soon Jeremiah will go back with me to take the records to him. We will pray for King Amon, that he will read them and take them to heart."

For Jeremiah, the journey with the documents came much too soon. Again, they were careful to begin loading the cart in the early dawn. Yet again, the light in Shelemaiah's window burned before they were ready to go, and this time he came out to them, hiding his face behind his nose rag.

"Hilkiah, what are you doing? Are you going somewhere with these papyri?"

Hilkiah said, "I am taking my son, my granddaughter, and my scribe to Jerusalem." Little Hamutal, along for the ride, clutched Jeremiah's robe.

Shelemaiah gazed intensely into Hilkiah's face. "If you were open about it, I would not ask questions."

"I am taking copies of some documents to the archives in Jerusalem, that's all."

Shelemaiah kept the thin line of his mouth shut.

Jeremiah, Baruch, and Hilkiah continued to pack the cart as though loading it up was as natural as breathing.

"Shelemaiah wants control," Hilkiah said. "He's like his father Hananiah. If he can't be called to be a prophet, he will call himself a prophet. I do not trust him." He finished placing the layers of copied documents in neat arrangements in the bottom of the flat leather box. "I suppose there is a use for such people. They keep us alert."

When the cart was fully packed, Jeremiah placed Hamutal high on one of the portfolios. Just as they brought the final documents through the door of the archives, they met Shelemaiah's son Irijah running breathlessly up the steps. The sweat from his brow pasted his hair in curls against his cheek.

"Oh, spare us this curse!" Irijah was shaking. Although more than twenty years old now, he still seemed boyish, the frail bones of his shoulders protruding in knobs. His thin arms waved like straws in the wind. "He's dead!"

Shelemaiah stood in the entry of the Anathoth archives watching Hilkiah and Jeremiah. He peered with concern at his son running toward them. He descended the steps, his robes bouncing. "What is it, my boy? Who's dead?"

"Amon, the new king, is dead. He has been murdered! They say it is Kamut and Pazael. A coup."

The heat in the air suddenly closed down upon all of them. In the quiet, the atmosphere seemed dense. Irijah continued, "No judge dares to touch Kamut and Pazael, and now they may have control of the military. Their men are stationed around the palace. There is no king now except Amon's little boy Josiah. No one except little Josiah."

"An eight-year-old king," Hilkiah said, stroking the leather portfolio. "Kamut and Pazael. I would not put it past them. We cannot take the documents to Jerusalem now."

A wave of shock and mourning shuddered through the city.

On a hot clear day in August, the sun so high that it seemed to burn a hole in the heavens, the crowds outside the court building jostled with one another for position, each onlooker craning to see above another's head.

At first, all the mob could see was a row of stiff officials standing like drowsy crows in their black robes on both sides of the archway. Shaphan, the new court secretary, had been chosen to present the verdict. This man of sense had been the one to convince the court they ought to conduct a proper trial of Kamut and Pazael. A farmer, Shaphan had spent most of his years in an obscure village nearby. His fairness and leadership ability had elevated him to the position of court secretary. The crowd hushed in anticipation of his appearance at the podium.

On this day of indictment, Beriah, Hilkiah, Jeremiah, and Baruch decided to watch from the archives in the upper room of the palace compound. Little Hamutal stood at the window, barely peering over the sill. A light breeze blew into the room.

Finally Shaphan strode forward, his long legs tangling his cloak. In his right hand he held the rod with the gold serpent. He raised it high in the air. "Guilty!" he cried out. The mobs cheered. Jeremiah prayed that this act of justice might be followed by others.

Because they didn't want Hamutal to see the actual execution on the following day, Jeremiah and Hilkiah arrived late to the palace. They hurried through the noisy crowds. Hamutal became curious when they climbed the stone stairway into the high chambers and saw the halls hung with colorful tapestries of red and yellow.

"They are flying flags in honor of Josiah, the new king," Jeremiah explained to his daughter.

One of the slave girls led them to the royal nursery door, leaned into the room, and beckoned to Jedidah.

Queen Jedidah dried her white cheeks with the back of her hand. "Oh, dear cousins," she exclaimed. "They stabbed him in cold blood!" Hilkiah put his arm around her shoulders, and she raised her eyes to him. "Amon was trying to make things right," she said. "Please don't misjudge him."

Light from the large windows at the back of the room laid huge bright patches of yellow on the plank floor. Scattered on the woven rugs and tables were toys: balls, games, twigs, and small bits of wood carved into tiny puzzles. Hamutal examined it all with a look of wonder.

Eight-year-old Josiah came running across the toy-littered floor to Hamutal. He stopped very close to her and gazed into her face. "Do you want to see a wooden horse?"

Hamutal hesitated and turned to her father for permission. When Jeremiah smiled and nodded, she broke away from him and followed Josiah to a brightly decorated rocking horse carved of cherrywood. The sun sparkled in the beaded tassels blazing with bits of gold and silver.

As the children left, Hilkiah turned to Queen Jedidah and said, "Your son is . . . do you remember Isaiah promised us a righteous king?"

Queen Jedidah looked at him with surprise through her tears. Her hair had been drawn tightly to the nape of her neck so that it pulled at her brows.

Hilkiah leaned forward. "Could Josiah be the one?" he asked the queen. "We'll petition the ministers to bring him to the temple. If you'll help us, we can educate Josiah in the ways that matter."

"But I fear the new chief magistrate, Pedaiah," Jedidah said. "You remember—the one whose daughter Zebudah is to marry Josiah?"

Hilkiah nodded gravely. "You mustn't worry about the officials just now. Surely they will be looking for some stability in this chaos. Perhaps you can help to win Chief Pedaiah's favor—convince him it'll be all right for the boy to receive some instruction from a scribe in the temple archives. I'll come to the palace with scrolls and writing tools. The little king must learn to read, and Jeremiah and I can teach him."

Josiah was happily showing Hamutal his exquisite wooden horse. He put his foot into the stirrup and leaped into the saddle. Hamutal stood beside him. He showed her how to rock the dazzling beast.

Hilkiah scrutinized the pair's preoccupation with one another. Turning to Jeremiah, he murmured, "Perhaps you are thinking what I am thinking?"

Jeremiah nodded.

"Of course . . . the little king has already been contracted to Chief Pedaiah's daughter, Zebudah of Rumah," Hilkiah said.

Jeremiah watched the boy place a piece of honey candy in Hamutal's tiny hand.

Later, driving the cart away from the palace, Jeremiah looked back at the walls as though trying to memorize them. There was a history told here in the layers of mortar and stone—a story of the struggle to design God's kingdom on earth, the quest to protect themselves and their posterity.

"I saw the gold horse," Hamutal babbled, sitting on her father's lap. "Josiah is the king. He said he is the king. He gave me pieces of honey. See?" She still had a piece of the honey candy clutched in her fist. "I played with Josiah, the king. I rode the gold horse. Did you see me ride the gold horse, Father?"

"I did," Jeremiah said into her dark curls. "Did you like the palace?"

"Yes, I liked the horse. I liked the sun on the floor."

Hilkiah leaned back from the reins, turning slightly to talk to his granddaughter. "How would you like to go there every day?"

"To see the king?" she asked.

"Yes, to learn from writings. To learn many things."

She paused and said, “Yes, if Josiah will teach me to ride the gold horse.”

“I’m sure he will,” Jeremiah said.

Chapter Thirteen

Eight-Year-Old King

An eight-year-old king. With a child on the throne, the court flew into chaos.

Scuttling for positions of power, those most responsible for public affairs, such as Chief Magistrate Pedaiah and his first assistant, Pashur, paid little heed to Hilkiah, who brought his family members to the palace daily to visit the young king.

The guards knew that Marika was Queen Jedidah's cousin and at first allowed her, with her husband Hilkiah, son Jeremiah, and the little Hamutal, into the nursery. But one day Chief Magistrate Pedaiah, father of the future princess, met the family at the gate.

"The members of the council noticed you have been coming to the nursery," he said. Chief Pedaiah was a huge, imposing man—with that extra large bald head angled slightly forward, giving him the appearance of an angry bull. His large body, decked out in striped silk and tassels, completely blocked the doorway. "We appreciate your concern over your little cousin's education," he continued. His deep voice rumbled around in his chest. "But there are certain things a king must be taught besides scriptures and history."

Hilkiah acknowledged Chief Pedaiah with a nod. "We understand that, Chief Pedaiah," he said. "I am certain those other studies will be taught by others in the court."

Still, Chief Pedaiah stood in the doorway, as though expecting them to produce a ticket for entry. "You needn't come again. The council is seeing to his education."

Hilkiah said, "You wouldn't want to neglect his education in God's ways." He paused. "It is my feeling, Chief Pedaiah, that this child may be the king we have been waiting for."

Chief Pedaiah was not illiterate. He, like most of the councilors, had probably read Isaiah. He looked past the family into the courtyard, as if pondering Hilkiah's words. He understood the scriptures.

"It cannot harm him to know of God's part in the history of Judah," Hilkiah continued. "That is what we are teaching him. If he knows the history of the kings, he may not make their mistakes."

Chief Pedaiah turned slightly at this speech. And as he moved, the little girl, Hamutal, rushed past his big legs into the stairwell.

"Hamutal," Marika called out.

In her eagerness, Hamutal climbed to the top of the stairs.

Chief Pedaiah stepped slightly away from the entry to look toward Hamutal. As he did so, Hilkiah, Jeremiah, and Marika slipped into the hallway and followed Hamutal up the stairs to the nursery. Chief Pedaiah was too large to move quickly enough to stop them.

Young Josiah greeted them with a sword in his hand, a long roll of paper folded together in the shape of a knife. He thrust it toward Hamutal as she slipped through the door. "I am a king," he shouted. "My father was a king. I must kill anyone who does not obey the king."

Jeremiah drew the boy aside and unfolded the paper knife. It was one of the pages they had prepared so that Josiah might study the alphabet. Josiah protested angrily, and Jeremiah quickly folded it back up and gave it to him.

Jedidah came up timidly behind her son. "Some of the council members have been here," she said. "Today they spent an hour teaching him to fight. There was nothing I could do."

Marika put her arm around her cousin's shoulders. "You did right to let them."

Submissive and cooperative, Jedidah was certainly a different mother from the questionable queens that graced Israel's history. Athaliah, who had ruled three or four generations earlier, had created chaos. When her father and mother, the wicked Ahab and Jezebel, were killed, she secured her eldest son Ahaziah's post by murdering everyone in line who might take his place. When someone killed that son she took the throne herself. To protect her appointment, she had all of her relatives murdered, even her own children. She would have killed her smallest baby, Joash, if his aunt and the priest hadn't hidden and protected him in the palace. Joash grew to be a good king who saved them all. This was what Hilkiah's family hoped for Josiah.

"You are the king," Hilkiah said, kneeling down beside the boy. "And yes, kings must learn to fight. But . . ."

"Chief Pedaiah and that other governor say that I must learn to use a sharp sword."

"Yes, that is fine. That is something you should do. However, a king does many things besides fight."

"What things?"

Hilkiah lowered his voice and held the boy's hand. "Oh, many things. He speaks to the people. He spends the money wisely. He encourages people to work hard, to learn to be frugal and virtuous. He's honest and kind—though he must sometimes be firm. You may become a great leader. What kind of a leader you are depends upon how well you've read and followed God's commandments."

"Hilkiah speaks truly," Jeremiah affirmed. "You must learn all you can about our people. About Adam, Noah, and Moses. And King David. All of us are related, you know. We are all one people. When Moses brought the people of Israel back to this land they found the people of Esau, Jacob's brother. We are also related to them. We are brothers and sisters. We go back thousands of years together, all of us. If you can understand who you are and honor your heritage, you will become very wise, and you will be a great king."

The boy had put down the sword and stood wide-eyed. "Can I ride the horses?" he asked. "Can Hamutal go with me to ride the horses?"

"As soon as we finish our lessons," Hilkiah told him. He guided the boy to his letters.

By the time the afternoon sun stood high and hot in the cloudless sky, Hilkiah was ready to go to the temple archives, but the children were still in jovial spirits. Jeremiah took them down to the stable at the end of the palace wall. While the horses stamped their feet in the dust and swept one another with their tails, Josiah rushed forward into the stalls, pulled the stool out and reached high for the flat blanket saddle and leather reins. Though the rising dust choked them, both children were excited about riding. Jeremiah took the two gentlest horses into the corral, saddled them, and lifted each child onto a horse. They rode in tame circles behind the fence, whooping with excitement. Josiah swung the ends of the reins in the air while Hamutal patted her horse's neck.

Jeremiah stood close by to protect his precious charges, while three or four of the palace slaves who worked in the sheds watched from under the leaning roofs. For a while Jeremiah did not notice the shadows moving across the yard, but when he turned slightly, he saw the silhouettes of two large men and a small child. One of the tall ones was Chief Magistrate Pedaiah, holding the hand of the beautiful girl with dark, shiny black curls—his daughter Zebudah. The other man was his assistant, Governor Pashur, whose furtive look seemed to measure everyone who came before him.

"We need to speak to you, Jeremiah." Governor Pashur glared out of the corners of his eyes. "Chief Pedaiah wishes to include Zebudah in the studies you are conducting." He glanced toward the children on horses. "Is this part of the study?"

"You could say it is," Jeremiah said. "And Zebudah is welcome."

The two officials nodded to one another while Jeremiah beckoned for the children to stop riding. He took the horses by their leather ropes and curled the ends around the top bar of the fence. Josiah and Hamutal stayed mounted

"Children, this is Zebudah of Rumah. Her father has brought her to the palace to join our studies."

"Hello, Zebudah," Josiah said. "Get on a horse and follow us around."

Zebudah hesitated. "I'm not getting up there," she said, holding to the edge of her father's cloak.

"Get the children off the horses and bring them to the nursery," Governor Pashur said. "We'll begin the history lessons this afternoon."

The children dismounted and followed Jeremiah and the other adults to the nursery, where the slaves set up a small table, placed flat bread on earthen plates, and poured goat's milk in small vessels. The little ones ate in relative silence, Zebudah looking askance at the children from under her dark curls.

"Don't you ride horses in Rumah?" Josiah asked Zebudah.

"No," Zebudah said. "I don't see how Hamutal can get up on one of those ugly animals. The horses can throw you and break your back."

"I love horses," Hamutal whispered almost inaudibly over her bowl of milk.

"Well, don't expect me to love horses." Zebudah retorted. "And if you keep making that sound slurping your milk, Hamutal, I'll go crazy."

When the meal ended and the lessons were to begin, Zebudah would not sit on the rag rug with the other children. She walked back to the window and pulled on the curtain, then sat on the table and rocked her legs back and forth. After a short time she said, "I heard this before." The others stared at her. "I'll get my father to take me home."

"Don't you want to hear about Moses bringing Jacob's family back from Egypt?"

"Moses and Jacob were supposed to be good," she scowled. "But then Joshua killed all the people on their way back to Jerusalem. My mother says her ancestors were slaughtered. Moses's people even killed the animals so nobody else could have them."

Jeremiah said, "You're right, Zebudah. It was wrong for Jacob and Esau to hate one another. They were brothers. Brothers and cousins should be kind to each other. Now Esau's family in Assyria wants to capture all of us here in Jerusalem. They want to come down and hurt us."

"Well, let them do it!" Zebudah wrinkled her nose. "Jerusalem is a wicked old place."

Jeremiah bit his tongue. "Will you be living in the palace, Zebudah?"

"We're going home now," she said. "I'm going back to Rumah to see my mother."

Chapter Fourteen

Lehi's Wedding

They did not see Zebudah until three years later when Josiah was almost twelve years old. It was the day of Lehi and Sariah's wedding.

Jeremiah avoided weddings if he could. Such events sharpened the tortured memories of his only love and its loss. Yet he knew he could not miss Lehi and Sariah's long-anticipated ceremony. Sariah was a cousin, so the entire family would be going. And the bride and groom had made a special point of asking Hamutal and Josiah to help carry flowers.

Hamutal was excited. Jeremiah would not disappoint her, although the event—to be held at the lavish estate of Lehi's kinsman, Captain Laban—might expose her to some of Jerusalem's debauchery. There were rumors that this household tolerated questionable behavior among the many wives and concubines who practiced pagan worship.

But it was decided that if both children stayed close to the family, attending would entail little risk, even for Josiah. Ever since King Amon's murder, Queen Jedidah had been very protective of her little king, seldom taking him out in public. Rumors of assassinations and murders continued to circulate among opposing factions. Still, the queen knew how much Josiah wanted to go. Because someone might recognize them, she wore a scarf over her face in disguise.

The family approached an inside gate. Laban's slave, Zoram, unlocked it. Bowing low as the crowd pressed up to him, the servant lifted the bulky lock, and thrust his shoulder against the blackened metal bars. Inside the courtyard there was a wash of color, and a spring fragrance in the air.

Jeremiah hurried the children past the obscene sculptures in the garden. But he needn't have worried. Hamutal was clapping with excitement at the yellow daffodils. Everything seemed to be in bloom:

fruit trees, hedges, flowers. The pathway to the main house led through rows of olive trees along retaining walls of polished stones with inlaid gems, strewn with spring seeds and the petals of white blossoms. They passed rows of yew, small shrubs of pine, and golden branches of forsythia laced with vines.

The main entrance to the house—a huge stone archway—opened up to a massive hall of polished marble. At the end of the hall, high windows looked out upon an astonishing garden. The carefully polished floor reflected the furnishings like a mirror. It seemed each potted plant, each chair, had been carefully placed to create an artistic effect.

Captain Laban was nowhere to be seen. Several women wearing bright-colored clothing and painted eyes stood about, bowing graciously to the guests. These women were Laban's wives and concubines.

In the center of the huge hall stood the bride and groom dressed in white linens, smiling and shaking hands. They looked radiant against the sparkling light of the windows overlooking the garden. Marika ran to her cousin Sariah and embraced her fervently. The groom, Lehi, his fingers laden with silver and gold, his tunic studded with rubies and gems, stood near his betrothed. He turned to her often with a tender smile.

Lehi extended a warm invitation to Hilkiah's family. "The ceremony will take place soon. In the meantime, please come in for some refreshment."

After the numerous guests were seated, slave girls brought trays laden with fruit wrapped in banana leaves. One of the girls bowed low to Hilkiah and said, "The master Laban apologizes. He is delayed."

While they waited, Jeremiah let Josiah take Hamutal by the hand and walk around the huge room to see the massive heads of rare animals on the walls.

"He is in a conference with men who want to talk about the threats from Assyria," Lehi offered as though it were something that happened every day.

Jeremiah stared at him. "There's someone here from Assyria?"

Lehi looked intensely at Jeremiah. "You didn't know this?"

"No,"

Jeremiah said. "What is happening?"

"They are negotiating—discussing the treacherous design of the Assyrians for the throne."

A disturbance in the hall hushed everyone. Reba, Laban's head wife, began passing baskets of white verbena to the children. In her booming voice of authority, she ordered them into the center of the room to form a half circle facing the dais. Dressed in scarlet, she wore at the back of her neck a thick black braid laced with pearls. Picking at children's clothes and giving them small sharp words of instruction, she said to the party, "Laban is busy. He will be here later."

When the musicians arrived, Reba ordered the proceedings to begin. As the priests raised the canopy, Sariah and Lehi stood with their backs to the garden, their faces flushed and beaming as Hilkiah pronounced the blessings of the sacred text upon them.

Laban never once showed his face for the wedding, so Reba took control of the festivities. Sariah and Lehi were surrounded by guests who planted kisses on their cheeks and presented them with lavish gifts.

The sun dipped behind the trees in the garden and shone through the central atrium, where palm trees stood silhouetted in fierce rays of gold. The dancing ended, and most of the guests left for their homes. The first wife, Reba, hurried forward, slapping her loose silver slippers along the bright floor.

The servant Zoram came to meet her from the hallway. "He's coming, my lady."

To the remaining members of the wedding party, Reba said, "Finally Laban is coming down. We hope it wasn't inconvenient for you to wait."

From the hallway came Chief Pedaiah, his beautiful daughter Zebudah, and other members of his family. Behind them came a swarthy man in a tall silk turban—Nabapolassor, the Assyrian ambassador from Babylon.

Zebudah, her perfect face glowing as white as the petal of a flower, glanced coyly at Josiah, who stood beside Jeremiah. She was thirteen years old, her visibly budding figure revealed beneath the silk burgundy cloak.

"I'm sorry my husband missed the wedding," Reba chattered to the guests who were leaving. She leaned upon the arm of her servant Zoram as though she would faint if he did not hold her up. "This is a critical time. Laban's business detained him."

It was not long before they saw Laban, a distant black shape swaying from side to side. He looked over the heads of the visitors and nodded toward them with glazed eyes. "The wedding. Yes, the wedding. There were some critical things to discuss with the ambassador from Assyria. I feel as though I have just fought and won a war."

"War?" Hilkiah moved toward him. He knew the Assyrians had wanted tribute. But war? "A talk of war?"

"Yes, war," Laban said. He raised his arm high and leaned it against the wall, looking through the white silk of his sleeve. "They wanted to come from Assyria to burn the city." He threw his head back and forced a smile. "All of you should know that while you were making merry, I have single-handedly averted war."

"Never mind him," Reba said as she hurried forward. "He has been having bad dreams lately."

"I convinced them they should rejoice with us, for the daughter of Esau's lineage will soon join the lineage of the kings of David." He slurred his words. "My wisdom has prevailed. Nothing will prevent the marriage of the two kingdoms—the family of Chief Pedaiah's wife Shali, the distant relation of Esau, to our young King Josiah here, promised forever to be royalty, one of David's kings. I said, yes, of course, Zebudah is promised to be queen. You knew long ago she was promised to be queen?"

Attempting to stand away from the wall, he faltered. "There are prophecies in the books that say we will be destroyed," he continued. A deep hiccup echoed in his chest. "But I have stopped the destruction. It is time to rejoice. Now there will be no war. The predictions in the books are lies. The prophecies say we are doomed, but they're not taking into consideration the strength of my militia."

He raised his chin. The people in the hush of the room heard his ragged breathing. "Or my power as peacemaker."

"You're stepping on your robe." Reba hiked it up behind him.

"We will prove ourselves to be strong," Laban continued. "And that is what will be written on the records. Do you know how important the records are? We are nothing without the records. I collect them, you know." Lifting his arms, he swung them wide across the house and the garden before them. His loose silk sleeves filled with the wind. "We will write our own victories in the books that follow Moses's records. Jerusalem has been saved by this marriage. I, Laban, the captain of thousands, have won the conflict. My legacy will live forever. I have saved Jerusalem."

Reba nodded as though it were all true.

"We are not sure what you're saying, Cousin Laban." Sariah's mother drew close to Sariah and Lehi. "We stayed to thank you for the use of your house for the wedding."

For a moment Laban stared into the sun-drenched windows. "You are welcome, my kinsmen. You are welcome, little Sariah and Cousin Lehi. Congratulations on your marriage."

Laban, who had once been a sleek, muscle-bound fighter, was now a thickset middle-aged man with brown spots all over his skin. His arms still looked hard, as though they could wield a sword and strike home every time. "We will be recruiting men for the forces. Yes, yes, I know you are a gold merchant, and a successful one at that, cousin Lehi," Laban babbled on, "but you must stand up for your country. You must join us. You must fight with us."

Laban leaned forward so far that it looked like he would fall on his face. He addressed the bride and groom. "When you climb into your marriage bed, my kinsman Lehi, you and your beautiful bride Sariah must make a son who will go to war with honor and glory."

Lehi lowered his eyes. Sariah grasped her new husband's arm and quietly pulled him away.

Chapter Fifteen

Tell the People

With Lehi's successful marriage as an example, Jeremiah wondered if he shouldn't try to find someone and marry again. But as he continued to pray and listen, he heard the voice of the Lord telling him not to take a wife. *The daughters who are born in this place . . . shall die of deadly diseases. . . . They shall be as dung on the surface of the ground. . . . They shall be food for the birds of the air and for the beasts of the earth.* It was a wretched promise for the children of Israel. Jeremiah's mission must be to concentrate on guiding Josiah.

But as time passed and Chief Pedaiah dominated the court, the boy king began to slip away from his dedicated teachers. It saddened Jeremiah to see the decline of the school—and, under the influence of a corrupt government, Josiah's decline as well.

Feeling helpless and angry, Jeremiah knew it was time to speak out as the Lord had long ago commanded him to do. If his father was waiting to present his writings to a more mature King Josiah, Jeremiah would be ready to present his own. In the empty afternoons, while Chief Pedaiah's men taught Josiah to fence and ride, Jeremiah began spending his time dictating to Baruch the alarming words of the Lord.

Baruch often quailed at what Jeremiah wanted him to write. "These are harsh words about Jerusalem. You are telling us that the Lord promises destruction. Will we be overcome by the Assyrians? Do you believe that the king's marriage to this girl with Assyrian blood will not solve the problem? Can the north country still be so firm in their hatred for us?"

Jeremiah's answer was that all of these messages were from the Lord. "Yes, I'm afraid the Assyrians will come. The marriage of our king to an Assyrian daughter is but a patch. The Assyrians act as an instrument of the Lord. It is not the Assyrians but the wickedness of this people that is at fault. It is we ourselves who have invited it. We must warn the king."

For thus says the Lord: The whole land shall be a desolation . . . Baruch wrote Jeremiah's prophecies carefully, shaping the words with the stylus on the sand-colored document. *Because of this the earth shall mourn, and the heavens above grow black; for I have spoken, I have purposed, I have not relented nor will I turn back. . . . All the towns are forsaken, and no one lives in them.*

Baruch protested, "But surely the people will listen to the prophets who are giving them warnings?"

"The Lord has told me even the prophets will die *as though devoured by a ravening lion.*"

Baruch asked, "Are you really going to show these incendiary writings to the authorities? Shouldn't you and Hilkiah first take the lost writings of Moses to the court?" He gathered a sheaf of Jeremiah's poems in his hands. "You know they won't pay attention to anyone—even Moses. The people do not want to listen."

Jeremiah placed his hand on the documents, pinning them to the table. "Sometimes I feel like setting these words on fire. At least they would be useful—as fuel for a bright flame."

Baruch gathered up the precious documents from beneath Jeremiah's hand. He tied them with a hemp rope. "I know who will listen to you," he said. "Come with me."

What Jeremiah remembered most about the honeycomb of apartments where Shallum and Huldah lived was the dark stairwell he and Baruch had climbed with the little rescued goat so many years ago. He also noticed there were no longer any decorative hangings on Uncle Shallum's empty walls.

Aunt Huldah's eyes followed his glance about the room. "We've given the artwork to our son Hanameel, who is building a new farmhouse in Anathoth. We wanted our grandchildren to live with beauty."

The years had not been kind to the couple. Huldah looked thin and drawn, her cheeks like the edges of a withered cabbage. Shallum was too heavy, his belly so large that it didn't allow him to sit comfortably. But his eyes still twinkled as he read Jeremiah's poetry, and he gazed at the young men with a reverent awe.

"These are very good," he said. "They are the truth. It's too bad you don't feel free to post them." He fingered though the half dozen or so papyri that Baruch had transcribed from Jeremiah's coarse handwriting.

"Post them?" Baruch said.

"Yes," Uncle Shallum mused, "perhaps without an author's name."

"I've brought them to you because no one else will read them," Jeremiah said.

Out loud Shallum read, *Backsliding Israel committed adultery, she defiled the land, and committed adultery with stones and with stocks.*

While she scoured a pot with a pad of straw, Huldah nodded.

Uncle Shallum continued to read Jeremiah's words. *Thus says the Lord: What wrong did your ancestors find in me that they went far from me, and went after worthless things, and became worthless themselves? They did not say, 'Where is the Lord who brought us up from the land of Egypt?' . . . I brought you into a plentiful land to eat its fruits and its good things. But when you entered you defiled my land, and made my heritage an abomination.*

For a moment Shallum read quietly, until he finally found a sentence that shook all of them with its power. *Your own sword devoured your prophets, like a ravening lion.* When he raised his eyes from the page, he said, "Yes, my son. I can see this now. If they knew you wrote these words, you would have reason to be afraid."

Huldah stood above them with the wool towel and the kettle in her hands. "May I tell you something, Jeremiah?" In spite of her withered appearance, her hands were still large, with fingers soft as round pads of cotton. She grasped the edge of the table. "For a while I have known that your daughter Hamutal will marry the king Josiah."

Jeremiah felt his mouth go dry. "But . . ."

His aunt put the palm of her hand up to stop him. "No, listen to me," she said. "It may not appear possible now, but the people talk. They are appalled that we are making a royal marriage bed with Shali's people, those who have come down to destroy us—to conquer us."

She stopped and pushed her hand across the table. "You have taught Josiah in the ways of truth and goodness. One of those truths is that the majority of the citizens themselves should make the decisions that will affect them all." She paused and lowered her head. In the light from the window, the color in her cheeks glowed. "Oh, I know. There is nothing we can do yet. Let Zebudah and Josiah marry. But mark my words, my dear Jeremiah. In your issue, there will yet be kings."

She turned her face to him, her eyes dark as deep water. "Do you remember, Jeremiah, how I asked if you might be the one who would save us?" Jeremiah remembered. "*He is prepared from the foundation of the world to die for us—to save us all.* It will be through the line of King David that he will come. And it will be through your line that kings of Israel will remain upon the earth."

Jeremiah thought back to that night he had heard God come to him in the garden: *Before I formed you in the womb I knew you; and before you were born I consecrated you; I appointed you.* He knew Huldah's words were true. He reached across the table, and with his rough fingers clasped her soft hand.

Chapter Sixteen

Josiah

King Josiah and Zebudah were married, and when the royal couple gave birth to a son, Jeremiah tried to shut out the words Huldah had told him about the destiny of his daughter Hamutal.

Bethany would be singing at the new baby's naming ceremony. "And the baby boy will be called Eliakim," she told Jeremiah. "Shali has ordered forty Israelite slaves from Assyria. Twenty to Zebudah's bedside—fourteen to do the bidding of the kitchen and the wardrobe, six to care for the new child while Shali and Zebudah go back to Rumah."

Jeremiah didn't understand. "What?"

"Mother and grandmother left the baby here so they could be free to reestablish important ties at home. But the baby Eliakim is well taken care of. Josiah is proud as a peacock that he, at age fifteen, has produced an heir to the throne."

Jeremiah and Hilkiah continued to teach Hamutal and the children of the palace. When they began to spend more time at the archives, they enlisted a third teacher, the sensible court secretary Shaphan, to help with the other children. Shaphan's young grandson Gedaliah came with him. Soon Hamutal, with her talent for academic studies, was helping the boy with his lessons. She loved tutoring younger students—although when Josiah left the school, her greatest joy went with him.

On one of the rare days Jeremiah attended the school, he happened to walk close to the high windows over the courtyard and catch sight of an unusual formation of the militia clattering in the square. He paused to watch, and then heard the noise of heavy boots on the stairs. He gestured to the children to keep quiet.

The door opened. It was Josiah.

After a long absence, the sixteen-year-old king had returned to the school. His cheeks were flushed. He held his sparring gloves in one hand, his sword at his side. The coarse dark hair of his head matched the stubble of his beard.

"Josiah!" Jeremiah wanted to embrace the young man he had taught and loved, but something in the king's demeanor told him no. "We're glad to see you."

Josiah looked like a man now. He dismissed his guards with a nod, then dipped his head in a polite form of respect.

Not a sound was heard except from a far corner where Josiah's two-year-old child, Eliakim, babbled to his nanny.

Josiah glanced only briefly at his child. With his head lowered, he began to walk among the shelves of toys. He reached the old wooden horse. "How well I remember this place," he said. Turning to Jeremiah, he asked, "Hamutal?"

"She's around the corner in the alcove by the window."

Indeed, Hamutal was bent over a scroll of the great tomes of Moses bound in leather straps. As Josiah walked toward her, she raised her eyes.

The young king stopped for an instant. "Hamutal." Courteously, he turned to Jeremiah. "May I speak to her?"

Jeremiah nodded.

"Hamutal, listen to me," Josiah said. "The people," he began, tipping his head toward the window of the court. "The people have demanded . . ." He cleared his throat. "Well, Hamutal. They have said that they want one of their own to be their queen."

The silence in the room seemed deafening. No one moved. The young king continued, "You know Zebudah is in Rumah with her mother."

Everyone knew this.

It seemed very sudden. He knelt at Hamutal's feet and took her tiny hand. "Will you . . . will you marry me?" He took the white hand and put it to his lips. "Oh, Hamutal. I have always loved you. I need you. Please be with me."

The king's second wedding was a quiet one. Only the most loyal members of the council were invited. The people gathered outside the courtyard to look through the gate at the wedding party as it passed from the sacred ceremony to the king's apartments.

Hamutal's face was hidden by a white linen hood embroidered with lilies. Only her dark curls were visible. The gown she wore was a simple loose *no'ahk bgadim* of new silk. A dozen children, dressed in yellow, carried the flowers.

Two weeks after the wedding, Hilkiah and Jeremiah were confronted in the inner court while lighting oil lamps at the altar.

Chief Pedaiah, his bald forehead glistening with sweat, stalked across the courtyard. "What has been done?" he thundered. "What have you clumsy infidels done?" His sandals hit the stones so hard they sounded like the padded feet of elephants.

"In the valiant governments," said Hilkiah, "the king is allowed to choose as many wives as he deems necessary."

"Necessary? We already have an heir to the throne. This will stir up our relations with Assyria. It looks like you wanted your own blood into the mix."

Hilkiah did not mention that his own blood had already been in the mix long ago in the court of King David.

"If there's a competing heir from Judah, it could cause civil war!"

"The marriage was proposed by King Josiah himself, not us. Zebudah has been spending much of her time in Rumah; the king deserves a companion. It was his request. He wanted to be with Hamutal. Zebudah's son, Eliakim, is still in line to be king."

Hilkiah and Jeremiah stood up from kneeling. "You need not be alarmed, Pedaiah. Your issue will be kings," Hilkiah said. "Please let us worship in peace."

When news of the wedding reached Rumah, Shali and Zebudah made a showing at the palace compound with a retinue worthy of the Queen of Sheba. They brought at least twenty new slaves, and four young Assyrian ambassadors, who were rumored to be Assyrian princes.

When Hilkiah and Jeremiah entered the palace classroom the following day, Shali was there. Still a svelte dark-eyed beauty, she had a way of gesturing seductively with her slender white hands. "You and Shaphan have been such good teachers. But you must be weary. I have brought these young men from Rumah to teach alongside of you."

Shali took over the palace. She settled Zebudah in the room next to the nursery, put the princes from Rumah in apartments close by, and ordered them to begin as instructors. She set up candles on foreign altars and placed a row of potted trees in the yard. Images and statues appeared everywhere.

Incense burners were placed on the sills of the windows and in sconces over the doors. The schoolroom was lined with large shelves bearing boxes of fresh, green-growing herbs. The worn Jewish scrolls were replaced with texts donated by the Assyrians.

King Josiah was spellbound with the new level of excitement, the extraordinary décor, and the new scrolls. He was fascinated by the replica of the goddess that now stood in the vestibule. Shali had explained to him that it would remind him of his own mother and of his wife who had borne him a son. They were a tribute to the women who gave life.

Shali taught King Josiah the basic tenets of her philosophy—that growth on the earth, trees from the soil of the earth, and the fertility of man and woman—were elements of a world worthy of man's attention and worship.

Alarmed at Shali's transformations, Jeremiah could be quiet no longer. He would post his messages anonymously on the palace walls. The texts pleaded for a return to the ways of the Israelite God. But the papyrus was always quickly removed.

When the pagan altars were installed, Jeremiah had dared to say out loud to Shali, "King Josiah is not acquainted with this method of sacrifice."

Shali said, "He learns quickly. He likes it. He is coming along fine."

Before long, she asked Hilkiah, Jeremiah, and Baruch to leave the schoolroom altogether.

The gold merchant, Lehi, agreed that Shali's actions were most troubling. He said, "Come stay at my house and work on your documents. I have many rooms." Although his household was busy preparing for the marriage of Sariah's sister to the young prophet Urijah, he had room for everyone. "And Hamutal's presence will comfort my wife Sariah, who as yet," he paused, "is still childless."

One of Lehi's rooms contained a large table cut from the cedars of Lebanon. Hilkiah, Baruch, and Jeremiah were welcome to copy records there. They continued to work over the discovered scrolls, translating them to careful, comprehensible language. The work was tedious, and Jeremiah would often retreat to the garden to clear his mind of stress.

One day, when his mother was visiting, he felt particularly weary. He wandered into the garden, where he noted Marika, Hamutal, and Sariah sitting together on a stone wall among the roses drinking cups of herbal water. The air in the garden was so fresh, the vines on the trellises so heavy with bees, that Jeremiah stopped to absorb the beauty before going to greet them. The women were deep in conversation. A bank of thick trees screened him as he waited, unwilling to interrupt their talk.

"It looks like Queen Zebudah is back with us now. For good."

"Why did she leave in the first place?"

"Her job was done. All she had to do was give birth to the boy. She left him to be raised by others."

"They say she has been ordered to get back here quick so she can have another one."

When Sariah's soft voice entered the conversation, Jeremiah heard a heavy sorrow in it. "For her it was so easy." Sariah's childlessness had been a great burden to her.

Marika stroked her cousin's hand. "Sometimes it takes much waiting, with patience and prayer."

Hamutal's eyes were bright with subtle laughter. "Not always a long time, Grandmother."

The two older women looked startled. "Hamutal!"

Hamutal nodded, her eyes narrow, but blazing with light. She covered her face with her hands as though to keep her words from flying through the air. "I wasn't going to tell. I wasn't."

Jeremiah stood riveted behind the leaves. His daughter would be the mother of royalty!

Chapter Seventeen

Hamutal

Jeremiah instructed the women that in order to avoid trouble from the court, they must keep the compelling news to themselves. Marika and her two youngest daughters settled in for a lengthy stay at Lehi's place. The women made much over Hamutal, giving her the right things to eat, brewing plenty of herbal drinks, and sewing tiny string shoes and swaddling clothes. Sariah and her slaves fluttered about her like hovering birds.

It was soon apparent, when Zebudah returned, that she would be having a second child. When again it was a boy, the kingdom prepared to hold a huge celebration, both in honor of the little king Eliakim's third birthday, and the birth of the new little prince, Johanan. There was much rejoicing, for this second prince would assure that Assyrian blood would be entrenched into the royal line forever.

Jeremiah worried about the growing evidence of Hamutal's pregnancy and the court's reaction to a third heir—this time from a daughter of Judea.

In the gray dawn after the extravagant celebration, while Jeremiah lay half awake in the apartment at the back of Lehi's home, he heard a voice calling him.

Peering through the haze of the dew in the garden, Jeremiah saw, just below the window sill, a head of flaming red hair. The intruder was Shaphan's grandson Gedaliah, grown into a young man.

"Jeremiah," Gedaliah whispered. To get to Jeremiah's window, he had climbed to the top of a lattice of roses. "It's Baruch, sir. It's serious. He wants to meet you at the waters."

Jeremiah quickly grasped Gedaliah's hand to help him climb over the sill and into the room.

"What is it, Gedaliah, my boy? What does Baruch want?"

"I think he's sick," Gedaliah said. "He's at the waters kneeling on the ground. He asked me to get you."

Jeremiah hurriedly dressed and followed Gedaliah out the door. Not another soul was in the streets. The dawn spilled over the walls with an oblique violet light. When they came to the courtyard they took a serpentine pathway through a maze of strewn husks and bones left from the night's festivities. There were shards of broken pottery lying everywhere, and pots of garbage from uneaten meals standing in accumulations of feces and urine. The scene of the party reeked with a fetid odor that had nothing to do with a child's birthday party. Jeremiah held his breath as he walked through to the waters.

Gedaliah withdrew as soon as they came to Baruch. The scribe was leaning over the fountain, covering his face with his hands. Jeremiah tried pulling him up, but Baruch stayed in the kneeling position rocking back and forth as though in great pain.

Jeremiah pulled back the curls that hid Baruch's eyes. "What is it? Please tell me."

"I have dishonored God," he choked. "Shali's slave girls . . . I am dishonored."

Jeremiah was surprised that Baruch had attended the festivities. Pedaiah and Shali's parties were always drunken brawls. Jeremiah remained silent for a moment, waiting.

"The enemies that took Israel a hundred years ago have all these years kept Israelite women as slaves," Baruch said through his tears.

Yes. Jeremiah knew this. It was so quiet he heard the waters lapping gently against the edge of the pool. "So the young daughters of Zion are slaves. There is evil in our midst, we know this. What more is there?"

"Shali's people brought these Israelite slave girls down from Assyria. She said, 'Relax. Relax and see how God's love is everything. Love is all. We will teach the boys to love.' And the Israelite slave girls . . . they are beautiful dancers." In a whisper, Baruch admitted that though he had not participated, he had watched.

Jeremiah looked out over the courtyard. The filth reminded him of a chicken yard in which a fox had done its ugly deeds. He took his hand from Baruch's shoulder.

Baruch shook with his sobs. The morning was slipping into light. Jeremiah took Baruch's elbow, lifted him, and walked with him back to the room in the archives where Hilkiah was already seated, copying records.

Hilkiah looked up, his gray eyes bright. “From the appearance of things, that was quite a celebration they had last night in the courtyard.”

Baruch walked slowly to the table where his work lay waiting for him.

“Baruch knows that firsthand,” Jeremiah said.

“Well, we’re not any of us Rechabites,” Hilkiah said. The Rechabites never touched wine.

“If I had not been drunk . . .” Baruch moaned.

“It is lax behavior and the evil of slavery that has brought disgrace into our kingdom. We would be wise to learn from the Rechabites,” said Jeremiah.

Reaching for his stylus, Baruch looked up at Jeremiah. “That is not all I must tell you,” he said. “Someone came to me. You would never guess who. They know about the pregnancy. Your daughter is in danger.”

“How do you know this?”

“You should take Hamutal to Libnah. You must not return to Anathoth. They are speaking against you—even one of your own brothers.”

Speaking against him? His own brother? He felt a stab of pain. Would it be cowardly to flee?

Wary of Baruch’s words, Jeremiah returned to Lehi and Sariah’s place that afternoon. The household was in disarray with the preparations for the wedding. As Sariah ushered him back to the garden, he almost tripped over toddlers trying to catch butterflies and wielding swords made of willows.

Hamutal sat on a bench under the hedge flowers, bent over a needle and thread. Marika was seated at another bench. Sariah’s sisters sat nearby, chatting about the coming nuptials.

In the far corner Lehi talked with Urijah, the groom. Jeremiah recognized him as one who had taught at the gate with Ezekiel and spoken out against the government. Jeremiah nodded to the young man. He felt unworthy to stand in the presence of someone who had the strength to preach on the street, when he himself—though he’d been called long ago—had not yet done so. Yes, he’d written many warnings. But so far he hadn’t opened his mouth.

As Jeremiah approached, Urijah greeted him. "Jeremiah. We have heard of the threats against you and your daughter." His sunburned brow glistened under his crop of thick, dark hair.

"Many priests," Urijah continued, "have read your prophecy of destruction. They say that King Josiah brings us peace, and your words that appear on the walls do nothing but cause dissension. I hesitate to tell you what the courtiers are saying. Do you want to know?"

Jeremiah nodded.

"Their statements are harsh. They're threatening to destroy you." He paused. *Let us destroy the tree with its fruit, let us cut him off from the land of the living, so that his name will no longer be remembered.*

Cut him off from the land of the living?

"Your posts are correct, Jeremiah. A compromise with Assyria is not the answer. Look what has happened because of it. They have foisted upon us their religion—or lack of it. Did you know what they are secretly throwing into the Valley of Hinnom?"

He knew, for he had been in the Valley of Hinnom.

Urijah looked away. "I too have come under fire."

"Urijah, you are very brave. To speak against the government at this time is dangerous. I hope you're aware of that."

Urijah nodded. "But someone must do it, Jeremiah."

Jeremiah looked away. "I would help . . ." He paused. "But it looks as though I must leave Jerusalem to save the life of my daughter and her child."

Chapter Eighteen

Libnah

Years later, when he was thrown into the pit, when he could not sit down against the wall without feeling the mud sucking at his elbows—during this most terrible of all times—he clung to the memory of his early days with Hamah and the baby girl Hamutal. Added to those memories, were the quiet months in Libnah with Hamutal, when they were in hiding. This time he had the joy of watching Hamutal hold the tiny Prince Jehoahaz in her arms.

Hamutal and Josiah's baby was named after King Jehoahaz, the son of Jehu, the Judean king of Israel who prayed to the Lord to deliver the people from Syria, and the Lord answered his prayers. "Perhaps in the same manner this king will deliver Jerusalem," Jeremiah said.

As the little boy began to walk, Jeremiah took him for many strolls in the compound. As the sun rose over the whitewashed walls of the olive orchards, he took the boy's hand and wandered out to watch the men working with the olive trees. Once he knelt with Jehoahaz in a hidden copse of blackberries and taught him how to pray.

As the child grew, Jeremiah warned him of dangerous wild beasts and evil men. The boy's black eyes widened when he heard the stories of Ahab and Jezebel and their wicked daughter Athaliah who killed her own children—except for the one baby they hid.

"If they hid the baby Joash," Jehoahaz wanted to know, "did they give him anything to eat? Did they ever open the door and let him see the sun? Did the soldiers rescue him?"

"If evil people rule the soldiers, nothing can be done until good people stand up and fight."

For their midday meal, Jeremiah brought cheese and bread in a burlap cloth. The boy tore the bread in oblong pieces and lined them up on a flat rock. The little ragged soldiers were then made to face formidable ranks of burned charcoal chips. Before he ate a piece of bread, he moved it forward, knocking off several of the enemy.

During the years Jehoahaz grew, Jeremiah spent much time praying and writing in the fields while he watched Latham's small herd of sheep. He didn't go to Jerusalem. If Baruch or his father wrote to him, he sent answers by messengers. Hamutal and Jehoahaz became his life. He vowed not to forget one precious moment of this time when he could hold his little grandson in his arms at Latham's feasts. Other afternoons he spent hours gathering olives or walking the fields, writing poetry.

It is He who made the earth by His power,
Who established the world by His wisdom,
And by his understanding stretched out the heavens. . . .
The Lord of Hosts is His name.

Jeremiah's favorite place to write was on a seat in a far corner of the garden under an old olive tree whose branches dipped close to him and quivered in the breeze. Surrounding the tree were beds of small flowering plants in bloom. Though bees also claimed this corner, they seemed to ignore him. The fragrance of the flowers so filled the air, the florid colors and aroma rewarded him with such pleasure that he was inspired to continue his writing. Often he leaned his head back and exposed his face to the sun.

His contentment was interrupted only by news of the desecration of Jerusalem. Urijah's reports lamented the apathy of the guards, who no longer made attempts to stop the hecklers from throwing filth at him. The smoke from the incense burning on the roofs was heavier than it had been since Manasseh's time. The fires of Jerusalem emitted acrid fumes that smelled of burnt sacrifice to counterfeit gods. Back streets were clouded with the choking vapors of smoldering lethal plants—or of human flesh.

Hilkiah wrote: *Do not come yet, Jeremiah. The temple is desecrated. There are new locks on several of the temple rooms. Shali has recast some of the gold and silver vessels from the temple and sent them to Assyria to appease her people. The priests are under firm instructions to keep away from the administrative part of the court now. The prophets in the streets suffer indignities and abuse.*

Trying to put Jerusalem out of his mind, Jeremiah concentrated on Hamutal and Jehoahaz. Yet when he retired to his chamber and knelt at the end of his cot, a flood of guilt overcame him. So far he had not begun to do what the Lord had asked him to do. He should be in the streets with Urijah and Lehi, stopping the evil.

And now the droughts were coming. There was enough water in storage for a while. The people had filled the cisterns during the winter rains. Yet the sun in Libnah began to burn every living thing. At first such light was welcomed. In the mornings the people awoke with a bright glare beating upon the fields, a warmth that seemed heaven-sent. But after a time, when the heat began to dry the little plants that struggled through the cracked soil, the resi-dents grew alarmed.

The first two years of exceptional heat were rewarded by just enough summer rain to slake the damage done by the wind. But the crops were almost half of what the farmers expected. And in the third year, there were no crops. In the fourth and fifth years, the land was without any vegetation, and in the sixth year, the fields had turned to powder.

The people had invited the disapproval of God. Jeremiah wrote: *Her nobles send their servants for water; they come to the cisterns, they find no water, they return with their vessels empty.*

The young men working in the orchards at Libnah came to the house sweating, their faces lined with worry. There was so little water in the streams, they could not fill the irrigation canals. The farmers . . . *are ashamed and dismayed and cover their heads, because the ground is cracked . . . because there has been no rain on the land. . . . Even the doe in the field forsakes her newborn fawn because there is no grass. The wild asses stand on the bare heights, they pant for air like jackals; their eyes fail because there is no herbage.*

Latham ordered his workmen to build a dam, but it took so long to fill the pond with water, they were required to dip bags made of the bladders of sheep into the mud to retrieve what water they could to nourish the olive trees and the animals. Night after night the animals from the wilderness came to drink what was left.

Although our iniquities testify against us, act, O Lord, for your name's sake; our apostasies indeed are many, and we have sinned against you.

One sultry night, after he had put his precious grandson Jehoahaz to sleep and dropped to his knees in prayer, Jeremiah felt a distinct presence in his room. He backed away from the cot and looked around in the dark. A small candle flickered at his bedside. He felt the presence of the Lord and trembled.

O Lord . . . I plead with you: let me put my case to you. . . . Why is the land ruined and laid waste like a wilderness, so that no one passes through? How long will the land mourn, and the grass of every field wither? For the wickedness of those who live in it the animals and the birds are swept away, and because people said, "He is blind to our ways."

Jeremiah listened, and heard the words of the Lord in his heart. *Because they have forsaken my law that I set before them, and have not obeyed my voice, or walked in accordance with it, but have stubbornly followed their own hearts and have gone after the Ba'als, as their ancestors taught them.*

The voice was as clear to Jeremiah as his own prayer. *Therefore, thus says the Lord of hosts, the God of Israel: I am feeding this people with wormwood, and giving them poisonous water to drink. I will scatter them among nations that neither they nor their ancestors have known; and I will send the sword after them, until I have consumed them.*

For the people of Judah have done evil in my sight, says the Lord; they have set their abominations in the house that is called by my name, defiling it. And they go on building the high place of Topheth, which is in the valley of the son of Hinnom, to burn their sons and their daughters in the fire—which I did not command, nor did it come into my mind.

The words he most feared came then—the Lord's indisputable command that he must go to the cities of Judah and speak out loud.

Proclaim all these words in the cities of Judah, or in the streets of Jerusalem. Hear the words of this covenant and do them. You shall say to them . . . cursed be the man who does not heed the words of this covenant.

For the next few weeks, Jeremiah took long walks into the hills with the sheep, tormented by his reluctance, baffled by thoughts of the potential danger facing him. He justified his continued stay in Libnah, knowing Urijah, Lehi, and the others were still speaking in the streets. He was not as good at speech as they were. He would do the writing, he said to himself. He carried stylus and papyrus in his sash to the slopes, diligently recording the words the Lord spoke to him. But was it enough?

While the drought raged, he continued to follow the sheep, even as they began to graze toward distant terrain. One day, from the crest of a rise, they moved down into a basin where a muddy stream lay beside a thicket of briars.

Water! A rare blessing for the animals. Cracking a broken stick from a bush, Jeremiah sat down beside the stream and stirred the dark pool. The movement of the water relaxed his tortured thoughts, and he fell asleep.

In the midst of his slumber he heard a riveting scream of terror. He awoke and saw the sheep scattering across the hills like a swarm of loose bees. He ran around the edge of the rocks just in time to see one of the sheep screaming in agony, flailing its legs about. The rattle in its throat struck him with terror.

A tawny-golden lioness stood over the ewe's belly dipping her jaws into its entrails. The cry from the ewe was cut short. Seeing Jeremiah, the lioness backed away, dragging the carcass in her mouth, dripping with blood.

He had heard there was a pride of lions in these hills, but he'd never seen them. The drought had brought them down. A little farther away across the sloping basin, another female, as sleek and graceful as the first, leaped into the running herd with abandon, snapping her jaws at the moving legs. Shrieks of desperation penetrated the air as the running sheep cried.

The lions pinned down one sheep after another. Jeremiah ran after them shouting and waving his arms. They tracked northward, leaving behind a scene of blood and carnage. The few remaining sheep ran south over the crest of rocks, bleating cries of panic.

The visit of the lions haunted him for days. He envisioned blood running in the gutters of Jerusalem; he saw giant flames burning in the streets. Even the bodies of the prophets lay torn and bloody by the gates.

Jeremiah could no longer stay in Libnah. He must return to Jerusalem and speak to the people.

Chapter Nineteen

Speaking Out

As Jeremiah made preparations for the journey, his eight-year-old grandson stayed close by his side. "Where are you going, Grandfather? I wish you wouldn't go."

The child followed his grandfather into his rooms to pack. He stood on one foot and then on the other, and dared to touch the scrolls and writing equipment that Jeremiah had laid beside his clothes.

"I must go and do as the Lord has commanded," Jeremiah answered.

Jehoahaz had been taught well about the Lord. "What has He asked you to do now, Grandfather? Hasn't He asked you to stay here with us and to write down the words He tells you?"

Jeremiah was strapping the sack with hemp while the boy drew his finger along the edge of the documents. Stopping his work, he knelt and pressed the boy's narrow shoulders between his hands. "I must go back to Jerusalem. The people will not read what I have written, so the Lord has asked me to go to the streets of Jerusalem and speak to them face-to-face."

"But you said they might kill you."

Jeremiah gazed for a long moment into the boy's dark brown eyes. "One cannot be afraid if he is obeying the commandments of the Lord."

Standing by the gate with her son, Hamutal tried to show courage as Jeremiah walked away. "Please be careful, Father."

After spending time away from Jerusalem for a while, he was always surprised that the city was busier than he remembered it. The crowds seemed more aggressive, less concerned about how they treated others in the congested streets. One of the first visits he wanted to make was to Lehi's house.

"My friend, Jeremiah, the poet!" Lehi greeted him warmly, though he could not hide his hesitation. "I'm glad to see you. But I must warn you right away. It's dangerous for you here."

Jeremiah stood almost a head taller than Lehi. He looked into the open foyer of the house, watching Lehi's slaves hurry back and forth.

Lehi turned and drew Jeremiah further into the large foyer, across the highly polished floors that mirrored the pots of flowers and gilded chairs. Lehi had found great financial success as a gold merchant. His many employees, slaves, and servants, moved about in the distance, softly padding though the halls.

Jeremiah asked where Sariah was, as she usually accompanied her husband, laughing and making much over their guests.

As Lehi walked with Jeremiah through the tile foyer, he said, "After all these years we have been offered God's supreme gift. We've hidden Sariah away. She is great with child."

"Wonderful! You are blessed for being so faithful."

The merchant pulled away from Jeremiah and went to the large window that overlooked the courtyard. The palm trees stood motionless in the heat. Rays of sun, beating down on the flowers, sparkled against the bits of gypsum and quartz in the stones on the far wall.

"If it were only popular to be faithful," said Lehi.

"Yes," Jeremiah said. "That's why I'm here."

"Urijah and I, Ezekiel, Daniel, Nahum—all of us speak, but it seems to do no good. Shali's power goes far. It has grown almost impossible to quote scriptures or to speak words of righteousness."

Jeremiah nodded. "The Lord is mindful. His judgments will bring difficulties: more droughts, more opposition. He is urging me to speak."

Lehi tugged at his beard. "You must be aware of how Shali hates you because your daughter married Josiah. A slave brought me a message that you were coming. When you entered the gates of the city, you were seen. They are waiting for you. There will be a hearing in the court."

Later, Jeremiah could not remember one step of his walk to the court with Lehi. He could not remember one word of their conversation. It was subdued, with some personal exchanges.

In the courtroom, Shaphan, the secretary, fingered through the papyrus documents lying on a table before him. On the dais behind him sat four other judges, their hoods covering their faces. "Come and sit down." He beckoned to Jeremiah.

Among the documents on the table were some copies of Isaiah's poetry lying next to copies of Jeremiah's own poems. He felt unsettled—seeing his work placed near Isaiah's—as though it were comparable.

"I was instructed by Governor Pashur to take your writings down from the walls."

Of course. Governor Pashur would have obeyed Shali's orders. Though the faces of the judges behind Shaphan were partially hidden, Jeremiah would not have been surprised if one of them were the glowering Governor Pashur himself.

"But when I read your poems, I had some of them copied," Shaphan continued. "Some of your poetry is very beautiful and might be placed alongside Isaiah's work." He shuffled through the papyri. "We don't object to these words about God. Your powerful poetry is inspiring. You persuade people to follow the commandments which are kept with the Ark of the Covenant."

Jeremiah waited uneasily.

"But I must tell you," said Shaphan. "It is passages such as these which inflame the court. You speak of the people of Jerusalem as *wanton: On every high hill and under every green tree you sprawled and played the whore."*

He continued, "You liken the people to a camel in heat: *a restless young camel interlacing her tracks, a wild ass used to the wilderness, in her heat sniffing the wind! Who can restrain her lust? None who seek her need weary themselves: in her month they will find her."*

He looked up with heavy eyes. "Murderers? Adulterers? *When I fed them to the full, they committed adultery and trooped to the houses of prostitutes. They were well-fed lusty stallions each neighing for his neighbor's wife.* Everyone goes after his neighbor's wife?"

Jeremiah stirred uneasily.

"I have been the court secretary now for many years," said Shaphan. "It is not always easy to walk the tightrope between the political powers and the will of God. I think you can see why we had to take down the documents you posted on the walls."

"I wish I could say that what I'm writing in those documents is overstated," Jeremiah said.

Lehi leaned over the table toward Shaphan. "Jeremiah merely wants to tell the truth in a way that will catch their attention."

"*A camel in heat*?" Shaphan read, his fingers tapping the pages before him. "*Therefore a lion from the forest shall kill them.* Jeremiah, surely you do not believe this? Surely you know how hard Josiah has labored to include and pacify the Assyrians. Your words about the north coming down like a lion and killing us—these are incendiary words."

"Perhaps he means it is peace at a great cost," added Lehi.

"But it is peace, nevertheless," Shaphan said. "A peaceful time is a time when many people may become wealthy. Even you, Lehi, have gathered to yourself a great estate."

"The Lord has blessed me," he agreed. "But therefore I pay more taxes."

Shaphan raised his eyes to Lehi and Jeremiah. "Our peace is costing a tenuous alliance with Zebudah's people, the Assyrians. And our future king Eliakim will have Assyrian connections. But Josiah is a good man who loves the Jewish people," he said. "He remembers you, Jeremiah, and is still fond of you. He knows that you are protecting his little Jewish son in Libnah. In fact, he would like for you to bring the boy to court someday. He will let you know when."

The king had spoken to Shaphan about Jehoahaz? Jeremiah took a breath, weighing every word. "Perhaps I will use language that is more circumspect. But tell King Josiah I care so much about Jerusalem that I cannot stay quiet."

An eerie silence fell over the courtroom. The partially concealed faces of the politicians slid behind their silk hoods like snakes retreating into their holes.

A few days later Shaphan sent a message that the king understood Jeremiah's concerns, and would allow street meetings.

The permission should have pleased Jeremiah. Yet suddenly the weight of responsibility overtook him. Was he a good enough speaker to hold attention? He had been hiding; he now could hide no more.

Jeremiah walked to the gate on the following day, carrying his papyrus copies of God's words in a cloth binding. He did not walk through the darkest alleys, but he made deliberate steps, as though he were challenging the strong presence of his adversaries. The air was clear, except for the thousands of incense burners still functioning on the roofs that issued cloudy wisps of smoke floating like sheets of gauze into the breeze. His caftan brushed the cobbles. In silence, people stood along the road to watch him as he walked.

"Jeremiah!" Urijah greeted him. The news of Jeremiah's return and trial had rippled through the entire city, easing the way for other prophets as well: Ezekiel, Nahum, and the young Daniel. When the gold merchant Lehi was free from his labor, he joined them.

Urijah told Jeremiah that the birth of Josiah and Zebudah's second son had made more of a difference than he thought it would. "These people don't stop and listen anymore," he said. "Why should they? When the second prince, Johanan, was born, they knew there were enough heirs to the throne to keep things the way they are."

"They cannot stay the way they are," Jeremiah replied.

For several months Jeremiah daily gathered his courage to speak to the lethargic crowds. It never got easy. Though all of the priests put their hearts into their preaching, they seemed unable to keep the citizens of Jerusalem from apathy and decline. The longer the city experienced some prosperity and peace, the less the citizens listened.

In the seventeenth year of Josiah's reign, Jeremiah noticed one man who always came with his head covered, as though trying to remain out of sight. While the others spit and cursed, this man often nodded his head. Once or twice after the speeches, Jeremiah stepped down from the dais to approach him, but the man hurried away.

Jeremiah walked around to the back of the group and came upon the hooded visitor from behind. When the man turned quickly, the hood fell from his face. It was Zoram, Captain Laban's personal servant.

"I am curious, Zoram, why have you come here so often, yet you never step forward to talk to any of us?"

Zoram bowed his head in respect. "I come to hear the truth. But because I'm in Laban's service I have heard secrets. There are rumblings in the military."

"About what?"

"You knew Shali has sent her favored ambassadors to Assyria?"

Jeremiah knew of Shali's ambassadors.

"But were you aware that they have now secretly taken some of our best Judean military trainers with them to train the Assyrian army?"

Jeremiah had heard that some of their best soldiers had been transported to Assyria. Everyone supposed it was to protect the border. But to train Assyria's troops?

"Now the ambassadors have gone to Babylon to win favor of the Chaldean kings. Shali and Pedaiah are trying to make friends with the devil. There is gossip that Assyria and Babylon are joining together to plan an attack."

Jeremiah stiffened. "Upon us?"

"I overheard it at the house. It is inside knowledge and hasn't been told abroad. King Josiah fears conspiracy, and he is frantic because we're not prepared. We are suffering from drought. Our armies have been digging wells and repairing walls. Our ranks have been weakened."

Jeremiah had been telling the people that destruction would come. But he hadn't known exactly how—except *from out of the north.*

Zoram bowed, his bearded chin quivering. He threw his cowl over his head and disappeared into the crowd. Scowling, Jeremiah watched him go. Shali was playing with fire. If those two powerful countries out of the north merged, they could snap up Judea as a child picks a coin out of the mud.

Jeremiah knew the answer was not in military might. But in repentance. Yet no one was listening to him. And Jerusalem was running out of water, money, and time.

Frantic to keep paying the tribute Assyria demanded, the priests opened up the temple for tours. Sick at heart, Jeremiah watched while the city's most disgusting rabble began forming long lines in front of the sacrificial basin, dropping their few coins on the courtyard, and slopping the liquor from the cups they carried as they bent over to pick up the money on the tiles. Climbing the steps, the roughnecks craned their heads to see inside God's house as they laughed and yelled, "Now we'll get an eyeful. It ain't no miracle. There ain't nothin' but sticks and stones."

Money did come in. The tour fund might have been helpful to repair the temple as well as pay the tributes, except that it was managed by Shelemaiah and his father Hananiah. Jeremiah was not surprised, finally, to learn they were embezzling it. He was mortified.

Turn now, every one of you, from your evil way and wicked doings. This whole land shall become a ruin and a waste. If such dishonesty were allowed to thrive, if Shali's covert stratagems were allowed to flourish, a terrifying future was in store. Jeremiah could sense it. *And these nations shall serve the king of Babylon.*

Chapter Twenty

King Josiah

Walking to the archives one day, Jeremiah saw Baruch running toward him. The scribe was panting, wiping the sweat from his brow. He carried a scroll in his hand. "Jeremiah, hurry. There is news. I was coming to get you."

Once upstairs inside the archives, Jeremiah could sense an unusual tension. All of the scribes, usually transcribing documents diligently, looked up from their work.

"What is it?" Jeremiah asked.

"A miracle," Baruch caught his breath. "Hilkiah!" Wide-eyed, he faced the high priest. "You must have hidden a copy of Moses's document in the money room!"

Hilkiah looked up from his work.

"It's a miracle. You know how many years it has been since we have wanted to take Moses's document to the king. And now! When the king discharged the embezzlers Shelemaiah and Hananiah, he gave the responsibility for the tour funds to the court secretary Shaphan, and it was Shaphan who found that copy hidden in the money room. And the miracle is that Shaphan has read it out loud to the king!"

Startled, Jeremiah felt his heart beat against his ribs.

"When the king heard the document, he tore his clothes and wept! And now he has sent this letter!"

Trying to steady his hands, Jeremiah grasped the scroll from Baruch and studied the seal of the king. He hurried to unroll the sheaves. There were two of them, and the outside sheaf was blank. Inside the scroll there was a short message from the king to the priests at the temple: Hilkiah, Ahikam, son of Shaphan, Achbor, and Asaiah.

Go, inquire of the Lord for me, for the people, and for all Judah, concerning the words of this book that has been found; for great is the wrath of the Lord that is kindled against us, because our an-

cestors did not obey the words of this book, to do according to all that is written concerning us.

"The king has read the document!" Baruch said. "He knows it's true. He wants to read it aloud in the temple to the leaders of Judah."

It was so quiet in the copy room of the archives that the thick air seemed to quiver. The large linen sheets that hung from the ceiling stopped moving.

Jeremiah didn't dare rejoice. It sounded too good to be true.

"The king has been thrown into confusion, concerned that Assyria and Babylon might both attack us. And he's tired of the drought," Baruch said. The scribe had grown a little heavier, but his round face was still framed by the black curls that hung against his cheeks.

Jeremiah glanced at his father. He saw tears well in the old man's eyes.

"Finally, the king has been humbled by the records that speak out of the dust," Hilkiah said.

Wary of this news, Jeremiah left for Libnah to see Hamutal and Jehoahaz.

It was on his return that he found, to his amazement, thousands of people and animals traveling in the opposite direction. When his mule pulled back from the congestion, a stranger, also on his way out of the city, stopped to help.

"Ishmael here to the rescue. Do you need my mule to give yours a little nudge?" the traveler said good-naturedly. "I don't mind turning around for a step or two."

"Thank you, my good man."

Ishmael led his mule in a half circle, fastening it to Jeremiah's animal to pull it out of its obstinacy. The cart held his wife and a small baby girl, who sought protection from the sun under a large parasol.

"I know you," Ishmael said to Jeremiah.

Jeremiah could not place him.

"I'm an acquaintance of Lehi," the man said. "You and I met fourteen years ago at Lehi's wedding."

"Oh yes!" Jeremiah remembered Lehi's wedding well. Although he couldn't remember Ishmael, he was most grateful for the man's kindness.

"My wife can't take the heat in the city," said Ishmael. "And now that there's so much dust, my wife gets very sick. We'll come back when it's all over."

"All over? What has happened?"

"Josiah the king," Ishmael told him. "A change has come over him. He removed all of the priests who were offering pagan sacrifices, destroyed all of the pagan objects, cut down the symbols of the goddess Asherah, and took down Topheth in Hinnom Valley, so that no one can sacrifice his son or daughter as a burnt offering to the god Molech. He published the laws of Moses aloud to the court, and he is determined to follow the ways of God."

Jeremiah listened intently. "Go on."

"It's been the most incredible month in Judah's history. When the king read the newly discovered book of Moses and saw how many laws we were breaking, he wept and tore his hair. He even sent officials to talk to the prophetess Huldah. She said that because Josiah has repented, he wouldn't have to see Jerusalem destroyed. Never before has there been a king like Josiah. He serves the Lord with all his heart, mind, and strength, obeying all the Laws of Moses."

Ishmael's words flew about in Jeremiah's head like moths. While they talked, Ishmael's wife sat patiently in the cart, holding the parasol with one hand, the baby girl wheezing in the crook of her arm.

They were still in the midst of a dry heat. Yet in the sky Jeremiah saw an unusual formation of clouds in the west. Could it be possible that God might bring them rain? "King Josiah had a great change of heart and has cleansed all of the Judean cities?"

Ishmael nodded. "He has removed the mediums, fortune-tellers, and pagan objects of worship."

Jeremiah took the man by the shoulder. "Ishmael, I appreciate what you've told me. May the Lord bless you and your family."

Jeremiah hurried the mule to the temple. His father Hilkiah was seated where he had sat for many years, the linen flags a colorful backdrop above his graying head. The archives were quiet. The slaves had been dismissed. The air was cooler, not just because it was dusk, but because the clouds that had moved in from the west had brought a sprinkle of rain.

"What has happened, father?" Jeremiah asked. "I've heard from a traveler to Jericho that Josiah has done an amazing thing."

"You've heard right. It is a miracle. The king is a repentant man."

"What happened?"

With the tips of his fingers, Hilkiah touched the papyrus that lay before him on the table.

And your eyes shall not see all the evil which I will bring upon this place.

"Josiah believed that if he cleaned up Jerusalem, if he made things right, the evil would not come," Hilkiah said.

They heard the sound of thunder in the skies. Hilkiah looked up through the high transom windows just under the vast ceiling in the room. "God is mindful of his people's needs—in times of punishment as well as in times of obedience."

Jeremiah watched the moonlight from the transom brighten his father's hair. Long ago he had taught Jeremiah the symbolic meaning of the Star of David—the womb and the male wedge joined together. And the upward thrust of the shaft of the cross that carried the shoulders of the man and woman toward God. Order could stand. Disorder bred chaos.

"Symbols are everywhere," Hilkiah said. "Our artifacts such as the Ark of the Covenant or Jacob's stone pillow are reminders. But heaven's glory is achieved only by obedience."

A letter, delivered by Shaphan's grandson Gedaliah, came to the archives. Holding the letter high when he came to the door, Gedaliah begged the guard to let him in.

Hilkiah remembered him by his red hair. "Gedaliah," he said. "What is it, boy?"

"I have an important letter for Jeremiah. It's from the king." The letter was fixed with gold wax and bore the imprint of the king's seal.

Jeremiah rose from his chair. It was highly unusual to receive a missive from the king.

Dear Jeremiah: Will it please you to meet me at the palace garden in three days when the sun is two lengths past midday. Please come alone. Josiah, King of Judah.

The king had never sought him out before! Perhaps he wanted to discuss Hamutal and Jehoahaz. Astonished, Jeremiah tucked the letter in his sash and turned back to the table.

When the time came for the appointment, Jeremiah walked through the large courtyard to the palace. Though the afternoon sun burned brightly, shadows played in the olive trees outside the palace wall. The birds were silent in the heat, and the guards at the doors of the garden were half asleep, standing like stone statues at the gate, their spears in their fists. When Jeremiah showed them the king's letter, they sluggishly stepped forward to open the gate.

The garden was empty. In the far shadows under the arches two figures came forward. One of them was a female dressed in a full black cassock with the hood covering most of her hair and shadowing her eyes. It was Shali.

Behind Shali, moving at a slow pace was the huge black man Ebed-melech, whose head rose above Shali's for what looked like a full two cubits.

"Well, Jeremiah," Shali said. "You have come as requested."

Jeremiah nodded in respect. "Honorable mother of our queen."

As they stood appraising one another, the leaves in the garden began to nod to a slight breeze. Even in the drought, the gardener had never spared water for these palace flowerbeds.

Shali had made a great effort to keep the beauty of her youth. But under the shadows of the dark hood, the age of her cheeks was visible. Her mouth was painted the same red, but the skin under her chin sagged into her hood. The long, bleached fingers she pulled from under her sleeves were followed by clawlike hands laced with thick blue veins.

"I received a letter from the king," Jeremiah said.

"I sent the letter."

"That was your writing?"

"Yes, of course." She said it without a trace of shame. "Jeremiah, my dear man, how often have you had an audience with the king?"

For a moment she took time to let her statement sink in. "There will be no audience with the king." She threw the hood away from her hair in a movement that looked like an old habit of flirtation.

She spoke with a level, determined tone. "Lately Josiah has asked about your daughter and her son. Not to me, but I have ways of discovering these things." Her chin lifted. "Josiah is never to hear about that woman and her son. Do you understand?"

Jeremiah felt her contempt like a stab of a knife in his heart.

"Nothing but good can come from cooperating with the powers of Assyria and Babylon. Yet you shout your frightening words." She raised her voice in warning. "We're approaching the marriage of Prince Eliakim. If your prophecies or your progeny should in any way interfere with the prince's ascension to the throne, there shall be such trouble as you will wish you had never seen."

She paused for effect. "My second grandson, Johanan, also stands in line for the kingship. There will be nothing available for your daughter and her issue. And if you interfere, I swear by the deities of my people, all of you shall suffer a wretched death."

Her words rang sharply on the air. Jeremiah glanced at the huge Nubian slave. His arms were as large as a man's waist.

Shali did not like Jeremiah's silence. "Do you understand, Jeremiah?"

"I understand what *you* want, honorable mother." He steadied his voice so that it wouldn't falter. "But I haven't inquired of the Lord to know what *He* wants."

Shali's face registered a cruel look of anger.

Jeremiah backed away, bowing graciously. "You have taken much trouble to give me your warning. For this I am grateful."

Shali stood with her graying hands on her hips. "Jeremiah, you're a marked man."

"I will consult with the Lord," he said.

Chapter Twenty-one

Cup of This Fury

After King Josiah read the discovered texts, his conversion was startling. He destroyed the pagan altars and decreed that the next Passover would be performed according to ritual.

On the fourteenth day of the first month, the animals for the festival were killed. Josiah further instructed the Levites, the teachers of Israel, to continue to safeguard the precious Jacob's Pillow and keep the sacred Ark of the Covenant Box in the temple rather than to carry it about as they had sometimes done.

To the families that kept their genealogy back to the children of Jacob, he said, "Take your places in the temple by kinship according to the responsibilities assigned to you by King David and his son Solomon. Arrange yourselves to be available to help each family of the people of Israel. Kill the Passover lambs for them. Make yourselves ritually clean and prepare the sacrifices in order that your fellow Judeans may follow the instructions which the Lord gave through Moses."

For the Passover feasts, King Josiah contributed thirty thousand of his sheep, lambs, and young goats, and three thousand bullocks. His officials also contributed many gifts.

Hilkiah and several other priests gave two thousand six hundred lambs and young goats, and three hundred bullocks to sacrifice during the festival. The leaders of the Levites contributed five thousand lambs and young goats and five hundred bullocks for use by the Levites as sacrifices.

After the lambs and goats had been killed, the Levites skinned them, and the priests sprinkled the blood on the altar. Each family group offered the animals according to the instructions in the Law of Moses. The Levites roasted the Passover sacrifices over the fire and cooked the sacred offering in pots, kettles, and pans, then distributed the meat to the people.

King Josiah had planned everything to the last detail, even the music. The musicians of the Levite clan of Asaph were in the places assigned to them. Bethany had been practicing a special musical composition for the occasion. The king had commanded that everything be done that day for the worship of the Lord, the keeping of the Passover Festival, and the offering of burnt flesh upon the altars.

For seven days all the people of Judea celebrated the Passover and the Festival of Unleavened Bread. Since the days of the prophet Samuel, the Passover had not been celebrated like this one. King Josiah, the priests, the Levites, and the people of Judah had come back to the law.

When it came time for the wedding of Josiah's fourteen-year-old son, Prince Eliakim, the court exploded with activity.

Standing on the horses' backs, the trainers rode the racing chariots through the city streets before Eliakim's marriage ceremony, restraining the animals with metal bits and long reins of leather studded with silver.

Eliakim and his bride Nehushta wore massive cloaks that resembled the wings of eagles. In place of feathers, leaves of hammered gold overlapped one another to the floor. The costumes were so heavy Nehushta had a little platform with wheels that rolled along under the fabulous wedding train to take some of the strain from her slender shoulders. The thirteen-year-old bride struggled beneath the weight until some of the slaves were enlisted to hold the garment up off the ground.

The flags that flew over the city were of gold cloth from Assyria. The wine was made from the best grapes grown in Judea. The row of banquet tables in the hall were so heavily laden that one of the tables slipped to the floor. Fowls were marinating and turning upon the spits to perfection. Fruits of every kind were heaped upon baskets with the grapes hanging like profuse jewels. Two hammered metal goblets sat at every place, one for water and the other for strong drink. One of the slave girls was assigned to cut small slices of lemon to keep the guests constantly supplied with drops of lemon juice in their water. Another slave kept the glasses filled with wine. The banquet was only for invited guests, but the wedding ceremony in the courtyard of the temple was open to anyone who could withstand the crowd and the heat.

Stepping down the narrow stairway that led from the archives to the courtyard of the palace, Jeremiah stopped on the middle landing. The dais was decorated with white flowers, each stem wrapped in silver. The canopy was so white, its brightness almost hurt his eyes.

Under an arch of white and silver flowers, he saw King Josiah and his wife Zebudah. Beside her were Shali, Chief Pedaiah, and Eliakim's younger brother, Prince Johanan, with the usual scowl on his face. Prince Johanan had already made a name for himself with his sword, killing every young fighter who had come up against him. The rumor was that his second-place claim to the throne had made him resentful. His face revealed guarded malcontent.

Rich and poor came to the wedding. Assyrian ambassadors and military dignitaries had seats near the dais, and on the edge of the courtyard was a group of Egyptians hiding their faces in richly brocaded silk.

Before the priest pronounced the ceremony, Bethany sang as her husband Beriah, the palace manager, played the zither. From her shoulders, a beautiful gown fell to the ground and pooled at her feet. Her face was framed by a burst of white lace that looked like the petals of a flower.

Jeremiah felt the music more than heard it, until he realized the accompanying words were taken from the verses of a song he had written long ago.

Thus says the Lord:
Cursed are those who trust in mere mortals
and make mere flesh their strength,
whose hearts turn away from the Lord.
They shall be like a shrub in the desert,
and shall not see when relief comes.
They shall live in the parched places of the wilderness,
in an uninhabited salt land.

There was a pause as the warning words echoed in the wedding party. But no one shifted. No one coughed. Bethany's voice rose, pure as a flute.

Blessed are those who trust in the Lord,
whose trust is the Lord.
They shall be like a tree planted by water,
sending out its roots by the stream.
It shall not fear when heat comes,
and its leaves shall stay green;
in the year of drought it is not anxious,
and it does not cease to bear fruit.

These were verses Jeremiah had shared with Baruch many years ago. As he contemplated them, he saw something unexpected. The king was looking at him. He stood frozen on the middle landing as King Josiah stared at him.

To be courteous, Jeremiah nodded. The king nodded in return. More than twenty years had passed since those school days when he had been Josiah's teacher. Jeremiah wanted to believe that things were better now in Jerusalem, and he could rest.

Chapter Twenty-two

The Love of His Life

On another of his visits to Libnah, Jeremiah found Latham's servants and slaves in an uproar. They were anxious about a missive that had come from Josiah's court. It was just a few words, but it had caused mayhem: *Prepare for the possibility that Egypt will be marching through.*

Egypt was coming?

Of course, if Egypt had heard the rumor that Assyria was colluding with Babylon to march southward, they would naturally be concerned. But to go on an offensive?

Even though the worried Shali immediately sent her ambassadors to the Egyptian army to secure a promise that Egypt would not attack Judea as they marched through, the trample of thousands of feet would devastate the land. In this time of unpredictable droughts, the farmers would be robbed of what little storage they had preserved. The animals would be cut down to serve as food. The military chariots and machines would tear up the roads.

Jeremiah prayed that the Lord would show mercy for his people. He wrote constantly, fashioning laments. Yet the Lord's answer was merciless. *I will call for a sword upon all the inhabitants of the earth.*

During the summer months in Libnah, Jeremiah again tried a long-ago formula of concentrating on the family and forgetting about Jerusalem. He had spoken in the streets. He believed he had done what the Lord had called him to do. He had given warnings. Now he would spend his days enjoying the companionship of his daughter Hamutal as they watched eleven-year-old Jehoahaz practice riding his beautiful horse.

The boy was going to be tall and very handsome. His dark brown hair, thick and straight, often fell in his eyes. His grandmother Abigail became his barber, coaxing him into a chair almost every week while she snipped and pulled. He hiked in the orchard with Jeremiah, sparred with his Uncle Chilian and any of the other uncles and cousins who visited the courtyard. Soon he showed great skill with the sword and knife.

When he turned twelve, the community rejoiced in the religious ceremonies that brought him into manhood. Jeremiah could not imagine greater feelings of love and pride than he had for Jehoahaz, his only grandchild. The boy's connections to the royal throne were seldom discussed. The two male heirs already in line for the throne made Jehoahaz's appointment next to impossible. And if Eliakim and the new bride Nehushta were to have a son, that son would follow Eliakim as king.

Neither Hamutal nor Jehoahaz ever saw or received any messages from the king.

But one dark night, Just before he was about to sleep, Jeremiah thought he heard Chilian's voice calling to him from the hallway. "Jeremiah! Can you hear me?"

Jeremiah rose from his bedding quickly.

"Get dressed at once and come to the front," Chilian said. "There are three men at the door with Father. They have commanded us to let them enter in the name of the king."

Stunned, Jeremiah was conscious of every echoing footstep as he followed Chilian along the vast corridors on the way to the front of the house. At the door, standing before Latham, were three cloaked men. One stood in the foreground, his hood hiding his brow. Behind him were the two who accompanied him: a black man, a full head taller, and another man whose dark eyes peered over a cowl that covered his mouth.

"My son-in-law." Latham nodded toward Jeremiah. "You wished to talk with him?"

Behind the woolen headcloth that covered much of his face, his eyes buried in shadows, the man in front spoke. At once Jeremiah recognized him—Josiah, the king. "Yes," the king said to Latham. "Please ask your servants to put up my horses and my men."

When Latham beckoned to the servants of the house to take the animals away, Jeremiah noticed that the black man was the same one who had been in the garden with Shali long ago. He did not turn his head as he walked out into the courtyard. The other man was King Josiah's assistant, Azaiah.

"King Josiah," Jeremiah said.

Uncle Latham did a double take.

"Yes, Latham. The king has come to your house," said Jeremiah.

Latham followed his men out to insure that accommodations for the soldiers would be made to the king's satisfaction.

After the men had left the foyer, Josiah turned to Jeremiah. "I have come to see my wife and my son. I beg you to leave this visit confidential."

A woman servant standing within hearing distance of the conversation, quietly turned and slipped down the hall, her robes shuffling against the tile.

Taken aback, Jeremiah stood before the young man he'd taught as a boy. The grown king, now twenty-seven, towered over him. They hadn't stood close to one another for a long time. The king removed his hood. Josiah's fine large head was thick with burnished curls. At his neck he wore a hammered-gold collar, and under the wool cloak, Jeremiah saw the silver vestment.

Josiah said, "I'm your student, Jeremiah. How sorry I am for the threats that have been made against you. And for the wrongs of the court."

Jeremiah bowed in respect.

"I'm caught between honoring the Assyrians—whom the courtiers long to appease—and the pride of our Judean heritage. I've been paying the price for peace. I read the book your father found in the temple and realized how far we have slipped from God's law."

"The Lord is heedful of your efforts: the cleansing, the Passover," Jeremiah said, ushering the king through the corridor to his quarters at the end of the hall. When they entered the room, he pulled a cedar chair to the table. "But I hear the heart of the court hasn't changed."

"There are still evils," said the king, his voice wavering. He lowered his eyes.

Jeremiah invited him to use this room, to rest, to stay for a few days. But Josiah shook his head. "They don't know I'm here," he said.

There was a small knock at the door. When Jeremiah opened it, the maidservant who had disappeared down the hall stepped aside.

In the muted dusk Hamutal appeared in the doorway. She looked as white as any angel, wearing a flowing gown that fell in ripples at her feet. At her neck she held the silk folds with her long slender fingers.

When Josiah saw her, he rose quickly.

"The boy is sleeping . . . or he would come," the maidservant said before she left.

Josiah reached out to take Hamutal's hand. "The love of my life," he said. "Oh, how I've wanted to be with you." Josiah took her hand and brought her into the room.

When Jeremiah saw Hamutal's radiant face, he slipped into the hallway and closed the door against the light.

The next morning, Jeremiah woke when he heard Chilian's voice outside the room. "Jeremiah! The king wishes a private session with you and Hamutal and Jehoahaz."

As he arrived at the front of the house, Jeremiah saw that Hamutal was bringing the thirteen-year-old Jehoahaz into the vestibule. Looking hastily dressed, the boy walked with a little shuffle.

When Josiah saw his son, his face glowed. "Jehoahaz," he said. His voice wavered. "My son."

"Father," Jehoahaz knelt at his father's feet.

"No, no, it is I who must kneel at your feet, for you will be king," Josiah said.

Josiah glanced at Jeremiah. "This announcement is something only the four of us must carry in our hearts." He looked at Hamutal. "You must promise not to breathe it to anyone."

He took Jehoahaz's hands in his and looked steadily into his face. "At this last Passover," he said, "when I destroyed the altars, many of the people were converted to righteousness. And now many have risen up to request that the next king be from the line of Judah, from David."

Josiah looked into the boy's eyes. "Son, how would you like to come and live at the palace?"

Jeremiah was not sure he heard correctly. "But the firstborn is Eliakim."

Josiah knit his brows. "Things are changing. The people are fearful of Assyrian and Babylonian designs."

Hamutal said nothing. Both she and her son had lived without Josiah for so long that he was now a foreigner—an emperor from a land far away. His clothes, the cloak with the gold trim, the armor at his breast, the silk hose and the soft leather boots—all of it was exotic and too exquisite for their world. Yet in Hamutal's face there was also a reverence, a love that defied any fear. If this was what Josiah would require, then this was what would be.

Still standing, Jehoahaz shifted his feet under his calf-length garment. He bowed his head.

"I knew that Hamutal would raise a righteous son," Josiah said. "Soon I will send for you."

Jeremiah stepped forward. "But is it safe, Josiah? We understand the feelings of the court. Your wife's family would go to any lengths to destroy a usurper to the throne."

"This is the choice of the God-fearing people of Jerusalem. And this is my choice," he said. "There will be substantial protection."

Hamutal stood behind the boy with her hands on his shoulders.

Softly Josiah blessed them. "God be with you, Hamutal. The will of God will prevail."

In the weeks after Josiah's visit, Jeremiah's life in Libnah seemed to be a miracle. Everything about the world he lived in—where he walked, where he sat—seemed to be illuminated. There was a new child growing in Hamutal.

Daily he became more aware of his customary tasks—his prayer, his hours preparing Jehoahaz for the priesthood—all of the routines that sustained him. He was grateful for every meal cooked in the kitchen, his washings, the garments the servants brought to him, and the stylus he used to mark the scrolls. He bent over his work every day, knowing how important it was.

Some time passed without any word from Josiah, and a change took place in Jehoahaz. The boy had spent many days wielding his sword and practicing quick turns with his horse. But as the king made no attempts to contact Latham's household, an anxiety arose in the boy. Sometimes he burst into unexplainable moments of anger. He knit his brows when he ate and kicked his foot at the table, up and down, up and down, nervously.

"You don't have to go to the palace if you don't want to," Hamutal told him.

"I want to go," Jehoahaz answered, scowling. "I'd just like to know when."

"Prepare today as though it will be tomorrow," Jeremiah said. "Every day is a day of preparation. You are learning now the most important lessons of your life—patience, honesty, kindness, the ingredients of good character, which are important virtues for any leader."

The boy's foot continued to bob up and down. "I've learned these things. Please. Just write to him," he begged. "Ask him when it will be."

Hamutal often expressed her hope that her first son would stay at least until the baby was born. And it happened that way. Indeed, the birth was a glorious event in Latham's household. The servants rejoiced with a huge gathering in which the women offered blankets and knitted clothes for the child. Hamutal gathered the family around her as though she would never let go.

Jehoahaz became moody and dark, resisting Jeremiah's lessons at school. Finally, Josiah sent a short note that read, "I am mindful of my son, Prince Jehoahaz. We're making preparations. Please have patience."

At that time Jeremiah and his grandson didn't know they would have to wait two more long years.

Chapter Twenty-three

Sons of the King

For the boy Jehoahaz, months passed like centuries. But one day, during the trimming of the olive trees, while the women were preparing the food for the midday feast, Latham's gardeners ran into the courtyard with exciting news. A large chariot flanked by soldiers on horseback was coming up the lane.

Latham scattered his servants quickly and asked them to bring Jehoahaz at once. Hamutal and Jeremiah came behind the prince, Hamutal holding the two-year-old Mattaniah in her arms and bowing her head, hidden by her veil.

Azaiah, the king's assistant, was accompanied by five soldiers in heavy chain armor. Azaiah wore a red cloak clasped by a large brass hoop. He didn't waste his words on pleasantries.

"The king wants both of his sons at court," he announced. He was a short man with a stubby beard and a head of coarse gold hair. His wrists were stacked with bracelets and jewels.

"Both sons?" repeated Jeremiah.

"He knows about the little child Mattaniah. His request is that both of them must be groomed in the palace to occupy the throne."

Hamutal's face grew white, and she gave a tortured cry. When Azaiah moved forward, she stepped back, clinging so fiercely to the boy that the little child struggled to be free.

"And may the mother come?" asked Jeremiah. "He has barely left her breast."

"It's not safe for Hamutal to come to Jerusalem. As it is, Josiah must hide the children from the hostile members of the court."

Hamutal would not give up the baby.

"Please, Mother," Jehoahaz begged. "I'll watch out for him."

Hamutal drew back, grief stricken. "If you go I'll miss you, Jehoahaz. But that's something we expected. I can't let Mattaniah go. No, no. I cannot do it."

"You needn't send any clothes or food. We're completely prepared," Azaiah said.

"Mother, please. There are soldiers waiting at the gate," Jehoahaz said.

"He's just a baby!"

As Azaiah tried to take the baby out of her arms, he wailed, his little face contorted.

"No, no, no," she screamed. "Not Mattaniah. He's only two years old. Please. Please."

Latham and his household had gathered in the foyer to watch. Abigail was on her way down the hall in her makeshift chair with wheels. Everyone had been alerted by Hamutal's cry. In the doorway stood two of the largest soldiers in full dress, their chain mail shining in the sun. They walked forward, the sound of the metal fringe on their armor striking the chains beneath their vestments.

Azaiah held Hamutal by the shoulders as one of the soldiers wrested Mattaniah from her. He screamed as the man carried him through the gate and into the waiting chariot.

"He'll be safe and happy with his father, the king," said Azaiah. "And if you have any rash thoughts about following us, Jeremiah, the king made it clear that you are to stay out of Jerusalem—or face arrest."

Hamutal fell into her father's arms, sobbing. Jeremiah held her. "Calm yourself, Hamutal. Please calm yourself. The boys need your strength."

Young Jehoahaz followed the visitors as though he knew exactly where he was going, his stride long and confident. The fifteen-year-old had been waiting for this moment for several years.

The family in the foyer watched him climb into the chariot, then turn and nod at the militia. They would be his to command someday. One of the soldiers, the metal on his tunic sparkling in the sun, smiled at something the boy said, and slipped his own sword out of the leather case he wore at his belt. When he gave the sword to Jehoahaz, the boy laughed and began to jab it in the air. The men laughed with him. He showed it to Mattaniah, who was still whimpering. In just a moment, however, fascinated with the silver on the handle, the little boy quit crying.

Jeremiah walked his daughter over to Abigail, who slid her chair close to a bench in the foyer and put out her arms. Hamutal buried her face in her grandmother's neck as the chariot drove away.

Chapter Twenty-four

The Cost of Peace

For almost two years, Jeremiah kept the king's order to stay away. But when he received a message from his aging mother that his father was ill, he knew he must go to Jerusalem. He tarried in his parents' house until he could acquire different clothing and disguise his beard with the red dye of the henna.

Fearful of going immediately out into the streets to teach again, he thought he would begin by talking to Lehi. When he knocked on the door, Giddel, Lehi's most faithful Israelite slave, opened it. Not a flicker of recognition crossed Giddel's face. Seeing the red-bearded stranger, he growled. "Who are you and what do you want?"

When Jeremiah revealed himself, Giddel fell on his knees. "Oh, Jeremiah, how we have missed you."

Lehi greeted him with open arms. "You think you can hide yourself, but I would know you just by the way you walk."

"I hope that isn't indicative of what the masses remember."

"The people have forgotten your preaching, Jeremiah. The only one who remembers you well is Shali. Josiah's cleansing and the repentance of the people lasted only a few years."

Sariah came into the room carrying a baby in her arms. Behind her were two older boys, and she led a toddler by the hand.

Lehi smiled, "We have been busy. Four boys now. Laman and Lemuel, and Sam. And this is our youngest, Nephi."

Sariah held the baby for Jeremiah to see. Baby Nephi gurgled and stuck his fist in his mouth.

"But why are we delaying our hospitality?" Lehi made an expansive gesture. "Come. Your parents are close enough for visits. We'd be honored by your presence in our house."

The roads from Lehi's house to the city were so familiar to Jeremiah he could have walked them blindfolded.

He decided to feel the city out by going first to the north gate. Taking time to look around, he saw many new buildings along the roads. Hundreds of animals and people jostled one another in the square. Vendors had set up smart-looking stalls where they created and marketed their wares. The potters entertained visitors as they shaped small and large vessels on their wheels.

The prophets Ezekiel, Urijah, and two others, Zephaniah and Daniel, were teaching at the gate. When no one recognized him with his red beard, Jeremiah found a place to sit on a barrel so he could listen to Urijah.

The days are surely coming, says the Lord, when it shall no longer be said, "As the Lord lives who brought the people of Israel up out of the land of Egypt" . . . but "As the Lord lives who brought the people of Israel up out of the land of the north and out of all the lands where he had driven them." For I will bring them back to their own land that I gave to their ancestors.

For my eyes are on all their ways; they are not hidden from my presence, nor is their iniquity concealed from my sight. And I will doubly repay their iniquity and their sin, because they have polluted my land with the carcasses of their detestable idols, and have filled my inheritance with their abominations.

Thus says the Lord, Urijah continued.

See, a people is coming from the land of the north, a great nation is stirring from the farthest parts of the earth. They . . . are cruel and have no mercy; their sound is like the roaring sea; they ride on horses, equipped like a warrior for battle, against you!

Jeremiah felt uneasy. These were exactly the words people did not want to hear. A man carrying a load of peat tied to his back lowered his head and spit in the sand. "People from the north? It's a time of peace, or haven't you heard? We're at peace with those people from the north."

Urijah was undeterred. "You will not escape the warriors," he shouted. "They shall hunt you down out of *every mountain and every hill, and out of the clefts of the rocks.*"

The man shouted, "This talk of war when there is no war. This kind of talk will make war happen. It's treason."

Ignoring the heckling, Urijah appealed to the Lord. *O hope of Israel! O Lord! All who forsake you shall be put to shame; those who turn away from you shall be recorded in the underworld, for they have forsaken the fountain of living waters.*

A woman carrying a water jar on her head stopped and narrowed her eyes in anger.

"The Lord," Urijah continued, "has promised to bring upon you *the day of evil . . . and double destruction.*"

"You lie!" the woman sneered. "Ha! You tell us the north country is going to come down and rip us away like they did Israel. But we have a contract with Assyria."

Dressed in a golden tunic, an officer, with a flank of soldiers, led a procession of women. They were laughing and stepping brightly through the crowds, tossing and flicking their scarves as though to carve a pathway for themselves. The sun glittered through the gold threads of the silk.

Jeremiah pulled back, wary of what was happening.

When the woman with the apple core saw the procession, she ducked away from Urijah and the heckler with the peat on his back. "Those harlots," she said under her breath. She tossed the apple core to the feet of the women as they minced by.

While the crowd waited, Jeremiah felt a tug on his robe. One of the girls had slipped to his side, her eyes wide with terror. "Save us," she whispered. "Aren't you from the God of Abraham? I plead with you." Then, as quickly as she had spoken, she stepped back near the others, continuing to prance. She flipped her dark scarf away from her burnished hair, and a yellow square of silk floated out to the end of her fingers. At that moment, a soldier grabbed her arm in reprimand and yanked her farther back into the group.

After the women passed, Jeremiah rose to stand by Urijah. His presence beside the young prophet tempered the noise at once. Surprised at the intruder, the crowd settled into a hush. Jeremiah was as straight and tall as he had always been. His hair might have had a bit of gray, but it only added authority to his already impressive stature.

With the power of the Lord in his voice, Jeremiah felt something he had not felt before—as though light flowed through him.

Hear the word of the Lord, you kings of Judah, and all Judah, and all the inhabitants of Jerusalem, who enter by these gates . . . for the sake of your lives.

Urijah pulled back in surprise, suddenly recognizing him. But Jeremiah put his finger to his lips to stop the prophet from saying his name.

Feeling empowered by the spirit of the Lord, Jeremiah began to speak.

Return now everyone from his evil way, and make your ways and your doings good.

The crowd was instantly silent.

"You're talking to the wrong people," yelled the woman who had thrown the apple core to the ground. "We are not guilty," she snarled. "We obey the commandments."

Jeremiah did not answer her for a moment. "Do you live God's laws? Do you obey *all* of the commandments? Do you take God's name in vain? The Lord has asked about the Sabbath day. Do you *bear no burden on the Sabbath day or bring it in by the gates of Jerusalem?"*

The crowd was so quiet, the only sound was their breathing.

"The Lord says," Jeremiah continued. *Do not carry a burden out of your houses on the Sabbath or do any work, but keep the Sabbath day holy, as I commanded your ancestors. Yet they did not listen or incline their ear; they stiffened their necks and would not hear or receive instruction.*

But if you do not listen to me, to keep the Sabbath day holy, and to carry in no burden through the gates of Jerusalem on the Sabbath day, then I will kindle a fire in its gates; it shall devour the palaces of Jerusalem and shall not be quenched.

There was total silence for a time. And then the buzz of murmuring rippled through the crowd. Anticipating repercussions from the impact of his words, Jeremiah thought it best to leave before anyone recognized him.

When he was able to retreat unobtrusively, he quickened his steps and strolled to the temple compound.

Six guards, dressed in uniforms of sparkling red and gold chains, stood at the entrance of the temple. "We have strict orders not to admit anyone who has no authorization," the chief guard said.

"May I see Baruch?"

"Who are you?"

"I am a relative of Baruch," Jeremiah said.

It was not long before Baruch, striding to the guards, recognized the red-bearded Jeremiah through the gates. When the guards opened the gate, Jeremiah ran to his cousin and embraced him for a long moment. The black curls hanging about the scribe's flushed cheeks were now gray. His shoulders seemed bent from his years faithfully spent preserving texts. Taking Jeremiah by the elbow, he led him past the militia to the compound.

Jeremiah said, "I may need your help to get into the palace so I may see my grandchildren."

Baruch looked aside and spoke in a low voice. "If you have an authorized clearance to the archives, there might be something we can do."

It was a few weeks before Baruch discovered a way Jeremiah could meet with his grandsons. Late one morning as Jeremiah copied a scroll in the archives, Baruch came to him quietly and said, "Follow me."

They went down the steps to the courtyard. There were so many priests and templegoers milling about the vast quad that no one noticed the two scribes. Baruch led him across the stone floor to the other side of the palace where there was a path to the waters. He took him down a narrow stone stairwell that Jeremiah had never seen before. It led to another compound of buildings inside the palace wall. An open field nearby was large enough to graze some of the king's livestock.

Beneath a low balcony on the hillside, Baruch bent so far over that he was barely able to get his legs under him. Jeremiah followed him, feeling his own fifty-one-year-old legs shake against his caftan. When they had passed through the opening to the other side, Jeremiah could see the reason for the tight passageway. He looked back upon three guards on the sidewalk of the palace garden. Surprised, he saw that one of them was the huge black man he'd seen twice before.

"Ebed-melech," Baruch said. "Queen Zebudah's favorite Nubian slave. He's guarding the entrance to the corral. He's formidable. No one can deceive him."

At the other side of the low barn buildings, dust rose from the ring. By climbing down into the arena, Jeremiah could see the fenced circle. Both of his grandsons were riding horses around and around close to the fence. Little Mattaniah was only five years old, yet he was throwing his reins in the air like his seventeen-year-old brother.

Baruch said, "I will go out into the yard and distract the instructors. Since there have been rumors of murder and intrigue against these princes, they watch them at every moment. But they won't follow the boys into the stalls. You won't have a lot of time."

Jeremiah waited, crouched below the window at the stall where Baruch had directed him. When Jehoahaz came to untie the saddle's leather straps, Jeremiah rose up and walked quietly toward the horse. He stood on the far side of the animal. When it snorted, Jehoahaz caught sight of Jeremiah. Fear crossed the boy's face, until he recognized this stranger.

"Grandfather," he said. "It's you!"

"I have missed you, my boy," Jeremiah said. "They won't let me into the palace."

Jehoahaz's face paled as he reached across the saddle to place the reins. He rushed forward. His arms went around his grandfather's neck, and he hung on for a long time.

They each had many questions, but there was not much time. When Jehoahaz called out to his five-year-old brother to come, one of the slaves came with him. Though shy at first, Mattaniah eventually came up to his grandfather and sat on his knee. He finally put his head with its light, strawberry-colored hair on Jeremiah's breast.

"I'm learning to be a soldier," Mattaniah said.

"That's good," Jeremiah answered. "It's good for you to learn to fight so that you can protect your mother from the enemies that would come upon us to destroy us. It's always good to be a soldier."

"Are there always enemies?" Mattaniah asked.

"Yes," Jeremiah said. "There are always enemies."

"If the Assyrians should turn against us," Jehoahaz said, "we must use the militia for complete protection. Father's militia is the best in the world."

Jeremiah did not tell the boy that there was no such thing as complete protection.

It was quiet in the vast, dark hollow of the stable. The slave ordered to stay by the five-year-old must have heard the conversation, but his expression stayed rigid, his eyes glassy with a stony gaze.

"Can't we fight them back?" Mattaniah asked.

"The best way to fight back is to obey God's commandments."

"Are you going to be with us now?" asked the child.

Jeremiah nodded. "I will come to see you as often as I can."

"My father is preparing me to be king," Jehoahaz said. "He says it is what the people of Judah want."

"I'm here to help," Jeremiah said. "We must prepare as carefully as we can."

Chapter Twenty-six

Stop the Egyptians

Though Josiah had taken all the precautions he could to hide his Jewish sons in the court, their residence was impossible to keep secret.

When Shali discovered Josiah had installed Hamutal's boys at the palace, she stayed in her chambers for a week and would not see anyone. One rumor surfaced that she wanted to kill them.

When her oldest grandson Eliakim produced the baby son Coniah, there seemed to be less and less possibility that Hamutal's boys could interfere. Shali came out of her quarters with her slaves and began to rebuild the pagan altars. No one stopped her.

On the rare days Baruch and Jeremiah were able to get through to the corral, they visited the military field where the boys were being trained to fight. If Jeremiah was lucky enough to see the princes, he kept his head covered when he talked to them. He attended to every word they spoke, no matter if most of it was about war.

"I knocked a dummy off a field horse," the vigorous young Mattaniah bragged.

"We're ready for war," Jehoahaz stated. "My father says no one will dare to come against our militia. We're the greatest in the world. So there will be no war. Jerusalem is protected by God. We have made peace with the Assyrians."

"What about the Egyptians?" Jeremiah asked him.

"We still pay taxes to the Egyptians. They want to fight Assyria, but not us."

"What if the Egyptian army cuts across our land to reach Assyria?"

"Shali has told them not to come."

For the time being it seemed Jerusalem's enemies were held at bay.

On a clear, hot morning, as Jeremiah, Urijah, and the other prophets were speaking at the gate, some Egyptian scouts arrived from Gaza with shocking news—the Egyptian king Necco had finished his preparations and was marching northward along the west coast to attack Assyria.

"There's no reason to be alarmed," Shali told those in the palace courtyard. "I've sent my ambassadors to make sure of Necco's intentions."

Shali's ambassadors returned with a message from the Egyptian king, Necco.

What have we to do with each other, King of Judah? I am not coming against you this day, but against the house with which I am at war; and God has commanded me to make haste. Cease opposing God, who is with me, lest He destroy you.

Still very much concerned, King Josiah announced that the brazen Necco sounded much too ambitious. Judean troops ought to protect Judah. And their supposed allies in Assyria would expect help. This meant confrontation. An alarm rippled through the city. The people climbed to their rooftops to burn incense and to bake cakes for the Queen of Heaven.

Chapter Twenty-seven

Josiah's War

Jeremiah returned as often as he could to the military field to catch a glimpse of his grandchildren. Recently, the officers had been recruiting more troops to prepare for the Egyptians. Jeremiah had to make his way through the turmoil of the dense crowds practicing their maneuvers, through rows of the metal shields glinting in the sun, the trappings flashing with bright gold-colored chains.

One day, as he stood alone behind the wall of the storage shed watching the maneuvers, the ranks seemed to be particularly animated.

"Grandfather!" Jehoahaz had come along the outer wall of the barn through the dense trees.

He was no longer a boy, but a large well-proportioned young man. He had a full head of deep auburn-red hair that shimmered in the sun. His suit of chains glistened like bright jewels. He carried a headpiece in his hands. "I must tell you good-bye."

"Yes, I know about stopping the Egyptians," Jeremiah said. "And, of course, Mattaniah will not be going with you."

Jehoahaz gave a slight laugh. "Not that he doesn't want to. He's a little fighter, that boy! But I must go. Father's determined to stop Necco from passing all the way through to attack our allies in Assyria, and I must help him."

When the yew tree by the wall shook in the breeze, the shadows on the surface moved as though some ethereal power were writing words of warning.

"Your father has dedicated himself to the protection of his people," Jeremiah said. "He tried instilling the laws of Moses into their hearts. Most of them didn't listen. Now he wants to stop Egypt's invasion, but I can't help feeling he should pay heed to Necco."

Jehoahaz laid his gloved hand on Jeremiah's arm and leaned over to kiss him on the cheek. "All will go well. Keep yourself safe, Grandfather. My father and I will be back soon."

After it was all over, Captain Laban broadcast at court that he'd warned Josiah not to go to the field of battle. Yes, he admitted that he had noticed in the ranks a strange well-equipped chariot that he hadn't seen before. He said to himself, "Who owns that chariot? I haven't seen that chariot on the battlefield before."

Laban claimed he made a special effort to draw close to this unknown vehicle and look into it. The occupant seemed to be a merchant dressed in a large striped-silk headdress which covered half his face as well as his hair. The man didn't turn toward Laban, but looked straight ahead with a narrow, determined gaze. He might have been a wealthy landowner or shopkeeper trying to make his way quickly through the crowds of men and animals.

Because he'd been busy fighting in the field with his men, Laban hadn't inquired further about the occupant in the chariot. But when the struggle—passing through two low hills just outside of Megiddo—came under a barrage of arrows, he saw several crippled chariots lying demolished in the road. The richly equipped chariot was among them.

When Laban rode to the damaged vehicle, he saw that the driver had been killed. Inside lay the man with a silk headpiece of many colors still wrapped about his head. He had been struck in the neck with an arrow.

"Help me. I'm wounded," the man gasped.

When Laban took the silk away to draw out the arrow, he saw that the man in the chariot was King Josiah.

"Never had I been so surprised," Laban reported. "Never had I suspected that Josiah would bring himself out upon the field of battle."

Quickly, so as not to risk his position, Captain Laban mustered horses to draw the vehicle to the side of the road. He leaned inside of the cab. The king was pleading so intensely, Laban could not refuse to help. Trembling, he carefully pulled the arrow out of the king's neck, unwound his own turban, and wrapped it around the wound to staunch the blood. He then ordered seven of his best field officers to accompany the king back to the palace.

The only prince on the battlefield aware of the king's situation was Jehoahaz. Sick at heart about his father's wounds, he helped Laban put the king into another chariot with a physician. Urging the horses to move at their most rapid speed, Jehoahaz drove a day and a half to get back to Jerusalem.

When they reached the palace, the king was still alive. They brought him into his bed chamber and placed him on the divan. Though his breath was uneven, and the whites of his eyes a dull gray, he asked for Jehoahaz. Begging for his son to stay with him every moment, he clung to the young man's hand with all of the strength he had left in his bloodless fingers. King Josiah, in the prime of his life, was thirty-nine years old. The physicians hovered over him with herbal remedies and prayers.

Jeremiah was surprised to get the message that Josiah requested his presence. Walking to the palace with his father Hilkiah, he hung in the background, waiting for the others to beckon him. Though the physicians were trying to keep the wounded king silent, a flood of anxious officials flowed through the palace asking what they should do. There seemed to be so many questions that could be answered only by the king.

The women, who had not been allowed to enter, waited outside the door, lowering their faces into their shawls. The guards limited the audience of the king to one or two others at a time, but as the day wore on, and the king grew weaker, some of the officials plowed through the guards with angry voices.

At last the king waved his hand to the guards. "I am sorry," he said. "Tell everyone to go except for Jehoahaz, the councilors, and the priests." He paused as though making a great effort. "Let the women come in."

The guards stood aside as Queen Zebudah rushed to her husband and knelt by the divan. Shali followed her daughter.

"Josiah, Josiah!" Zebudah cried out. "Oh, my husband! Please don't leave us!" She sobbed against his hand. Her tears wet his fingers. "Oh Heaven, spare him. Spare him."

Jeremiah and Hilkiah had moved to the edge of the room to be out of the way. Jeremiah noticed that Shali was no longer the astonishing beauty she had been. She was now a great-grandmother—she had a great-grandson, Eliakim's baby, Prince Coniah. Her hair seemed like gray wire, her profile like an old knife. Over her shoulders she wore a red tunic laced with gold thread, and on her feet, sandals with laces wrapped around her ankles. She had aged. Yet her brazen eyes were as deep and vital as they had ever been.

"Don't tire him," Shali said to her daughter, Zebudah. "He has important business yet." Zebudah drew back, her eyes red from crying.

"Yes," Josiah said weakly, scanning the visitors in the room. He had requested the council stay with him for a specific reason. There was the sound of slow breathing in Josiah's throat—a sound of gasping to get the breath he needed to live. "Please," he said. "Jehoahaz, come to me."

The concerned son, now twenty-three years old, knelt at the side of the divan and lowered his head against his father's hand.

"No, no," Josiah said. "Stand up. You are to stand."

Jehoahaz stood. But he clasped his father's fingers and lifted them to his lips.

"Jehoahaz is now the king," Josiah said so clearly that the court couldn't help but hear. Chief Pedaiah and Governor Pashur made audible sounds of distress in their throats.

"No, no, father," Jehoahaz said. "You are the king."

Shali leaned against the foot of the divan and faced the dying man. Her hands, tight as the talons of a hawk, clutched the foot of the bed. "You have forgotten that Eliakim is the eldest! He's still on the battlefield. Do you remember him, your son Eliakim? And his new son Coniah?"

"God bless Eliakim for fighting on the battlefield for the safety of Jerusalem and Assyria. It is well." Josiah gave a jagged cough that rattled his throat. "But I trust Jehoahaz to lead the people in the ways of God."

Jeremiah stepped forward. He stood beside his grandson and placed his hand on Josiah's brow. "Oh blessed king," Jeremiah said. When he spoke, the sound reverberated in the chamber.

"I have done what God wanted me to do," Josiah murmured. "I go to our God."

There was not a movement in the hall. Jeremiah stood beside his grandson, the new king, Jehoahaz, while the son held in both of his hands the limp wrist of his father. Life was draining away.

The court was silent. No one stirred—until Governor Pashur moved forward. With a reluctant stare from dark eyes under his heavy brows, he laid his tapered fingers on the king's bedcover. "We will honor the king's dying request," he said. "We shall make Jehoahaz king."

There was a buzz of voices. Pashur had won the approval of the council. But Shali's eyes turned the color of ashes. She tightened her fists. While the priests tended to the body of their king, she glared at Governor Pashur, who took her hand in a firm grip and led her away. As he hurried her into the recesses of the temple offices, the spectators in the bedchamber could hear her wailing angrily.

Afterward, when Shali and Zebudah finally came to the balcony, the people reached out their arms to them. Some of them tore their hair and clothes. Many women paced up and down, shedding fierce tears, pounding the lower wall of the palace, shaking their heads with grief.

Word of the death spread quickly that afternoon; thousands from the hills and cities around Jerusalem gathered to attend the impressive ceremony. From Ammon, Edom, Moab, Jasher, Maacah, they dragged their carts and parked outside the gates. Hundreds of gifts poured into the temple, some with crude writings expressing sadness and regret. Yet many of the mourners stated how grateful they were that Jehoahaz was to be their king.

Chapter Twenty-Eight

The Throne

The coronation took place on the day after the funeral. The court secretary, Shaphan, brought the council and priests together inside the temple and read the inaugural documents.

The priests anointed Jehoahaz with oil. Immediately after the anointing, the twenty-three-year-old king of Judah made a solemn announcement. He said he must continue his father's mission by returning to the battlefield and stopping Necco's campaign against the Assyrians. He would leave early in the morning. If anyone wished to join the ranks with him, he would welcome them.

Jeremiah dreaded Jehoahaz's departure. He suspected that Pashur had already known honor would take the new king back to the battlefield. Jeremiah tried not to let himself imagine treachery . . .

When Jeremiah and Lehi awoke in the morning, they could hear the rumbling of the hooves of horses and the tramping of many feet. Walking outside to the street, they watched the informal collection of hundreds of recent recruits eager to defeat the Egyptian battalion that had killed their king. There were slaves who wore garments so thin they were torn in many places. Their weapons were rusted carving knives, their sandals so worn they had to be tied to each foot with rope. Some old soldiers wore military uniforms they hadn't put to use for many years.

The reports coming back from the battlefield were not good. The final report came from Josiah's second son, Prince Johanan. Riding a swift horse into the palace yard, he waved a tattered flag. His voice echoed against the palace walls as he shouted, "We've made peace with the Egyptians! And Eliakim is king!"

When Jeremiah heard the commotion in the courtyard, he glanced at his father, Hilkiah. The older man was nodding off—which happened more and more often as he bent over his copy these days. Without disturbing him, Jeremiah rose quickly and walked to the windows. He looked down into the courtyard.

"We've stopped the Egyptians!" Johanan cried out. "They've made Eliakim king. They call him Jehoiakim."

The feisty Prince Johanan, a stocky man with rough, short sideburns, rested the bottom of the flag pole on the pommel of his horse's saddle while he grabbed the middle of the pole and whirled it in a circle.

"What are you telling us, Johanan?" One of the council members in the yard approached him.

"Necco captured Jehoahaz at Hamath and took him prisoner to Egypt."

There was a murmur through the crowd. Someone howled, "Do we belong to Necco now?"

Johanan whipped the flag with confidence. His brother had been restored to his rightful place as king. "We are still Judah. Long live Jehoiakim, the firstborn—the true king!"

Chapter Twenty-nine

Warnings and Consequences

Jeremiah followed Hilkiah to the apartment close to the temple. Marika sat curled in a leather chair before the window in her bedroom, grieving for her great-grandson. Bent over with her head in her hands, she was tearing her hair. Small wisps of it lay on the floor at her feet.

"Mother, Mother," Jeremiah said in a broken voice. "Please, my gracious and lovely mother, do not risk your own health for this tragedy."

She raised her face to her oldest son and reached for him with an unsteady hand. "There are criminals in the court. Now my grandson has been taken to Egypt."

"Perhaps Necco believes that if he has Jehoahaz in captivity, Jerusalem will continue to pay more tribute."

"But Eliakim as king?" Marika looked away. "There are rumors that he has fathered at least a hundred babies who have ended up as sacrifices at Topheth."

"We cannot prove that," Hilkiah contended. "Do not speak like this, for it will reap upon us the terror of the court." He came to his wife, leaned over the back of the chair and put his gnarled hands on her shoulders.

Marika bowed her head. "If only the people would turn from their wicked ways."

Hilkiah kissed her hair. "We haven't much time left on this earth. We must work to change what we can change."

During the day, Jeremiah stood at the archive windows and looked down on the olive trees bending in the wind. When the leaves turned over, the colorless gray undersides flickered in the sun. He must hold himself together in the winds of this life when darkness buffeted his heart. He must stand steady because his work was not done. He knew he must continue to speak in the city.

Trying to finish some of the copy work in the archives, he spent hours helping his father and Baruch gather scraps of papyrus, bits and pieces of writings, and placing them in a leather bag. His father sometimes glanced over to his table and smiled. It had been a matter of good-natured banter between Hilkiah and Baruch that Jeremiah had written enough verses to stuff a feather bed.

Outside on the street, Jeremiah grew weary hearing the councilors and self-proclaimed prophets rejoice because they had "procured the peace." To save their official titles they prostrated themselves before the Egyptians and promised to pay the requested tribute. They also began to return to pagan ways and commit unspeakable atrocities in the temple of God.

Jeremiah was sick at heart.

But in the prophets of Jerusalem I have seen a more shocking thing: they commit adultery and walk in lies; they strengthen the hands of evildoers, so that no one turns from wickedness; all of them have become like Sodom to me, and its inhabitants like Gomorrah.

One day while Jeremiah visited at the marketplace with Lehi, an official named Elishama approached them. He was flanked on both sides by two priests.

"Jeremiah," he said. "I think you know why we are here. King Jehoiakim has sent us to stop you."

"Yes, we have heard some rumors," Jeremiah answered.

"You are asserting lies about the prophets and the government officials."

"They are not lies."

"What you have been teaching stirs up trouble," Elishama said. "You call us monstrous names, and liken us to a pile of rotten figs! We are now pawns of Necco of Egypt, and he is threatening to collude with Nebuchadnezzar. Surely you must understand. When the people believe what you tell them, they become troubled and angry. Some of them will not pay their taxes. When you tell them that Jerusalem will be destroyed, you discourage them. Some of them say, 'Oh well, if Jerusalem is to be destroyed, we will not need to honor the king or pay the tribute.'"

"Is this about money?" Jeremiah asked.

Elishama waved his hands as though bothered by a pesky fly. Lowering his voice, he said, "No. It's not about money. It's about treason."

"Treason?" Lehi whispered. "They're calling it treason?"

Jeremiah's face felt hot. If he could not speak the truth, what could he do? He asked Lehi to accompany him on the way home. As they walked through the shops, Jeremiah stopped at the potter. The man's business had been suffering lately because taxes were so high the people had no money to buy his vessels. Standing behind the potter at his wheel, Jeremiah watched the mud fly.

"I'm sorry. I didn't see you." The potter looked up.

"I wish to buy one of your large jars," Jeremiah said, pulling money from his purse.

Jeremiah carried the jar upright in his arms so the lid would not fall off the top. As he and Lehi walked through the streets with the huge pot, some of the elders and older priests who'd been out in the marketplace began to follow them. Soon they'd attracted a murmuring crowd.

The throng continued to follow them as they headed straight for the potsherd gate out to the Hinnom Valley. His anger fresh, Jeremiah stood on an outcropping of rocks and raised the jar high in the air. How well he remembered what happened many years ago in this valley! He looked out over the deep ravine. As a young man he'd dared to climb down into this pit and find the corner of Hamah's green robe.

Jerusalem, Jeremiah cried out the Lord's words. *In this place I will make void the plans of Judah and Jerusalem, and will make them fall by the sword before their enemies, and by the hands of those who seek their life. I will give their dead bodies for food to the birds of the air and to the wild animals of the earth. And I will make this city a horror, a thing to be hissed at; everyone who passes by it will be horrified and will hiss because of all its disasters. And I will make them eat the flesh of their sons and the flesh of their daughters, and all shall eat the flesh of their neighbors in the siege, and in the distress with which their enemies and those who seek their life afflict them.*

Jeremiah lifted the jar high into the air. He threw it with great force against the stones at his feet. The clay burst into hundreds of pieces. Hitting the sharp rocks, the lid lost a pie-shaped piece and rolled like a wheel up and over the craggy boulders into the muck below.

So will I break this people and this city, as one breaks a potter's vessel, so that it can never be mended. In Topheth they shall bury until there is no more room to bury. Thus will I do to this place, says the Lord, and to its inhabitants, making this city like Topheth.

Many of the people who witnessed Jeremiah's anger followed him back to the temple. Lehi stood beside him as he walked into the courtyard.

When he heard heavy footsteps, Jeremiah didn't even turn his head. He stood patiently while the strong hands of young guards took his arms and bound them at his back. He walked quietly between them, scraping the soles of his sandals on the courtyard's stone floor. He lowered his gaze as he passed flanks of officers. They were taking him to the courtyard where prisoners were often chained before they were lowered into the palace dungeon.

Jeremiah looked up and saw the window of the nursery where he had often stood watching the crowds. The chief officer rapped him sharply with the flat edge of his sword. "Keep moving, Jeremiah," the officer growled.

"You know the reason for this, I presume?" one of the other officers asked him.

Jeremiah did not answer.

"Speak up!" the guard slapped him hard across the face.

"I do."

"Tell me what this is for."

"King Jehoiakim believes it is treason to tell the people the truth."

Again the guard beat him across the face. "The truth? That we are *camels in heat* and will be destroyed? You're telling lies. And your lies are causing trouble." He hit Jeremiah again. "You're saying inflammatory things about the officers and priests who have given their lives to keep the peace."

When Jeremiah raised his head he could not see the guard except through a blur. This time the officer struck him with a terrific blow to the temple, and blood trickled into his ear. His knees buckled. The guard let him collapse half-conscious against the wall, while several other guards threaded thick hemp rope through a large ring riveted into the rock.

Braced against the wall, Jeremiah was too weak to bring his legs out from under him. He sat back on his heels, with his head fully facing the hot sun sinking across the western sky. His hands were numb, his wrists raw under the rough rope.

The guards had fastened him to the wall that faced the courtyard. He seemed to be alone, but from around the corner through the gate came the sounds of other prisoners sneezing and spitting. Undoubtedly they were also bolted to the walls.

The guards barked harsh commands at anyone who tried coming near. When a ten-year-old boy pushed through the ranks with a bit of bread for Jeremiah, the officer in front snarled at the youth, "Forget you ever knew him."

In excruciating pain, Jeremiah leaned against the wall and closed his eyes. He did not concentrate on the pain, but on the prayer in his heart.

Finally Baruch had heard the news and hurried to the scene. Although he could not draw close to Jeremiah, he paced outside the ring of guards. Lehi also walked around and around, moving to a new position whenever the guards blocked his vision.

Baruch's face was drawn and tense with anxiety. "This is Jeremiah," he told the guards, "the teacher of God. He should not be treated harshly. Please, you don't understand. He is a priest, a holy man. He speaks and writes the words of God."

"We have our orders," they said.

When twilight came, the desert cold seeped along the stones. Jeremiah managed to pull his legs out from under himself and rest his back against the wall. Baruch circled the area, helpless to do anything.

Pain kept Jeremiah awake. A cat crawled along the top of the wall and jumped to the pavement below. Doors opened and shut in the maze of rooms deep inside the temple.

He must have slept in the early morning, for he hadn't noticed the dawn. When he opened his eyes, light poured into the courtyard. People were preparing to visit the farmers' markets at the gates; he saw women carrying clay jars on their heads as they made their way to the waters. No one looked at him. Only one guard now stood where there had been five or six the night before.

Jeremiah tried to concentrate on the memories that had always sustained him: Hamah, the baby Hamutal, his mother and father, his grandsons Jehoahaz and little Mattaniah.

About ten in the morning, doors to the temple opened. Several officials came out into the yard. Patches of sun passed over the wall and lighted the stones in the courtyard. When the sun hit the walls, the city became an oven, radiating heat. Several priests came into the yard. The man in front was Governor Pashur.

"Jeremiah," he said. "You have a devoted following. It seems there are important people who like you."

Jeremiah looked up.

Governor Pashur turned back to the guards. "Let him go."

One of them leaned over and cut the thick hemp with the sharp edge of his sword.

Rising slowly with tremors in his knees, Jeremiah stood in front of Governor Pashur and steadied his feet. He said, "The Lord did not name you Governor Pashur. The name he has given you is *Terror Everywhere*."

The man recoiled at these words.

The Lord has named you not Pashur but "Terror-all-around." For thus says the Lord: I am making you a terror to yourself and to all your friends; and they shall fall by the sword of their enemies while you look on. And I will give all Judah into the hand of the king of Babylon; he shall carry them captive to Babylon, and shall kill them with the sword.

I will give all the wealth of this city, all its gains, all its prized belongings, and all the treasures of the kings of Judah into the hand of their enemies, who shall plunder them, and seize them, and carry them to Babylon. And you, Pashur, and all who live in your house, shall go into captivity, and to Babylon you shall go; there you shall die, and there you shall be buried, you and all your friends, to whom you have prophesied falsely.

As Jeremiah turned to leave the courtyard, Governor Pashur got his voice back. "I will do a little prophesying of my own," he said. "You will suffer greater reckoning. This will be nothing. You will look back upon today and wish I would come again to unbind you in such a timely manner."

Jeremiah turned toward the lodgings of his parents with painful, halting steps. At the apartment he drank a flask of water and lay on the divan while his mother, Marika, cradled his head in her lap, weeping, and wiping the dried blood away.

Chapter Thirty

Urijah

Jeremiah chose to spend more and more of his time in the archives beside his frail father. Hilkiah was determined to keep accurate account of all that was happening. Jeremiah stayed with his aging parents in their small dwelling.

One day at the marketplace, he found Lehi with his hood pulled far over his face.

"What's going on?" Jeremiah asked him.

"The king has pronounced death to treason."

"Death to treason?"

"And it is the prophets he calls treasonous. I've told my brother-in-law Urijah to flee."

"Has he gone?"

"He has gone into exile—I believe to Tahpanhes in Egypt. They're looking for him everywhere. It's time for me to leave as well," Lehi said. "My family and I are in danger."

"Where would you go then? Would you follow your Urijah to Egypt?"

"We'll go into the wilderness."

"The wilderness? Where into the wilderness?"

Lehi looked off into the distance. "Oh, I don't know. I've heard there's a way south and east into a land of milk and honey."

Jeremiah wondered where Lehi got the idea of such a place. "In the wilderness there's danger."

"I know," he said pensively. "I'd have to be prepared. I'll have to study it out."

"Well, perhaps, if the Lord has told you in your heart that you should leave, you should leave," said Jeremiah. "If we hear a commandment from the Lord, we must follow, even though it seems to make little sense."

Later, in the archives with Baruch, Jeremiah brought up the disappearance of Urijah.

"It's true," Baruch said. "And a unit of the militia has gone to Tahpanhes to bring him back. The gossip among the priests is that Jehoiakim will put Urijah to death for what he has told the people."

"Exactly what has he told the people?"

Baruch raised his eyes and said, "Just what you're telling them."

The walk between Hilkiah's apartment in the temple complex and the archives was not much longer than five hundred yards. But for the next few weeks as he walked that distance, Jeremiah kept his head covered. No one paid attention to him. He made the journey each morning, praying that the temple guards wouldn't notice him.

One morning, as Jeremiah left his parents' home, he saw many more people in the square than usual. Young people were seated in a crescent against the entrance to the courtyard, and women stood with their backs to the walls, dangling their laundry baskets on their knees. He was surprised to see several of the king's guard pacing the streets in their most formidable military dress. Another group dragged a prisoner through the archway. It was Urijah.

Above the courtyard, King Jehoiakim stood on the balcony with his jealous brother Johanan. On the king's other side was Jehoiakim's thirteen-year-old son Coniah, the next heir to the throne. The young prince stood as straight as a rod. Beside Coniah was Jeremiah's own grandson—all the issue he had left after Egypt's capture of Jehoahaz—the young prince Mattaniah, who'd recently become engaged to marry one of Shaphan's daughters.

Mattaniah had grown tall and lean. Even from a distance, Jeremiah saw Mattaniah's penetrating gaze. The boy's most striking feature was his thick auburn hair—so much darker now than it had been in his childhood, that it seemed to resemble a mop of sheepskin dipped in rust-colored dye. Anyone in the court could see that he was a match for any king who'd ever lived. Jeremiah had heard rumors that when the prince sparred at court he usually won; and with his pleasing smile, he had gained favor with everyone, including the king, his court, the priests, and their children.

The guards took only a few moments to take Urijah up the steps to the dais. He stood looking up to the heavens, his eyes steady. There was no attempt to cover his face. As the closest guard tightened Urijah's hands behind his back, another kicked him in the back of his legs until his knees buckled and he was forced to kneel on the stones.

"Oh my Father, God of Abraham," Urijah cried. "Accept my soul."

The chief executioner took his time drawing his sword from his scabbard. Urijah's young wife clenched her hands until they were white. Her sister Sariah stood close by, her eyes shut.

Suddenly, at the tap of a wand, one of the guards pushed Urijah's head down while the chief executioner swung his sword high. It whistled as it sliced through the air and struck Urijah at the back of his neck.

Chapter Thirty-one

A Sword

Urijah's execution stopped the street meetings. Some of the prophets feared opening their mouths ever again. But, now, unlike his former tendency to be reticent, Jeremiah could not stop the words that tumbled from his lips. He asked Baruch's help to write everything down.

I must shout, "Violence and destruction!"
For the word of the Lord has become for me
a reproach and derision all day long.
If I say, "I will not mention Him,
or speak any more in His name,"
then within me there is something like a burning fire
shut up in my bones;
I am weary with holding it in, and I cannot.

With each wave of words the two of them recorded, Jeremiah became more determined to continue speaking out. Despite the possibility the councilors might execute him, he knew he must obey the Lord's commandment to speak the truth.

For thus the Lord, the God of Israel, said to me: "Take from my hand this cup of the wine of wrath, and make all the nations to whom I send you drink it." They shall drink and stagger and go out of their minds because of the sword that I am sending among them.

Baruch raised his eyes at these words.

"Write them, Baruch."

Baruch dutifully bent to the stylus and drew the letters on the papyrus. The words were harsh, and he was afraid for Jeremiah.

Then drink, get drunk and vomit, fall and rise no more, because of the sword that I am sending among you.

"See, I am beginning to bring disaster on the city that is called by my name, and how can you possibly avoid punishment? You shall

not go unpunished, for I am summoning a sword against all the inhabitants of the earth," says the Lord of hosts.

The Lord will roar from on high, and from His holy habitation utter His voice; He will roar mightily against His fold, and shout . . . against all the inhabitants of the earth.

He is entering into judgment with all flesh, and the guilty He will put to the sword.

Finally Jeremiah could hold back no longer from speaking out again, and he returned with Lehi and Baruch to speak near the temple. He knew several unsympathetic priests were standing at the pillars, listening.

"Be careful, Jeremiah," Baruch touched the stylus to the surface where he was writing.

The wind sighed in the palace towers. A strong gust blew the awnings over the garden wall, knocking down potted herbs, spilling their contents onto the stones below. Lehi hurried to put them back in place.

Wail, and cry out; roll in ashes . . . for the days of your slaughter have come—and you shall fall . . . and there shall be no escape.

When I called you, you did not answer, therefore I will do . . . just what I did to Shiloh. And I will cast you out of my sight, just as I cast out all your kinsfolk, all the offspring of Ephraim. I called you, but you didn't answer.

Jeremiah was never sure exactly who grabbed him, but he felt the pressure of several hands. One of the men said, *Why have you prophesied in the name of the Lord, saying, "This house shall be like Shiloh, and this city shall be desolate, without inhabitant?" You will surely die.*

People were packed so close around him, Jeremiah could hardly breathe.

One of the priests cried out, "*This man deserves to be sentenced to death because he has spoken against our city. We heard him with our own ears.*"

Jeremiah would not be stopped. *It is the Lord who sent me to prophesy against this house and this city all the words you have heard. Now therefore amend your ways and your doings, and obey the voice of the Lord your God, and the Lord will change His mind about the disaster that He has pronounced against you.*

Someone laughed. "God can change His mind, eh? Well, He's not standing in front of us to tell us how He changed it."

Jeremiah continued, *But as for me, here I am in your hands. Do with me as seems good and right to you. Only know for certain that if you put me to death, you will be bringing innocent blood upon yourselves and upon this city and its inhabitants, for in truth the Lord sent me to you to speak all these words in your ears.*

Suddenly there was another gust of wind. Lehi stood in the background against the pots of dill and savory. The plants stirred.

Shaphan and his father pleaded with the mob. "*Do not deal with him in haste.*"

Shaphan, who stood above the milling crowd, stopped in front of Jeremiah and spread his arms wide. His son, Ahikam, even taller than his father or grandfather, stood with him. They created a barrier. There was a hush in the crowd as Shaphan spoke.

"Remember the father of Manasseh, King Hezekiah?" Shaphan said. "The Prophet Micah told Hezekiah and Jerusalem that the city would become a pile of ruins. But the king did not put Micah to death." Shaphan spoke with persuasion, though the crowd continued to murmur. "*Hezekiah changed toward the Lord and the Lord spared him. This man spoke to us in the name of the Lord. He should not be put to death.*"

Shaphan and his son stayed immovable. Only the edges of their caftans waved in the wind. The priests let Jeremiah go and backed away. Baruch came to the side of his friend, and Jeremiah slumped against his arm.

Chapter Thirty-two

Out of the North

Jeremiah went underground. Hiding his face in his hood, he walked quickly from his parents' home to the temple archives. He did not attend any public events, not even the spectacular wedding of his grandson Mattaniah. He watched the marriage procession from the archive windows.

As the years passed, Jeremiah rejoiced secretly when he heard the news that Mattaniah's wife Dolazah gave birth to another child. Soon the prince had four sons and a little daughter. Jeremiah cheered in his heart for his great-grandchildren, though he dared not attend any celebrations or send any messages.

With Baruch's help, Jeremiah focused on his work. Both dedicated scholars, they developed a plan to collect, abridge, and compile the best documents, history, and poetry into one massive compendium. Also, Jeremiah's special project was the collection and production of his own writings. The many hours of rewriting and assembling consumed him.

"These poems of Habukkuk's are well-written pieces," said Baruch. "And we should include the prophecies of Zephaniah and Nahum also."

"We must include all of Ezekiel," Jeremiah said. He laid everything out for Baruch to look at. Some of the documents were unreadable. But Baruch had a talent for parsing and summarizing. Jeremiah held the scrolls apart while Baruch examined the text.

The two of them worked day and night with little sleep. Jeremiah oversaw the production of his own poems and treatises as recorded by Baruch. His compendium dealt with his calling, with Hezekiah's aqueduct, histories of the political climates that existed during the reign of each king, Urijah's execution, and the history of wars and hostilities.

Though some of the prophets still spoke in the streets, Jeremiah did not. For the time being he felt his work was to record and preserve the documents. The only connection he had with the people was an occasional visit from Ezekiel or Daniel. He was particularly impressed with Daniel, who, as a boy with a special love for all living things, would not eat flesh. It was Daniel who ran up the stairs one afternoon and burst into the room with the news that Egypt was defeated.

"What is it?" Jeremiah put down his stylus and rolled up the scroll.

"The Assyrians have overtaken the Egyptians at Carchemish!"

Hearing a rising hubbub below in the courtyard, the scribes began to make out the chant of the gathering crowd. "No more Egyptian taxes!" One voice rose above the others. It was the old prophet Hananiah, exulting in the outcome. "Assyria is triumphant. And Assyria is our ally!"

Standing at the window, Jeremiah watched the celebration with a despondent heart. He knew this was not good. For if the rumors were true, Assyria was forging an alliance with Babylon. And the combined conquerors would follow Egypt, hot on their heels. And Nebuchadnezzar was a warmonger who compelled even the wild animals to bow down before him.

His conjectures were correct. After the Babylonian and Assyrian armies had defeated the Egyptians, they didn't stop, but boldly chased the fleeing Egyptians southward into Judea. Terrified, the thousands of families in the small country towns packed their carts and began to make their way to Jerusalem.

Chapter Thirty-three

The Words of God

Jerusalem was alarmed. Feeling pressure, Jeremiah struggled to get his documents of warning ready for Jehoiakim to read. It seemed ironic that he fostered the same desire to speak to the king that his father once had. Perhaps this time—with the danger of advancing refugees and the foreign armies that followed them—Jehoiakim might listen.

Sometimes Baruch, who had dedicated all of his life to writing the words of God, looked up with fear. "Do you understand this will almost certainly bring trouble?" he asked.

"This is what the Lord wants the officials to know," Jeremiah said. "But they will not accept these words from me. So, Baruch, you will have to read them."

Baruch's hand trembled on the scroll. "You want *me* to read these to the council?"

"Yes," Jeremiah said. "You know they'll reject me. Go to Shaphan and ask him to let you have an audience with the councilors. He should admit you to a hearing. Then go to the king. The Lord wants the people to hear these things. Perhaps they will turn from their evil ways."

"Shaphan?"

"He's the only sensible one."

"I've heard rumors that Jehoiakim disliked his sensibilities, and has let him go."

"Or one of his sons," Jeremiah said.

Baruch took Jeremiah's scroll with him to the court. He was not surprised that the rumors had been true. King Jehoiakim had replaced the court secretary Shaphan with his henchman, the wrestler Elishama. Only one of Shaphan's sons—the tall Gemariah—still remained in office. When Baruch petitioned Gemariah, the son reacted with a look that briefly registered fear. He said he could make no promises, but he offered to meet Baruch in his office to decide if they could take the documents to the king.

Baruch entered Gemariah's apartment with some hesitation. He swallowed hard when he saw who was in attendance. Elishama sat at the far end of the room in the chair most decorated with insets of gold and brass flowers.

Baruch knew Elishama, Elnathan, Governor Pashur, Chief Magistrate Pedaiah, and a rabble-rouser by the name of Jehudi. But four for five officials in the room were strangers to Baruch.

Gemariah introduced Baruch and then said, "Read the scroll to us."

Baruch read:

You have not hearkened, nor inclined your ear to hear. Because you have not heard my words, Behold, I will send and take all the families of the north . . . and will bring them against this land, and against the inhabitants thereof, and against all these nations round about, and will utterly destroy them . . .

When he paused, someone growled, "Read on."

Baruch lowered his face to look at his sandals.

Moreover I will take from them the voice of mirth, and the voice of gladness, the voice of the bridegroom, and the voice of the bride, the sound of the millstones, and the light of the candle. And this whole land shall be a desolation, and an astonishment; and these nations shall serve the king of Babylon seventy years.

"Serve Babylon seventy years?"

There was more in the scroll about the intentions of the new king, Nebuchadnezzar, and what would happen to the people after seventy years of captivity. The council listened.

"Did Jeremiah dictate this to you?" Elishama intoned.

Baruch answered. "Yes. I wrote what he said on this scroll."

Elnathan stood. It had only been a few years since he'd fetched Urijah from Egypt to execute him for treason. Dressed in purple silk with gold chains at his throat, Elnathan looked older since Urijah's beheading. His hands were white. When he spoke, his mouth drew into a tight line. "If it were up to me, I'd tell you to flee with your life. But it's possible the king might . . ." He didn't finish, but paused, narrowed his eyes, and stroked his chin. "All right. At least we can ask. We'll send Jehudi to get the reaction of the king. You must wait here."

Jehudi looked eager. He left with two other officials to ask permission of the king.

When Baruch followed him with his eyes as though he would like to go, Elnathan scowled at him. "You should hide yourself. You'll never be welcome in the presence of the king. But I'll let you wait here until Jehudi returns."

When Jehudi and his cohorts finally came through the door, they glanced at Baruch with looks of disdain. Baruch felt fear seize him briefly. But Jehudi nodded, "Yes, you may bring the scroll."

"But you must stay here," Elnathan growled to Baruch. He rose from the chair, and with a show of his power, he swung his robe in an arc. Then he turned to follow Jehudi.

But Baruch was not daunted. When they were in the hall, he fell behind them as they chatted noisily on their way to the palace. When the guards opened the huge doors into the foyer, Baruch slipped past as though he belonged to the party. The sound of his footsteps ringing against the marble and cedar arches blended with the clatter of the others who walked ahead.

As the massive doors to the throne room opened, Baruch stood out of the way behind a pillar, surveying the scene with awe. He'd never been inside the palace. The large arched windows were hung with silk drapes tied with brass and gold. Imported, richly woven red and gold rugs lay on the polished tile floors. At the end of the hall was a huge fireplace flanked by carved lions. The shimmer of the blue and yellow fire cast an eerie glow on the cheeks of the king.

Surrounding the silken divan where the king reclined, many slaves waited for orders. Young princes and princesses, servants, concubines, and his most recent mistress milled about and favored his requests without hesitation. A slave waved a canopy of gold and silver above his head.

It was Elishama who first spoke to the king. "You gave Jehudi pemission to bring the scroll for your perusal," he said. "Would you like us to read it?"

It seemed that King Jehoiakim was in a trance. He moved his fingers slightly.

Without waiting for an audible answer, the man named Jehudi coughed and unrolled the papyrus. Baruch hid behind the pillar. While Jehudi began to read, the king demanded a cup of wine. After he took a few sips, he dropped the cup on the floor. A slave immediately fell to his knees and wiped it up.

Jehudi's strong voice began to quiet everyone in the room.

The Lord shall roar from on high. . . .
Against all the inhabitants of the earth . . .
the Lord has a controversy with the nations. . . .
He will give them that are wicked to the sword,
says the Lord.

The king beckoned Jehudi closer. He looked at the scroll. Out of the leather sash he wore at his waist he drew a sharp little knife. He thrust the blade at the edge of the papyrus, forced a cut, and then with his white hands, he ripped off the piece that had just been read. Leaning back on the divan, the king threw the piece of papyrus into the fire.

The king turned to Jehudi. "Keep going," he said, waving his hand.

Jehudi continued to read. Each time the official finished reading a page, the king asked to take a look at the scroll. Carelessly pulling it toward him with one hand, with the other he took the small knife, thrust the edge of the blade upon the papyrus until it was rent, then with both hands grasped the two sides of the papyrus that flanked the cut, and tore the piece of the document away. Each time he tore the ragged piece of scroll away, he tossed it into the fire.

Baruch turned to leave. He had seen enough. He took one last look at the huge hall. It was unlikely he would ever see such luxury again.

Chapter Thirty-four

Invasion

Heartbroken by the destruction of the scroll, Jeremiah mourned for a short time and then pulled himself together. He couldn't let his own sorrowing obstruct his mission to proclaim the words of the Lord. He immersed himself in the task of restoration.

He was busy with this work when the Egyptians came. He could see faces of terror among the citizens. The pressure of dealing with the Egyptian army, the drought, the hungry migrants from the country, as well as Jehoiakim's recruitment of the farmers and slaves to the weakened militia—all of these problems had left the economy crippled. And the people were destitute and afraid. They rightly feared the hungry Egyptians. The foreign soldiers began forcing them to give up their meager supplies, taking freely from the coffers and demanding more.

Then came the criers shouting the news that the Assyrian and Chaldean armies were not far behind. On the morning the dreaded troops arrived, people scattered, fearing that the Assyrian army would plunder with even more force than the Egyptians. And finally, behind Assyria, they knew the invading armies of Nebuchadnezzar would be ruthless.

Jeremiah feared that Nebuchadnezzar would enter the temple and strip it of the Ark, the gold, the sacred tablets. Perhaps even Jacob's hallowed rock pillow would be in danger. He and Baruch designated a spot on the mountain where they could conceal the artifacts.

The approach of the armies was as the people feared. The intruders wanted as much as they could get. And Nebuchadnezzar's soldiers were ravenous.

On a day when there seemed to be more military disturbances in the square than usual, both men covered their heads and left the compound. Jeremiah hired a cart to take the concealed Ark and

Jacob's stone with them. They included documents in the covered load they took to the hill. They shut them away behind a rock cairn.

On their way down the mountain, they noticed a huge crowd gathering at the Fish Gate. A massive camp had been set up, filled with people from Jerusalem.

Lehi approached and said, "Nebuchadnezzar has lined up all of the architects, construction engineers, mathematicians, and artisans, and forced them to pack up their belongings for a journey to Babylon. The only reason I'm not in that camp is that we went underground."

"Underground?"

"Because I've foreseen this, we had already packed up everything. So I was able to hide most of what was in the house down in the cave beneath my floor," Lehi said.

Jeremiah didn't know what to say.

"It seems that Nebuchadnezzar stops at nothing," Lehi continued, "He conscripted thousands of young men to serve in his army, even those from noble families. The Chaldeans took our best, most intelligent, to serve in their court. Even Daniel was taken to go with them. Nebuchadnezzar promises he'll treat Daniel and the young noblemen like royalty."

In the weeks of the terrible upheaval that followed, Jeremiah roamed freely. In the midst of chaos, the crowds left him alone. He peered into the faces of those who were chosen to travel to Babylon, and were, for all purposes, now Babylonian slaves.

"You'll come back," he said as he made his way through the rows of tents. "Work hard in Babylon. Cultivate your gardens. Have children. Live righteously. Obey the Lord your God and you'll save your lives."

Jeremiah tried to get into the palace to see if his grandson Mattaniah was still in the city. He asked people on the street if they knew what had happened to Mattaniah or his four boys and daughter. But no one knew.

Jeremiah hadn't been close to Mattaniah all these years, and he knew very little about the great-grandchildren. He knew Mulek was the oldest—a talented, handsome young man. But he knew nothing about the other three boys or the redheaded daughter, Scota. These were his own kin, Jeremiah lamented. And he didn't know them.

"We can't let you in," the guard at the palace said. "But the royalty is safe. All of the princes, Coniah and Mattaniah, and their young families hid with Jehoiakim in the dungeon. Mattaniah has six children now. His wife Dolazah gave birth to a second daughter while they were underground."

Without access to his grandchildren or great-grandchildren, and with a heavy heart, his feet like lead, his legs and back aching from age, Jeremiah continued his work of restoring the remaining portions of scroll that Jehoiakim had burned. He also made new copies of some of the documents he'd hidden in the hill. There was still much to be done. He wanted to organize and preserve all of the words Baruch had copied from the speeches he'd given in the square.

Chapter Thirty-five

Leaving

The candles sputtered, and the light in the small apartment of Jeremiah's parents grew dim. Marika had put curtains over the window when Hilkiah complained about the glare. The shadows on the walls flickered and danced their spectral rhythms while Marika worked at the basin to prepare the vegetables for a thin stew.

Jeremiah stayed beside his father's bed even in the night when the old man's pain kept him awake. Jeremiah stroked his father's hands, praying this illness would pass. His mother walked about aimlessly, drawing the *tse'ifim* over her eyes, murmuring prayers of hope, pleading with the God of Abraham, but Hilkiah's health did not improve.

"We will die without seeing our grandchildren." Marika often crossed to the window and held her eyes from the light.

"You must continue to tell King Jehoiakim to pay the tribute," Hilkiah said to his son. "Nebuchadnezzar is ruthless. But if the people continue to be obedient to the Babylonians, their lives will be spared." If he spoke too much, his breathing grew ragged, and then he would break into a harsh cough. A coughing spell often shook his body so vigorously, it sent the blood to his face.

For three years King Jehoiakim faithfully paid the tribute Nebuchadnezzar demanded. But in the fourth year, because there were so many extra families to feed in a time of drought, he rebelled.

With his last breath, Hilkiah urged Jeremiah to tell Jehoiakim to pay the tribute.

Jeremiah nodded when his father spoke. "I will, Father. Please rest now."

"Tell him today."

"They will not listen to me, Father. Most of them have shut their ears to what the Lord has told them to do."

Hilkiah tightened his fingers on Jeremiah's hand. "But you must tell them, nevertheless."

"If my grandson Mattaniah ever becomes king, I'll talk to him," Jeremiah said. "But that time may never come, since Coniah and Johanan are next in line for the throne."

"Pray for it, my son," Hilkiah breathed. "Surely God will listen to you."

Because his father was so weak, Jeremiah didn't wish to finish the conversation. But his father would not let it rest. "Mattaniah will be a great king," he murmured.

Jeremiah didn't tell him that with so many years in court Mattaniah had learned the traditions of his half brothers. All of the royals seemed to be arrogant and bullheaded. But someday, Jeremiah prayed, someday, if Mattaniah were king, surely he'd be a merciful ruler who desired to save the oppressed. He hoped Mattaniah would worship the God of Abraham.

"Father, please rest," he urged.

Hilkiah's death was a blow. Jeremiah stayed with his mother and held her while she sobbed. Her hair had turned silver, and her skin was as soft as the petal of a rose.

King Jehoiakim didn't pay the tribute. And an angry Nebuchadnezzar moved forward to punish him. He brought a substantial number of new recruits he'd forced to join his ranks. After making camp about a mile from the city, thousands of Babylonian soldiers marched unchallenged up to the gates while the people looked on helplessly. The militia didn't even try to stop the hundred men who marched into the palace and arrested the rebellious king.

Jeremiah and Baruch followed while the militia marched the king through the city, through the gates, outside into the field. Suddenly Jehoiakim broke away into a run. More than five thousand of Nebuchadnezzar's men were standing in the surrounding fields, holding the Judeans hostage. A hundred or more surrounded the king. Those closest to him grabbed him and pummeled him with fists.

When Jehoiakim kicked furiously with his feet, one of Nebuchadnezzar's men struck him through the heart with a large blade. Jehoiakim fell to the ground in the dust, then jerked like a dying beast. He lay gasping, his mouth filled with dirt.

Jeremiah remembered the Lord's words to him: *Jehoiakim . . . shall be buried with the burial of an ass, drawn and cast forth beyond the gates of Jerusalem.* This had come to pass.

When Nebuchadnezzar crowned Coniah king, in the tradition of conquerors, he changed the boy's name to Jehoiachin. And he continued to set up more camps outside the walls as he waited for the young king to pay the tribute.

Jeremiah hid with Lehi in his dugout. It was dark and crowded. The two oldest boys, Laman and Lemuel, who often berated their father's judgment, insisted on going out to the streets to discover what was going on. They took the slave Giddel with them. They hurried back to the dugout when they saw Nebuchadnezzar's guards approach. The only news they gathered was, "No news."

"The army is waiting for Coniah to pay the tribute," Laman said.

But the Babylonians couldn't wait forever.

Jeremiah hid underground with Lehi's family for three long months, during which time they received reports of another huge siege in which many people were gathered up and forced into the camps outside the gate. The only one they dared to send to the streets to find out what was happening was the slave, Giddel.

When he returned with the news, Giddel had a difficult time speaking. "Nebuchadnezzar is not a patient man," Giddel said. "Jehoiachin could not pay the tribute, so the cruel king brought his Babylonian army into the city and ravaged it. They have taken Jehoiachin, his wives, his children, and his mother Nehushta, and thousands more of the intellectuals and business leaders. They've taken all of them back to Babylon."

Hearing Giddel's report, the women in Lehi's family cried out with agony.

Jeremiah tried to calm himself. "Who have they placed as king?" he finally asked.

"Mattaniah. They now call him Zedekiah. His sons have been installed as princes. But they couldn't find the oldest, Mulek. His father sent Mulek across the seas to safety."

Mattaniah! Jeremiah's heart stopped. Mattaniah had been crowned king! The grandfather was not sure how he felt. The tragic circumstances overpowered his joy.

"Don't believe this appointment is the end of our troubles," Lehi said. "From the rumblings I hear, Mattaniah will always be in danger. Prince Johanan has organized a group to usurp the throne. He'll do everything he can to unseat the king and grasp control of the kingdom."

Jeremiah knew the political unrest was extreme—not only the peril of Johanan's jealousy, but the inexperience of the young Mattaniah. The boy didn't seem ready to be king. He hadn't been raised by Hamutal. The sweet days when he was a tiny boy on a horse with his brother Jehoahaz had passed into history. Now Mattaniah was accustomed to political power, strong drink, and women. Mattaniah, the new King Zedekiah, had many wives and concubines. Every day that Jeremiah mourned Jerusalem's weaknesses, what he most lamented was the moral destruction in his own family.

Tentatively, Jeremiah began teaching in the streets again. On his walk to the archives every morning, he dared to talk for a few moments to those who would listen. Always, he watched across the military fields or peered into the corral at the compound, praying that he would see his great-grandchildren with their mother or nurse. But his glimpses were long-distance, and rare. He felt abandoned.

Even his good friend Lehi seemed unapproachable at times—as though he had secrets he couldn't divulge—not even to his friend Jeremiah. One morning Jeremiah saw that all of the carts that had always been parked in front of Lehi's house were gone.

He knocked on Lehi's door. As the dawn light began to rise, he rattled the great wooden knob, but no one came. After waiting about ten minutes, just as he was about to turn away, the door opened a crack and a ruddy face peered through. It was Lehi's loyal slave, Giddel.

Giddel had stayed long past his service limit of six years, choosing not to take his freedom. "Jeremiah?" he said. "Is that you?"

"Yes, Giddel. Where have they gone?"

"They left in the middle of the night," Giddel said. "And I don't know where. No one is supposed to know."

Before Giddel withdrew into the entryway, he smiled. "He gave my family this house."

Lehi had given his house to a slave?

"Lehi knew I would take care of it."

Jeremiah wondered if Lehi was planning to come back. At one time, he'd told Jeremiah he was going, "into the wilderness."

"And he gave me my freedom with a decree," Giddel added. "God has been good to us," the freed slave said in parting. "God bless you, Jeremiah."

Jeremiah wished for all slaves to receive such blessings. On his way to the archives he could not stop thinking about the Judeans who were now slaves in Babylon.

"Lehi's gone," he said to Baruch.

"Lehi?" Baruch asked. "Where has he gone?"

"Not Egypt." It would be too dangerous to go to Egypt—although he believed some of the people had earlier escaped to Tahpanhes.

"He just disappeared?"

"Listen to me, Baruch." He paused to regain his jumbled thoughts. "Lehi didn't want his family in captivity—to serve as slaves in Babylon."

Baruch was listening. "Are you saying there's a chance the Babylonians will come again to enslave more of our people?"

"Yes."

"Do you mean that all of us will be slaves?" he asked. "Surely Nebuchadnezzar won't return and take all of us."

"All of us."

Chapter Thirty-six

Free the Slaves

Not long after Jeremiah discovered that Lehi had gone, a rumor circulated that Lehi, Sariah, and their four boys had been murdered. There were some rumors that because Giddel had taken the house, he was the one who'd committed the crime.

No one found any bodies. And no one who knew Giddel and his family believed the rumors—that is, until another murder shook the city. The guards had been called to Captain Laban's home because his servants found the captain lying naked in a pool of blood. Robbed of his clothes and his sword, he lay where all could see him. His severed head had rolled away from his body and left a red smear on the tiles.

Laban! People wondered why Laban, one of Jerusalem's greatest military captains, had not been protected by his ranks of slaves and soldiers—unless his slaves had done it. When the household discovered his slave, Zoram, had disappeared and that valuable ancient documents had been taken from Laban's archives, there was fearful shrieking in the streets against the slaves.

"Zoram did it," Laban's wife, Reba, told the authorities. "Why don't you lazy dogs get on your camels and chase him down?"

The entire city took unusual care to monitor their slaves, revoking privileges, sometimes beating them into submission. As he walked the streets, Jeremiah found that people were terrified of a slave uprising.

One day when he turned on a road leading to a small empty lot, he found, hiding in the corner in a bank of weeds, an old discarded, brittle ox yoke.

Lifting the heavy yoke and settling it on his shoulders, he knew he looked ridiculous. As he came out into the marketplace, several people who knew him asked him why he was wearing an ox yoke. He told them that it represented bondage, that the Lord had asked him to tell the people there should be no more slavery in the city. If they didn't obey the Lord in all His commandments—if they didn't release the slaves—there might be more murders. And with their continued disobedience, all of them might be taken to Babylon to serve as slaves for seventy years.

The self-proclaimed prophet Hananiah came after him through the crowd. "Don't listen to his lies!" he cried out. "If we release the slaves, there'll be chaos! The Lord said he'd break Nebuchadnezzar in two years and bring the captives home." Under his breath through his teeth, he sneered, "Fraud!" In a fit of anger he grasped the edges of the yoke on Jeremiah's shoulders and yanked it up so hard that it scraped past Jeremiah's cheeks, nearly taking his head off.

Jeremiah never knew how much his antics with the yoke, his speeches in the marketplace, the disappearance of Lehi and his family, or the murder of Laban influenced the king to free the slaves. But suddenly a miracle happened. The issue of slavery reached the sensibilities of the young king.

In the fourth year of his reign, Zedekiah decreed that all of the slaves, both male and female, were to be released.

Prince Johanan, whose luxurious new mansion was kept by hundreds of slaves, resisted. He proclaimed he could release neither his household slaves nor the guards who were overseeing the dungeon under his scribe's house on his large estate. His complaints and threats forced Zedekiah to appropriate additional funds to pay for wages.

Still speaking in the streets, Jeremiah praised Zedekiah. The king had taken hold of his position with honor and a sense of responsibility. He prayed that his grandson would continue to grow into his office with grace.

The ancient covenant that released the slaves every six years had been honored by an old ceremony. The body of a bull was cut in half and placed in the temple. The officials had walked through the two halves of the bull and covenanted to release their slaves. Under Zedekiah's rule, the court performed the same ceremony as a covenant, only with replicas of two bull halves, both made of brass.

Zedekiah's experiment to release the slaves lasted less than two weeks. As the days passed, tensions multiplied. No one had anticipated how much their everyday lives were impacted by the labor of their slaves. Cleaning, food preparation, transportation, and construction tasks came to a halt.

But the most difficult problem was that the slaves didn't know how to be free. They gathered in the square with their families, laid out their meager belongings, and sat on their old blankets. They had nothing to eat, so relied upon the charity of the men in the temple. They ate the meat that was sacrificed at the altars.

Most soon went back to their masters and begged to be reinstated. At first the masters paid them wages and asked for rent and money for food. After a few months, the slaves moved back into their old quarters furnished by their masters. And soon they were doing their old jobs.

Jeremiah stayed with his widowed mother, Marika. He sat by her bed, rubbing her aching arms or fanning her face with a large reed fan.

She wouldn't listen to his claim that he had failed. "Don't let the failures of the people break your heart."

When the officials walked between the two halves of the bull they'd made a covenant. Now they had broken it. Jeremiah could not keep his silence. This time the Lord's message to the people was most difficult.

You had done right in my sight, in proclaiming liberty every man to his neighbor; and you had made a covenant before me. But you turned and polluted my name, and caused every man his servant, and every man his handmaid, whom you had set at liberty . . . to return . . . into subjection. Therefore . . . you have not hearkened unto me, in proclaiming liberty.

Jeremiah's voice faltered. He was weary from telling the people these words, and knowing they'd refused to listen.

Behold . . . I will make you to be removed into all the kingdoms of the earth. . . . The hand of the king of Babylon's army will return to this city; and they shall fight against it, and take it, and burn it with fire: and I will make the cities of Judah a desolation without an inhabitant.

Jeremiah's latest preaching brought the council's attention to him once again. The council decided they must take action and examine the documents that Jeremiah and Baruch were writing. But they were slow.

By some miracle, Jeremiah was allowed to continue speaking in the square.

Chapter Thirty-seven

The Ministers

Nebuchadnezzar didn't care that Jerusalem and the surrounding cities were drying up in the drought. He demanded his seven thousand five hundred pounds of silver and his seventy-five pounds of gold. He was building hanging gardens for his wife—a lavish environment that would remind her of her childhood mountains. Her new palace would be constructed according to a vision he saw in a dream— tile floors inlaid with gold and silver, with pillars standing as high as the pillars of the temple, topped with jewels.

Finally Zedekiah had no more gold, silver, or resources to pay tribute to Nebuchadnezzar. The drought and the task of feeding the freed slaves made it impossible. Just as the farmers had come to the city to escape Nebuchadnezzar's army, they now came because of the drought. They sat on mats they laid out in the streets. With their children crying for food, they wandered about hopelessly. Jeremiah and the priests administered to the hundreds and thousands of families as best they could.

A woman listening to Jeremiah looked up through the gate as a small boy ran toward her. The *tse'ifim* fell from her hair. Quickly she pulled it up and covered her face. She put her arms around the boy, and he whispered in her ear.

"Jeremiah, tell the priests that Nebuchadnezzar's army is coming down from Riblah again," the woman said. "My boy saw them over the hills in the north pass."

The boy had seen the army, all right. Jeremiah suspected it would be the largest Babylonian army yet to come down across the hills. And it was. In the next few days, as the vast militia circled the city, Jeremiah grew nervous and morose as he watched them begin to build mounds close to the walls. He knew they had learned these skills from the brilliant engineers of Jerusalem they had kidnapped and forced to build the mountains for Nebuchadnezzar's hanging gardens. It wasn't long before a few stray arrows began to sail over the buildings. He didn't know how long it would be before the mounds gave the vast army easy access to the streets.

As the city became increasingly alarmed, an emissary from the king approached Jeremiah. "Zedekiah wants a message from you."

Jeremiah hesitated. "Zedekiah?"

"He believes the military will need help." The man paused. "And the Egyptian army is on its way. They're angry with Nebuchadnezzar for plundering in their territory." The messenger looked down and spoke quietly. "He's asking you to pray for him and tell him whether or not we should get the Egyptians to help us, or even go to Egypt to get away from the Babylonians."

This was the first time Jeremiah's grandson, King Zedekiah, had ever asked for his opinion.

Jeremiah took a moment to reply, knowing the answer would not be popular. Shaking his head his head slowly, he spoke sorrowfully. *The Egyptians will not be a help to us. Behold, Pharaoh's army . . . shall return to Egypt into their own land.*

"Is there anything else you wish to tell Zedekiah?" The emissary still averted his eyes.

And the Chaldeans shall come again and fight against this city, and take it, and burn it with fire. Thus says the Lord; deceive not yourselves, saying, "The Chaldeans shall surely depart from us." For they shall not depart. For though you had smitten the whole army of the Chaldeans that fight against you, and there remained but wounded men among them yet should they rise up every man in his tent, and burn this city with fire.

Chapter Thirty-eight

Captive

For a short time Egypt's indecisive movement toward Judea threatened the Chaldeans. Though they didn't pull out, Nebuchadnezzar's nervous generals seemed to relax the pressure on Jerusalem. Slowly, more and more Judeans took the liberty to risk walking past the Chaldean camps, venturing outside the city walls.

For a long time Uncle Shallum's son Hanameel had urged Jeremiah to come to Anathoth. There was a particular field Hanameel wanted his cousin to buy. Jeremiah had put it off because he would have to travel outside the gates—past Nebuchadnezzar's camps. But as the crowds heckled him, one of the themes was, "You urge us to go peacefully with Nebuchadnezzar, to save our lives, yet you have no property. You don't have a family, you don't have a house you have to leave. We would sacrifice too much!" He believed that if he bought the field, he would demonstrate to the people that he had faith they would return someday. Uneasily, he began his journey to Anathoth.

As he reached the gate of Benjamin, he caught his breath. When his old enemy Irijah saw him, it was too late to turn around.

Without hesitation, Irijah dashed toward Jeremiah, his face twisted in anger. He screamed, "Stop, Jeremiah! You think you can desert Jerusalem!"

At the same time Irijah screamed, two other guards pulled Jeremiah back to the gate of Benjamin. They pounded on him like lions ready to tear him apart.

Jeremiah tried to pull away, but Irijah grabbed his sleeve and clung to him. "Headed for Nebuchadnezzar's camps, are you? I knew it! How much do the warmongers outside our gates pay you to tell our people we'll be forced to go to Babylon and serve as slaves for seventy years?"

The men hurried forward, beating him as they tied his arms with strong hemp rope. Jeremiah felt the sweat pour down his face. He tasted the salt of it on his lips. He was no longer a young man. The pounding on his shoulders and arms brought him so much pain he wanted to cry out.

The guards walked him to the palace. Zedekiah wasn't present, but Prince Johanan was. Watching the disturbance, the prince growled, "Take him to the dungeon under my scribe's house."

Jeremiah didn't struggle as they led him to the huge gate of Johanan's estate. The jealous Prince Johanan, angry to be left out of the kingly line, had insisted on luxury. He built the house and the dwellings of its caretakers with the taxes that should have been paid to Egypt and then Babylon. With the labor of many slaves, he'd constructed a lavish residence. The arches above the front foyer reached almost as high as the tops of the temple. The tiles on the courtyard were inlaid with shells from the Mediterranean Sea. The wood on the porch had been imported from the faraway islands called Eire where the Phoenicians had sailed for many hundreds of years, carrying wood and metal back on their ships to build the temple and homes in Jerusalem.

Inside the compound a covered walkway led to the scribe's house where the dungeon lay underground. Through a small foyer laid with squares of cedar, a door led to the prison below. As the slaves and guards pushed and pulled Jeremiah toward the stone stairway that spiraled into darkness, the sandal on Jeremiah's right foot shook loose on the stone step. When he bent to retrieve it, the officers jerked at him harshly, forcing him to abandon his shoe.

At the bottom of the stairs was a hall flanked by iron gates. Each gate led to a small, dark, five-foot-square cell. Only one small window, about six inches square, let in light at the end of the row.

Jeremiah fell awkwardly to the floor. He remained quiet, praying that God would help him withstand the onslaught. A guard shut the iron gate with a clang.

Jeremiah welcomed the silence. When he heard the guards climbing the staircase, he felt relief. He was alone. There was nothing in the cell—no chairs, no blanket, no rug. There wasn't even a dish for food. When the door above had been shut, and the dungeon was almost totally dark, Jeremiah spent a few moments orienting himself. The cell was almost six feet high, and five feet square. He was closed into a dark box.

"Jeremiah?" came a voice. "I heard them call your name."

Jeremiah was startled. The voice came from somewhere close-by. "Who are you?"

"I am Giddel."

Giddel? Lehi's slave? Jeremiah heard the sorrow in his voice. "Why are you in this place?"

"They accused me of drawing up false ownership papers for the house and murdering Lehi's family and Laban."

"What really happened?"

I tried to tell them about that night Laban was murdered. They thought I was lying."

"I'll listen. Please tell me what happened the night of Laban's murder."

"The boys came back."

"The boys came back?" Jeremiah repeated. "What boys?"

"Lehi's boys."

"And then what, Giddel?"

"He needed up-to-date records to take with him."

Laban had recently hired the scribes in the archives to bring his materials up to date. He owned a complete record of Isaiah's work. He added some of Jeremiah's own poetry to them.

Jeremiah leaned his head against the stones. So Lehi's family needed a set of complete records? Jeremiah remembered that Lehi urged Laban to sell him some of his several copies. Laban had refused. But, separated from the written laws of God, Lehi would have been desperate. He often said, "Without teachings from the past, the next generation is lost."

"And Zoram went with Lehi," Giddel said. "Zoram didn't kill Laban, but no one knows who did."

Jeremiah wondered what happened to Lehi and his family. He supposed he would never learn the truth.

There was no light except from the small opening at the end of the corridor. Twice a day the guards came into the hallway with little pottery gourds of thin gruel, a mixture of oats and rye. Each prisoner was allowed to sip out of the gourd for two or three minutes.

On a smooth section of stone, Jeremiah dug with his ring, carving out the number of days he spent in the dungeon. He could tell when night came only because the entire place was pitch black. In the morning, weak light again began to filter into the hallway, and the midday light illuminated the granite stones to a silver sheen.

He counted eighteen days spent in the dungeon. He might have been forgotten there forever, except that someone had bragged to the court that they captured Jeremiah. On the eighteenth day, a messenger came to the dungeon with a message that Jeremiah was to see the king.

Unwinding his bruised body from the floor of the cell, Jeremiah walked unsteadily to the iron gate. He was elated when the jailor unlocked the latch, but he discovered he could hardly move. All of his bones ached.

Zedekiah was seated at a table. One other person stood in the room in back of the king—Shaphan, the former court secretary, the grandfather of Zedekiah's children. Shaphan didn't speak during the interview.

When the guards closed the door, Jeremiah stood teetering. One of his sandals had been lost. His body and clothes reeked from his eighteen days in prison. The king glanced briefly toward him, then lowered his eyes to his reading.

This was the first time Jeremiah had been accepted in a private audience with his grandson. He waited.

"Come to the table." Zedekiah didn't raise his head.

When Jeremiah approached, Zedekiah looked up and narrowed his eyes.

Zedekiah didn't explain the action of the priests against him, or try to justify Jeremiah's prison sentence. He asked a simple question. "Is there any message from the Lord?"

Jeremiah curbed his desire to call out his grandson's name. He wanted to go to him, take him in his arms, and weep with him. But there was no opening from the king for such a gesture. Zedekiah had asked a question, and Jeremiah would have to speak the truth. He prayed that the king would listen.

"There is an answer from the Lord." Jeremiah wavered, for he knew the answer, and it was not pleasant. For a moment he was quiet. *You will be delivered into the hand of the king of Babylon.*

There, he had said it. And the power of the words sent his feelings spinning in a thousand directions, as unmanageable as a fire burning out of control.

Zedekiah didn't move. He narrowed his eyes and gazed at Jeremiah for a long time. "I've let you preach in the streets for ten years. But your negative prophecies do not inspire the militia to save our province."

Jeremiah gathered his strength. *How have I offended you, or your servants, or this people, that you have put me in prison? Where now are your prophets who prophesied unto you, saying, the king of Babylon shall not come against you, or against this land? Therefore hear now, I pray you, O my lord the king, let my supplication be accepted. . . . Do not cause me to return to the house of Johanan, lest I die there.*

Zedekiah stayed silent. The man must have been aware he was in the presence of his grandfather. But the king's responsibility was to the major consensus of the kingdom and to the valor of the troops. He studied Jeremiah for a few moments before he spoke. His face registered a stern determination.

"All right," he said. "Shaphan, order Jeremiah to be locked up in the courtyard." Finally, Zedekiah lowered his eyes. "And please," he said, "please, Jeremiah . . ." It was the first time he'd called Jeremiah by his name. The sound of it rang in the room. "Do not disable our war efforts."

As Jeremiah walked with Shaphan to the door, he turned to risk one more word. "They've imprisoned the slave Giddel, and he is not guilty," Jeremiah said. "Please let him go."

Shaphan took Jeremiah by the elbow and led him to the door. When it opened, the guards stepped up, flanked Jeremiah, and led him outside and to the courtyard wall at the palace square. Jeremiah had been locked in this spot once before. But this time there was no rope. A heavy chain fastened to a huge ring bolted into the rock walls chafed against his ankles, and thick irons rubbed against his wrists. He hadn't had a chance to bathe or change his filthy robe. Leaning against the wall, he prayed. "Dear Lord, oh, God of Abraham, please have mercy upon me."

Chapter Thirty-nine

Zedekiah

Outside the walls of the city of Jerusalem, thousands of enemy soldiers swarmed the rising Babylonian mounds. Zedekiah's guards and militia still talked with the bravado of lions. "We will defend ourselves," they said. "It is our might that will protect us."

And no one dared to say otherwise—except perhaps for Jeremiah, who, though he was in chains, continued his message. "Without attention to the Lord's words," he said in a low but powerful voice, "there will be disaster."

Still fastened to the courtyard wall, Jeremiah woke in the morning from his bed on the stones. His limbs throbbed with pain. A young woman came to him with a child in one arm. In the other she carried a pillow of straw covered with burlap. When she knelt to him, he felt as grateful for the gift as he imagined Jacob felt for his pillow of stone. But as he reached out to take it, one of the guards kicked it out of his grasp.

The chief guard brought him a small loaf of stale bread every day. Jeremiah kept it hidden under his cloak to protect it from the small hungry boys who played around the prisoners and taunted the guards.

In the afternoon and evenings some of his followers came to the palace square to talk to their prophet. They stood packed in the courtyard and begged him to tell them what they should do. His message was always the same.

Behold, I will give this city into the hand of the king of Babylon, and he shall burn it with fire.

Baruch stayed close to Jeremiah with his sheaves of papyrus and a few scrolls. He brought his stylus, and they worked together on the same tasks they had been performing in the archives. Jeremiah and Baruch had made a kind of peace with the guards. But when the members of the council saw that Baruch was writing down the words of Jeremiah, they pulled him away from the courtyard and took him to the king.

Baruch did not resist. He cooperated fully, taking the archival records with him. The councilors who read them complained to King Zedekiah that Jeremiah's prophecies smacked of treason.

He that remains in this city shall die by the sword, by the famine, and by the pestilence.

"These threatening messages encourage people to give up, Zedekiah," said the officers. "Are we supposed to leave the city, kneel before the Babylonians, and throw down our arms?"

The king's face registered nothing. Baruch was surprised when Governor Pashur read a more positive passage from the writings. "He does prophesy: *Judah shall be saved.* There is a promise made to the people of Israel and Judah, that David's descendants will always be kings."

When Governor Pashur was finished reading this scripture, Zedekiah's countenance changed. David's descendants would always be kings? That would be his descendants. He leaned forward, lifted his elbow to the arm of the throne and gazed intently.

"This prophecy assures that your progeny will always be kings, so it contradicts the statement that we will lose this battle," Governor Pashur said. "And Jeremiah's following words confirm that the kingdom will last forever."

Have you noticed how people are saying that I have rejected Israel and Judah, the two families that I chose? And so they look with contempt on my people and no longer consider them a nation. But I, the Lord, have a covenant . . . with Jacob's descendants and with my servant David. I will choose one of David's descendants to rule over the descendants of Abraham, Isaac, and Jacob. I will be merciful to my people and make them prosperous again.

"Doesn't this say that we will be forever in a covenant with one of David's descendants and that we will be prosperous again?" Governor Pashur asked.

No one answered him. The king said he needed time to think, and he waved Baruch and the councilors out of the room.

Not even three days passed before Governor Pashur, accompanied by top-level guards clanking with armor and weapons, came again to the courtyard where Jeremiah was chained to the wall. One of them was the huge black man, Ebed-melech. Governor Pashur announced that Jeremiah was ordered to see the king.

Jeremiah had been sitting so long against the stone wall that he could barely stand. When Ebed-melech unlocked the chains with the huge iron key, Jeremiah reached out his hand for help. Ebed-melech grasped his arm and brought him to his feet. When he stumbled, Ebed-melech steadied him. On the arm of the huge black man, Jeremiah made his way to the palace and down the corridors to the throne room. At the entrance, Jeremiah's knees felt weak. He glanced at Baruch who had come with them, carrying his writing materials.

When they reached the throne, Governor Pashur demanded that Jeremiah repeat his treason to the king.

Jeremiah swallowed and steadied his voice. "It is the Lord's will that you hear these words."

Zedekiah, I will give this city into the hand of the king of Babylon, and he shall burn it with fire. And you shall not escape out of his hand, but shall surely be taken, and delivered into his hand; and your eyes shall behold the eyes of the king of Babylon, and he shall speak with you mouth to mouth, and you shall go to Babylon.

There were rumblings in the council. Zedekiah listened quietly to their angry voices.

Someone in the background said, "Does Jeremiah dare to give such a death sentence to our kingdom?"

With a rough hand, Governor Pashur grabbed one of the scrolls from Baruch. "Listen to his threats, oh king," he barked. *Deceive not yourselves, saying the Chaldeans shall not come again, and fight against this city . . . for though you had smitten the whole army of the Chaldeans that fight against you . . . yet should they rise up every man . . . and burn this city with fire.*

In the stillness, the rumblings among the men rose in volume. The king sat up straighter and leaned forward on his throne.

"You remember the letter Seraiah recently sent from Babylon?" Governor Pashur continued. "He told us the Judeans will be returning in a year. So Jeremiah is a false prophet. His words just stir up trouble."

The king sat up straighter and leaned forward on his throne. "Well," he began, deferring to the councilors who'd begged him for action.

Finally one spoke up. *We beseech you, Zedekiah, let this man be put to death: for he weakens the hands of the men of war that remain in this city, and the hands of all people, in speaking such words to them . . . . This man does not seek the welfare of the people.*

The room fell into dead silence. Zedekiah pulled at his robe to release it from the leg of the chair. He settled himself for a long moment, knitting his brows. When he finally opened his mouth, his words were deliberate, yet edged with nervous discomfort.

"Very well, then." Zedekiah caught his breath. He assessed the faces in the circle. This was not the first time the councilors had brought charges against Jeremiah. Nothing had ever been done. But Seraiah had indeed sent the letter from Babylon affirming that the Judeans would return in a year. If the captive people did return, Jeremiah's prophecies were false.

"All right. Very well," Zedekiah repeated. The group was silent while the king looked intently at Jeremiah, his eyes narrowing. Then he waved his hand to the councilors. *Behold, he is in your hand: for the king is not he that can do anything against you. Do with Jeremiah what you will.*

Jeremiah flinched. Pashur and his father Malchiah, along with Shelemaiah and his sons rushed forward to hold him steady. It seemed a hundred claws strained at the irons on his arms and legs. With his feet and legs bloody from scraping the stones, he was half-carried, half-dragged to Malchiah's well. They bound him around the waist with a thick rope and stood him against the wall while they conferred in murmurs. Finally two guards lifted his feet, scooped him up, filthy robes, single sandal, and all, and held him over the edge of the abyss.

Jeremiah gasped, finding it hard to get air. The odor from the well was foul. The guard with the rope held Jeremiah for a moment and then slowly released him into the pit. As his body scraped the sides of the well on his way down, he could hear them talking. They talked about what Nebuchadnezzar was doing.

"I've counted eight mounds," one man said. "They are too far from the walls to be effective."

"But have you seen that now they're building them closer to the walls?"

As the words of the men above him faded, Jeremiah felt the difficulties of the city also slip away. Smeared by algae and scum, he felt pain as he bounced against the rocks of the well. When he hit the mud, the powerful odor of rotten garbage slammed into his lungs. He felt a jerk as the men removed the ropes. At first there seemed to be a firm footing below his feet, but as he tried to steady himself, he began to sink into the sludge.

"Oh dear God," he cried out. "If this is my death, please take me into thy hands. If this is the end of justice, please have mercy on Jerusalem."

Jeremiah saw the light fade when the night came. He saw the light above in the opening of the well when the dawn came. There was no other way to measure time passing. There would be no bread thrown to him. He'd been left to die.

When he heard voices above him, he cried out to them. He was sinking farther, his weight digging more deeply into the grime. He was so weary that he leaned against the wall and dozed from time to time. When he saw another dark sky, he knew he'd been in the well for a full day. Then another, and another. He cried out, trying to hold himself above the muck to breathe.

Just before the next dawn, as his thighs sank so far into the sludge that it began to reach his waist, he heard the brush of hands on the wall. He lifted his chin with great effort and saw a dark shadow against the blue sky—the silhouette of a man's head.

"Help me."

There was no answer, though he heard several voices far above him in Malchiah's courtyard. The household seemed to buzz with some kind of activity. And soon, in just a few moments, down into the well came a ragged clump of old clothes, twisted and tied together to form a circle.

Jeremiah looked up. The face in the sky was pitch black. The clutch of tied clothing bobbed up and down. Finally, the voice at the top said quietly, "There's an opening in the rags. Put your arms inside."

It was Ebed-melech.

"Hurry."

Jeremiah pulled the circle over his head and placed it under his arms. The tether of plaited garments lifted him slowly. There were three other guards helping Ebed-melech. The task was a slow, daunting one. The mud was so heavy over his feet that he could barely suck them free. He'd lost his other shoe. No matter. His spirit soared.

When he was close to the top, Ebed-melech said to him, "I went to the king. I interrupted him at court by the gate of Benjamin and told him that what they did to you was wrong. He sent me with these three men to take some old clothes out of the palace store-room and pull you out of the well. There's no bread left in the city. You would have died of starvation. We'll soon be under siege. They keep building those ramps outside into higher and higher mounds, and soon they'll be up to the walls."

"Ebed-melech." Jeremiah forced the words. "The Lord is going to destroy this city. It cannot be helped. But his message for you is that he will deliver you."

You shall not be given into the hands of the men you fear. For I will surely deliver you, and you shall not fall by the sword because you have put your trust in me.

Ebed-melech pressed Jeremiah's arm, his eyes glistening as he turned to join the men at the wall. He placed a hand on the sword that dangled at his side.

There was little the militia could do while they waited for Nebuchadnezzar's army to scale the walls. Soon there was a great pounding noise as the powerful Assyrian and Chaldean troops battered the walls again and again to break them down.

A guard came to Jeremiah and unlocked the iron chains around his wrists and ankles. "The king wishes the guard to bring you to the temple," the man said. He held Jeremiah up on his feet.

When they reached the entrance to the temple, the guard left, and two others brought him in through the gate before they released him and stood back in the shadows. Behind one of the columns stood a man in the feeble light. He wore a large wool hood over his head. It was Zedekiah.

Jeremiah wanted to run to his grandson and gather him in his arms. He would have called him Mattaniah and held him close.

After a moment, Zedekiah drew near to the prophet. He spoke through a rasp, as though he had trouble breathing. "I haven't been wise. I should have consulted you all these years," he said. *Jeremiah, I will ask you one thing; hide nothing from me.*

For a long time Jeremiah hadn't known the heart of Mattaniah, his grandson. So many words of the Lord had reached this king without bringing any resolute action. At the king's words, Jeremiah trembled. *If I declare it unto you, will you not surely put me to death? And if I give you counsel, will you listen to me?*

Zedekiah straightened under the hood. With a gaze that looked much like his grandmother Hamah's often piercing scrutiny, he steadied his eyes toward Jeremiah. *As the Lord lives, I will not put you to death, neither will I give you into the hand of these men that seek your life.*

Jeremiah wanted to trust this man. There was still time for Zedekiah to make a choice.

Thus says the Lord, the God of hosts, the God of Israel, If you will go forth unto the king of Babylon's princes, then you shall live, and this city shall not be burned with fire . . . and your house shall live. But if you will not go forth to the king of Babylon's princes, then shall this city be given into the hand of the Chaldeans, and they shall burn it with fire, and you shall not escape out of their hand.

Zedekiah stood for a long time, finally murmuring, "It sounds like surrender."

It was probably as Jeremiah suspected. Zedekiah had never really been in charge. He was still a young man—and afraid.

I am afraid of the Jews that are fallen to the Chaldeans, lest they deliver me into their hand, and they mock me.

Jeremiah perceived the fear that his grandson so clearly fought. His voice rose, *They shall not deliver you. Obey, I beseech you, the voice of the Lord, which I speak to you. . . . It shall be well with you. Your soul shall live.*

The pounding against the walls suddenly escalated. King Zedekiah shuddered. He turned his face toward the guards, listening in desperation to the thumping.

Finally, Zedekiah leaned close to Jeremiah's face. *Let no man know of these words, and you shall not die. But if the princes hear that I have talked with you, and they come unto you . . . then you must say to them, I presented my supplication before the king, that he would not cause me to return to Jonathan's house, to die there.*

Zedekiah turned away and pulled the hood over his head. It was an abrupt ending with no visible results. As the king walked away, guards came from the shadows to accompany him.

A large group of councilors and officials appeared as though by magic out of the temple. They'd been watching closely what went on between the king and his grandfather, and wanted to know everything that he and the king discussed.

"Tell us what the king said," they demanded.

"I was begging him not to send me back to prison to die there." Jeremiah repeated the king's instructions.

Suddenly, just outside the temple, there was a huge crash of tremendous force against the city walls. A great cry rose up from the women as they ran in the streets after their children.

Chapter Forty

Journey

On the ninth day of the fourth month of Zedekiah's eleventh year as king, Shaphan and his grandson Gedeliah brought a group of officials to the courtyard. The retinue also included several highly ranked militants of the Babylonian army: Nebushaz-ban and Nergal Sarazer, and finally Nebuzar-adan, the commanding officer of the Babylonians. Jeremiah tried to rise from the stones to show respect, but the chains restricted him. He could barely hear their discussion, so he was astounded when Gedaliah used a set of irons to unlatch the bolts that fastened him to the wall.

Though Shaphan's hair was streaked with gray, he was still an imposing figure. The young Gedaliah, who'd brought messages to Jeremiah long ago, was now a grown man. He knelt and fumbled with the locks.

"We are moving all of the prisoners," he said. He left the chains on Jeremiah's wrists and feet, but he finally managed to pull out the bolts. While he was close to Jeremiah, he said that when Zedekiah's family had tried to escape, they were captured. There was the possibility that Prince Johanan would try to usurp the throne.

"The city is broken up," Gedaliah said. "And all the princes of the king of Babylon came in." Gedaliah reported that Zedekiah had tried to take many soldiers with him and escape the Chaldeans, but, as they fled out of the city by night, by way of the king's garden gate that led out to the meadows, the Chaldean army pursued them and overtook them in the plains of Jericho. *And when they had taken him, they brought him up to Nebuchadnezzar, King of Babylon, to Riblah in the land of Hamath, where he gave judgment upon him.*

Jeremiah froze. His gaze settled on Gedaliah's weary eyes.

"It is over," Gedaliah said. And then he leaned closer to Jeremiah with another piece of unexpected news. "But you knew we had saved the oldest son, Prince Mulek, didn't you? We finally smuggled him onto a ship going to Egypt, and from there it will sail to the isles of the north."

Jeremiah waited while he heard the click of the locks that fell from the other prisoners. Shaphan and Gedaliah, moving slowly down the courtyard, whispered the message of their new ruler, Nebuchadnezzar, to the Judean captives. All of the Judeans must leave Jerusalem. Jeremiah noticed that the Babylonian guards treated Shaphan and Gedaliah with high regard. It was apparent that Shaphan had listened to the Lord's words and made peace with the Babylonian captors.

In the road outside the courtyard, the conquering army had drawn up many large ungainly wooden carts fitted with cages in which they proceeded to put the Judean prisoners. They lifted Jeremiah into the high bed and locked him to the bars.

Behind the carts, hundreds of stragglers carried bags and blankets and herded many animals. They carried their little children on their shoulders. From his position in the cage, Jeremiah saw a sea of people, both behind and in front, following the Babylonian forces out of the city. They were headed north, in the direction of Rumah. Behind them, great gray clouds of smoke billowed into the sky as the palace and the buildings in the courtyard square went up in flames.

Once the entourage reached Rumah, Jeremiah could hear the people of Israel singing the mournful chants and hymns they'd sung since the time of their bondage in Egypt. When the sky fell dark around them, he saw the winking fires built by every family. The light danced on their faces to the rhythm of the dirges they sang. As the camps settled down, Jeremiah and the other prisoners ate handfuls of grain out of the coffers of food that some of the travelers brought with them.

In the middle of the night, the commanding officer Nebuzaradan, his vestments jangling, stooped down to wake Jeremiah. At first the officer did not remove the chains Jeremiah wore on his wrists and legs, but let him hobble forward awkwardly. When they were far enough away from the Israelites, he finally bent forward to divulge his message above the hubbub of the guards.

"You're a fortunate man, Jeremiah. Nebuchadnezzar knows how hard you've worked to spare the people from their stubbornness. He asked me to let you go." He began to fumble with the locks on the chains.

Jeremiah looked up, puzzled.

"The Lord your God threatened this land with destruction and now He has done what He said He would do," Nebuzar-adan said. "All this happened because your people sinned against the Lord and disobeyed Him. You tried to tell them to repent. Now I'm taking the chains off your wrists and setting you free."

When Nebuzar-adan unlocked the heavy iron, Jeremiah flexed his hands.

"If you want to go to Babylonia with me, you may do so," the commander said. "And I'll take care of you. But if you don't want to go to Babylon, you have the whole country to choose from. You may go wherever you wish. Nebuchadnezzar has placed Shaphan's grandson, Gedaliah, in Mizpah to serve as governor of the remaining towns in Judah. You may go to him and help him restore Judea. Or you may return to Jerusalem—wherever you think you will be safe."

Nebuzar-adan gave him two loaves of bread and a small leather purse with money in it. Jeremiah gazed from the faces of his captors to the hills beyond, breaking with the dawn. "May God be with you," Nebuzar-adan said.

Overcome with emotion, Jeremiah stood speechless for a few moments before he voiced his gratitude.

Hiding the bread in his cloak, he turned southward. The road was heavy with the morning traffic of Assyrian chariots moving back and forth along the nearly hundred-mile distance from Rumah to Mizpah. Jeremiah was grateful for the knowledge that the remaining Judeans and their new governor, Gedaliah, were congergating until it would be safe to return to Jerusalem.

While he walked, there was time to think. Jeremiah felt a strange sense of joy, not only that he was free, but that Nebuchadnezzar and his chief officer had shown compassion upon him.

Gedaliah was a good choice for governor. He was young, eager, and open to the belief that Nebuchadnezzar would be fair.

Though he knew he'd be walking almost a hundred miles, Jeremiah felt stronger than he had for a long time. Conscious of the passing chariots, he glanced at farmhouses along the way with an eye toward asking the farmers for help if there was trouble. He slept uneasily at night, finding a grassy spot in some stand of trees, holding the bread and purse close under his chest, and pulling his cloak over his head.

On one such night, close to the end of his journey to Mizpah, he woke hearing two voices close-by. He was hidden in a copse of trees near the road, hoping no travelers would spot him. When he raised his head, he saw some dark figures walking toward him. Quickly he dug a small pit to bury the purse. When he saw their faces, he could see they were young men, and he backed into the shadows. But it was too late.

"Hello," the young man in front called. Advancing toward the trees, he waved his hand. "No need to be alarmed. Is your name Jeremiah?"

Puzzled, Jeremiah raised his head. He was looking east, and the sun had begun to roll over the hill. The light dazzled his eyes. "Who is it?" he asked.

"You don't know us. Melech and Ben Aman. We're messengers from the military camp outside of Mizpah. Some people from Rumah told us you were on your way south. The chief captains, Ishmael and Johanan, wish to speak to you."

"Ishmael? Johanan?" Jeremiah dug up the purse and placed it in his sash, tying it close to his waist. He sat up on his haunches, looking at the visitors, hesitant to engage in conversation until he knew more.

"We're from the armies of Prince Johanan and Ishmael of Ammon."

Jeremiah's breath stopped. This was what he'd feared. Johanan had joined with some man named Ishmael and they'd raised an army. Prince Johanan was out to take power.

"The Babylonians killed most of the priests. Only a few escaped to fight with Johanan and Ishmael."

The other young man, Ben Aman, stood tall above Jeremiah and put his thumbs in his girdle. "Did anybody tell you what happened to Zedekiah and the priests and officers?"

Gedaliah said only that Nebuchadnezzar passed judgment upon Zedekiah. He wondered what that judgment might have been. "Tell me."

"They took all the soldiers and the king's family north to Riblah, then tortured the boy princes in front of their father Zedekiah, until they were dead. They gouged out the king's eyes and threw him into a dungeon."

Jeremiah felt a wave of nausea. He rose to his feet.

"Nebuchadnezzar killed more than sixty Judean priests and councilors. He beat them to death in the courtyard. Only the man Seraiah escaped to Johanan to tell the truth about Nebuchadnezzar's evil reign. And now Babylon's king is trying to impose his sovereignty upon Judea."

Melech brought his arm up to stop his companion from talking further. "Johanan wants you. We think you ought to join us. We're the only Judeans who refuse to surrender to Nebuchadnezzar. There are two good-sized camps—one under Johanan and one under Ishmael."

He pointed to the east. "Ten captains, many soldiers, all ready to band together against the evil Babylonian tyrant." He paused. "We're ready to go except that Johanan and Ishmael are in disagreement. Johanan wants to take his camp to Egypt and Ishmael wants to return his camp to King Baalis of Ammon, to return to the hometown of his wife. When Johanan heard you were on the road he wanted to ask for your help."

Jeremiah waited for something he couldn't name—a feeling. All he could perceive was a sense of mistrust—or foreboding. He bundled his bread closer to his body and kept his eyes fastened on their faces. He wanted to ask Melech and Ben Aman where Zedekiah's two girls were: Scota and Tamar. But he thought it best to keep quiet.

"I'm sorry I cannot come with you," he said.

"They said you were not a traitor. They thought that you might help us," said Melech. "At least you could support Johanan as king."

"But if Zedekiah is dead and Nebuchadnezzar has appointed Gedaliah as Judah's governor, I must go to Mizpah."

"Gedaliah?" Ben Aman said. "That pawn of Nebuchadnezzar? He's nothing but a puppet of the Babylonian empire—and must be taken out."

Again Melech tried to calm his partner with a raised arm. "Gedaliah and his Judean officers in Mizpah still bow before Nebuchadnezzar. They claim they're the remaining legitimate Judeans because they have the artifacts and Zedekiah's daughters with them. But these daughters cannot take the throne. They're helpless girls. Johanan is a rightful king. If we can gather enough loyal Judeans we can prevail over Nebuchadnezzar's control, and go to rebuild Jerusalem."

So! Zedekiah's daughters were in Mizpah with Gedaliah. Perhaps Baruch was there also. It was time to hurry to Mizpah. When Jeremiah moved to the right, Ben Aman moved in front of him.

"Oh, you want to leave, do you? Are you sure that's the right thing?" Melech asked.

"Nebuchadnezzar has given me freedom of passage," Jeremiah said. "I beg you young messengers to let me return to the Governor of Judah at Mizpah. Perhaps I can convince him to negotiate peaceful arrangements with you."

Melech backed away. "Gedaliah, eh? Well, he's already invited us to a meeting there. Both Johanan and Ishmael said they may go. But Gedaliah is not royalty. He cannot be king of Jerusalem."

Jeremiah took another step forward. "Thank you for thinking of me," he said. "And perhaps, if you change your mind, I'll see you at Gedaliah's meeting in Mizpah. God be with you."

He turned away from them, praying they would let him go. And they did.

As the young men turned to move east, where the camps were located a few miles from Mizpah, Jeremiah began again toward Gedaliah's camp and did not look back. When he turned to see if anyone had followed him, the road was clear.

Chapter Forty-one

The Daughters

Sometimes the texts from the other prophets rang in Jeremiah's head. He repeated them by heart. Isaiah had written: *The Lord . . . will yet choose Israel, and set them in their own land: and the strangers shall be joined with them, and they shall cleave to the house of Jacob.*

It didn't take long for Jeremiah to reach Mizpah. Along the way he washed himself in a stream of water, and dried his ragged cloak in the sun. Worn and weary, he asked a shepherd boy the way to the governor's house.

It was the most prominent house in the area, surrounded by a tall golden-colored wall. Peering through the front gate, he marveled at the grand structure. Some generous citizen of Mizpah had lent their mansion to the governor of Judea for a temporary dwelling until the buildings in Jerusalem could be reclaimed.

Jeremiah leaned against the iron gate of the great house to wait for someone to let him in. A servant finally came and took him down the walkway and through the huge front door to the inner room where he found the new governor, Gedaliah. The tall and slender grandson of Shaphan was seated at a large round table. For several years, the young man's auburn hair had acquired strands of gray. His lean face was lined with the ravages of the siege. Behind him three arches framed an overgrown green garden surrounded by a rock embankment.

Several other leaders sat with Gedaliah around the table, their faces in the shadows. At first Jeremiah didn't recognize any of them except the governor, whose flaming red hair, though deepened in color, had always given him away. But as Jeremiah looked more intensely around the table, he recognized Baruch.

"And we have your scribe here, Jeremiah," said the governor.

Baruch came forward with his arms outstretched.

Baruch's curly hair looked disheveled, as though it had not been taken care of for months. Gray wisps surrounded his face. But his eyes were still piercing brown. He was dressed in the same coarse robe he'd worn in the archives of the temple. When Jeremiah embraced him, he could feel the leather packets of documents the scribe was carrying under his robe.

Jeremiah wanted to ask him what had happened to the library, and to the artifacts. The messengers on the trail had mentioned that the Ark and the pillow and the documents were with Gedaliah, and Jeremiah believed Baruch would have been the only one who could have retrieved them from the cave, and he would probably be the one who knew where they were now.

"We heard you had a free passage out of Rumah," Baruch said.

"I lost track of you. I wondered if I'd ever see you again," said Jeremiah.

Gedaliah introduced Jeremiah to the officers around the table. "We'll make a new world, Jeremiah. We have, in safe custody, the daughters of Zedekiah."

Jeremiah nodded. It was as he'd hoped.

"Our hearts are heavy with the deaths of Zedekiah's sons," Gedaliah continued, "but King David's line will be preserved. The promise of God will be kept. The gold of the Ark is lost, but we have the precious tablets and Jacob's pillow stone. The kings of David will be crowned over this stone. This is a safe haven. We've brought many of the people who were scattered in Ammon, Moab, and Edom to this place. All of them hope that the kingdom of Judea will be restored to peace."

Jeremiah hoped for that same peace. As Gedeliah continued, he nodded.

"Tonight you must dine with us. We're bringing many people together—several from Babylon—even men from the group under the command of Prince Johanan and Ishmael. Although these two are unwilling to bend to our conqueror's will, they need help to resolve their differences. They're at each others' throats. But the war is over, Jeremiah. It's time for reconciliation. We may look at each other as human beings. We're joining one another in a pledge of peace."

Gedaliah led Jeremiah to the table. "This is a new world, my friend. And you helped to make it happen. You told us to accept the northern armies—and that if we worked for them and honored their requests we'd save our lives."

He paused and pointed to the overgrown garden visible through the arches. "And you were right, Jeremiah. The Lord has blessed us. We'll return to Jerusalem with the artifacts and rebuild the city. You and the other prophets have spoken the truth."

Jeremiah was invited to sit at the head table, but as they waited for the others to be seated, his eyes grew so heavy that they began to close. He was only slightly aware that Gedaliah beckoned a servant to set up rooms down the long hall for him.

"Who's coming to dine tonight?" Jeremiah asked as he excused himself from the table.

"Johanan and Ishmael. And we had a messenger from another group of eighty or more supporters from Sheshem, Shiloh, and Samaria—some of whom will arrive later. They may not make it to this dinner, but I've sent a messenger back to invite them for tomorrow. The messenger said they've shaved off their beards and torn their clothes as they mourn for their rebelliousness against Nebuchadnezzar. Now they wish to support us in working with the Babylonians."

Suddenly there was a commotion in front of the house. An older, stocky, muscular man stood in the doorway. Dressed in the uniform of the Judean army, he wore a metal hood with two red feathers protruding from a small mound at the top. His eyebrows came together in front as though he wore a permanent scowl.

"Johanan!" Gedaliah exclaimed. "You're early. But have you come alone? I thought there were ten officers all together."

There was a tense silence in the room in the presence of the graying prince. His lean calves were wrapped with gray woolen leggings bound with leather. He looked fit for battle. His horse stood just outside the open front door. Its neck was white with lather.

"Gedaliah," Johanan said. "I would invite you one more time to bring your people to support me. We must build the true kingdom of Judea. I'm the next in line for the throne. Ishmael's plan to go to Ammon will fail us. Who will help us in Ammon? We must go to

Egypt. We need your support. If you join me we can convince Ishmael to rally under my leadership."

"Surely this is not right. We received a response to our invitation earlier—that you and Ishmael were happy to come and dine with us in peace."

"There isn't much time," Johanan said. "I believe Ishmael wants to rise up against the rest of us—you included."

Tall and lean, Gedaliah was much like his mild grandfather, Shaphan. "Johanan, you must be mistaken."

"There's not much time," he said. "Let me go, I beg you, and I will slay Ishmael, the son of Nethaniah, and no man shall know it."

The color in Gedaliah's face faded. He reached out for Johanan's arm. "Come, Johanan. You speak falsely of Ishmael. We hoped to dispel your differences tonight in good fellowship."

The prince would not budge. He stood with his leather-wrapped legs apart, as though he'd been built into the stone floor. "Tonight," Johanan stammered. "I've warned you . . ."

Standing in the shadows, Baruch whispered to Jeremiah, "We must get away from this house. My cousin Bedan will take us in tonight. We must go quickly. There's something of great importance we must take with us."

As they walked through the kitchen, Baruch spoke a few words to two young girls at the sideboard. As though on cue, they reached for two heavy, cylindrical, barrel-like wooden crates that were generally used for waste. One end was covered with fish netting pulled tightly over packed garbage.

Glancing at Jeremiah, Baruch enlisted his help with the heavy containers. One of them seemed to weigh two hundred pounds. With great effort they carefully tipped the barrels over on their sides and began to roll them. Two kitchen boys helped roll both barrels out toward the back. Jeremiah thought they would stop at the refuse bin—filled with other barrels and boxes full of melon skins, chaff, and rotting food. But Baruch worked his way through the back gate.

Jeremiah struggled with the weight of the barrels. Finally, sweating, he gazed directly at Baruch. "Is it what I think?"

"Shh," Baruch said. "Yes. The tablets and the pillow."

Jeremiah was stunned. "I can't believe no one else knows."

"Oh, they know all right. They know we have them. They just don't know where."

Resting occasionally as the sun slipped away in the west, both Baruch and Jeremiah rolled the barrels down the street into the back part of town without being recognized or confronted. The streets were burning with hot sand. Only a few struggling desert plants grew along the edges. With the exception of the grand house behind them, the homes were small stone huts with brush roofs and dark doorways.

Baruch took Jeremiah to such a hut with a dirt floor where they rolled the barrels behind the house into a patch of weeds. Coming around to the front door, Baruch knocked softly. Baruch's cousin Bedan welcomed them. The flames from the small cooking fire filled the house with light.

"This is my cousin and good friend, Jeremiah," Baruch told them. "He's hoping to return to Jerusalem with those of us who'll go back someday."

Bedan was a roughhewn shepherd with a wizened, sun-darkened face. "I pray for Governor Gedaliah's welfare. He may be able to help us return to Jerusalem. But did you know the king and all of his sons are dead?"

Jeremiah wondered how much this citizen of Mizpah might know. "But there were two daughters. Do you have any idea where the daughters have gone?"

Bedan narrowed his eyes.

"It's all right," said Baruch. "You can talk. This man is a priest and a prophet of God. And what's more, the girls he seeks are his great-granddaughters."

Bedan looked at Jeremiah with a suspicious gaze. "The daughters are here in Mizpah," Bedan said in a low, tentative tone. "Down the street in a hut like ours there's an old man and his wife who've been caring for them these past few weeks. They're acquainted with my daughter Dinah, who works at the governor's mansion."

Jeremiah leaned forward. "And you know where these people are?"

"I could show you on the morrow."

Just before Bedan and his family were ready to put out the fire and go to bed, they heard a fierce pounding against the front door.

Bedan opened it to see his daughter Dinah standing on the doorstep, crying.

Jeremiah recognized her as one of the kitchen girls who'd tried to move the disguised barrel out to the bin earlier in the evening. She was shaking with fear, her eyes dilated and her breath heavy.

"Dinah, what is it?" Bedan went to her.

"Murder," she cried, her face white. "I hid," she gasped. "Then I ran out, but Betta . . . they killed everyone in the kitchen."

"How many cutthroats were there?"

"I don't know," she sobbed. "Ten or so."

"We must find them," Bedan urged.

"No," she said. "Blow out the lamps! Save our lives."

Bedan blew out the flames in the house, and all of them sat at the rim of the room in darkness and silence. Eventually, they slept in what space they could manage to occupy.

They did not light a fire in the morning. All day they stayed cramped inside the tiny house illuminated by a few streaks of sun that came through two high windows. Restless and troubled, the family spent much time praying.

They prepared no new meals, but ate only the remainder of the corn they'd cooked the day before. The mother made small pinched balls of the grain and placed them on a plate. The children helped their mother prepare the food. And after the meager meal, they played peg games in spaces not much bigger than a handkerchief. It was a long day.

Finally, as they waited for the sun to go down, Bedan stopped in the middle of a sentence. He gestured to the children to hush. He thought he could hear a terrible scream. When it was quiet, all of them heard a shrill screech.

"Someone's in trouble," Dinah said.

The room was so quiet, they could hear the baby's congested breathing, when suddenly there was a faint knock at the door. The children ran to their mother's knees and groped for each other's hands, their faces frozen with fear.

All of them froze when they heard a sob through the door. And then a thin voice. "Please, please let me come in."

Dinah sat up swiftly from her place beside her mother. "Father," she cried out. "It's Betta!" She gathered a cloth around her shoulders and hurried to the door. "Betta! Betta! I prayed for you!"

When Dinah opened the door, the girl Betta leaned upon it with a loud wail. "They are all dead," she moaned. Dinah hurried her inside the room. Betta clutched the dark brown woolen cloak on her shoulders.

"What happened?" Bedan asked.

"Dinah probably told you. Yesterday we saw ten men come in the door and murder the governor and the councilors with knives."

Jeremiah sat forward.

"They called the leader Ishmael. He and his men stayed in the house all day. I hid in one of the empty trash barrels under some chaff and peered through a chink in the bin. I couldn't get away. Then in the evening a large group of eighty or more beardless men came to the gate of the house. They wore hair shirts and they'd cut themselves to repent and prove loyalty to Gedaliah. From the doorway, they saw the bodies Ishmael had murdered. They gasped with alarm. But Ishmael entreated them to come in. And then . . ." Betta choked back a sob. "It was the murderer Ishmael himself who went to them crying and beating his shirt, bawling and groaning as though beside himself. He deceived them, shouting, 'The men have been murdered. Please come in to see what someone did to Gedaliah.' I didn't move. When all the beardless men finally got into the house, Ishmael and his men rushed upon them and stabbed them with the same knives they used on Gedeliah! Only ten of the eighty escaped. All of the rest were killed!"

For a moment, the silence seemed to shake the room.

"Do you know where these murderers are now?" Bedan asked.

Betta wiped the tears from her eyes. "I think they left in the direction of Gibeon. I watched them go before I dared to leave my hiding place. I knocked on every door along the road before I came here. Curious people are swarming all over the house now. They're going outside the city to find Captain Johanan and tell him what has happened."

Jeremiah rose to his feet. He felt his heart hammering in his chest. No one was safe here! He beckoned to Baruch. "Do you think you could get your cousin to show us the home of the king's daughters?"

Bedan's eyes widened. "You didn't recognize her?"

"Recognize who?" Jeremiah looked puzzled.

"Here is the daughter," Bedan said to him. "Betta." The girl turned. "Here is your great-grandfather."

"Scota?" Jeremiah asked.

The girl put her finger against her lips. "Shhh."

Chapter Forty-two

Egypt

When he opened the door and walked out on the street, Jeremiah looked up to the sky. It was pure blue with not a cloud. The air was fresh, and he breathed in just to feel alive.

But the dust in the streets foreshadowed some evil. There were cries and screams from the grand house of the governor. Women, tearing their hair, ran in all directions. Several men on horseback herded people like cattle, not allowing them into their houses. Ishmael's rogues commanded the residents to drag the dead bodies from the governor's house across the village green and throw them into an open pit.

When Bedan's children followed him to the door, Jeremiah put out his arm to stop them. Two or three other horsemen had rounded up a group of people inside the square in the middle of the town. The wives of the dead were howling; the few men remaining in the town were trying to comfort them. When one of the men tried to break free, a man on horseback thrust a sword down into his neck, cutting away his head.

Jeremiah backed into the house and stood at the door with his head down, listening. No one could leave. Scota would have to stay here, though she expressed great anxiety about rescuing her adopted parents and her little sister.

"They're gathering the rest of the people up as prisoners," Baruch said. "There aren't that many of us left."

Jeremiah faced the family before him. "We must go with them," he said. "We must obey every request. They're taking over the town."

Baruch nodded. "Put the children in your wagon, Bedan. Pack those barrels first."

They drew the cart to the back of the house behind the bushes to pack the artifacts away from curious eyes. After half an hour, they entered the house again to eat, but did not light a lamp.

It wasn't long before a soldier rapped at the door with the hilt of his sword. "Everyone out!" he shouted. When no one answered, he kicked at the door. As Bedan cracked open the door, the soldier kicked it open. "Get out of here and into the square."

Jeremiah beckoned the family to come out. He turned to the soldier and asked, "Can you tell us where they're taking us?"

"With Ishmael. To King Baalis of Ammon," the soldier barked. "You're his prisoners now." When he saw that Jeremiah and the others were cooperating, he rode off, slapping his horse with the ropes.

Bedan carried his youngest child while his wife gathered what food they had into large sacks. She tied some of the sacks up under her robes to hide them.

The road was clogged with people. All of the citizens were on the road with their wagons, packed to the top with as much as they could carry.

Ishmael from Ammon was easy to recognize. He was mounted on a restless white stallion, his regalia sparkling gold and silver in the sun. He was the grandson of Elishama. Jeremiah wondered how this son of priests had gone so wrong. Had he also killed Prince Johanan?

They followed the group northeast. Jeremiah watched Scota as she held Dinah's hand. The two girls bent their heads together as they walked. Every once in a while, Scota raised her eyes anxiously and looked over the crowd.

Finally, she burst away from them and ran to the edge of the road to an old woman covered with a dark blue cloak. An old man, wearing a black cap, walked beside her. The couple held the hands of a little girl between them. The child was about ten years old. Her skin was as fair as the breast of a white dove, her eyes and brows black. The hair on her head sparkled with red and brown highlights.

"Tamar! Tamar," Scota cried out. "Nanah and Pahar!"

The man on the horse at the edge of the road cut Scota off. Scota waited at the edge of the stream of people until the old woman and the old man brought Tamar into the roadway. Scota ran to the old woman and gave her a great hug. Then she hugged the man she called Pahar. She took Tamar's hand and walked with her into the crowd.

When Jeremiah was able to move close to them, he knelt in the roadway and pressed Tamar's small white hands between his palms.

"Your grandmother was my daughter," he said. He was afraid the horseman would interrupt them before he could talk to her. The group was moving so rapidly that he had to stand. But he slipped his right hand through her tiny fingers. "I'm your great-grandfather. I could never come to see you. I was in prison while your father was king. But I've loved you all this time."

Tamar's eyes were bright with understanding. She didn't try to remove her hand from his. She looked up at him with the flicker of a smile. Though she didn't speak, she matched his footsteps evenly as they marched along.

"We call them Betta and Calli," Nanah said. "Sometimes they use their real names with each other, when no one else is around."

Most of the captured citizens grew weary, walking the miles toward Gibeon. Anxious for water, they had almost reached the large pool near that place when a ripple of some disturbance ahead of them slowed their march.

The girls backed up, and Bedan's wife, with the heavy bread sack under her cloak, sat in the road to nurse her baby. The children asked for some bread, and she reached into her cloak to find a crumb for them. A horseman scowled at her, but did not stay to reprimand her, because he seemed anxious to be on his way to some trouble down the road.

"What is the trouble ahead?" Baruch asked Bedan.

"I don't know," Bedan said. "But I'll go to find out."

On his return, Bedan's face was distorted with anxiety. "It is Johanan's army ahead," he said.

"Johanan!" Jeremiah exclaimed.

Baruch looked anxious. "What's going to happen?"

"So Johanan is still alive," Jeremiah responded. "He may break up Ishmael's grasp. Then we would be in Johanan's power and forced to go to Egypt."

It was indeed Johanan's army. There was a ripple of excitement in the crowd. The word was passed along that Johanan's army would save them from Ishmael's drive to Ammon.

Ignoring Ishmael's soldiers, the crowd ran toward Johanan's militia. When Johanan's soldiers saw Ishmael's men, they began to yell and gallop toward the murderers, shouting angry obscenities. But seeing their numbers, Ishmael's force quickly swung their horses in the opposite direction and rode away. No one went after them.

Johanan's camp that evening exploded with excitement. Shouts and exclamations could be heard far into the night. The hopeful prince announced that soon they would receive instructions.

That afternoon they reached Chimham, near Bethlehem. It was with joy that everyone found places on the ground to sleep. The people of Chimham and Bethlehem brought bread and fruit to the travelers. Those who had learned music began to sing. The songs were like magic as the moon and stars slid over the hills. Most of the songs were the beautiful words of Isaiah. Baruch had memorized many of them. And his voice was strong and steady.

Fear not; for I am with you:
Be not dismayed; for I am your God:
I will strengthen you; yea, I will help you;
Yea, I will uphold you with the right hand of my righteousness.

Jeremiah slept well. In the morning, as he woke, he heard some voices close by. When he looked up, he saw Johanan standing above him. Behind Johanan were Azariah and several other officers of the forces. They stood away from their leader, but waited respectfully for him to accomplish his purpose.

"We're honored that a priest such as you travels with us," Johanan said. "We have a request."

Jeremiah rose from the ground to meet the motley party. He studied the leaders. Others began to gather behind Johanan and his officers, pressing forward to listen to Johanan's petition.

His pleading words rang out so all could hear. *Please do what we ask you. Pray to the Lord our God for us. Pray for all of us who have survived. Once there were many of us; but now only a few of us are left, as you can see. Pray that the Lord our God will show us the way we should go and what we should do.*

Jeremiah had never trusted Prince Johanan—the jealous brother who'd always wanted the throne. But Jeremiah felt he ought to take Johanan's words on good faith.

Finally he answered, *I have heard you; behold, I will pray unto the Lord your God according to your words; and it shall come to pass, that whatsoever thing the Lord shall answer you, I will declare it unto you; I will keep nothing back from you.*

When Johanan spoke, he sounded sincere—even humble. *The Lord be a true and faithful witness between us, we will obey the voice of the Lord our God that it may be well with us.*

For more than a week, Jeremiah prayed sincerely to learn the Lord's will for Johanan. During that week in the camp, there was a stream of unending celebrations. All of the people of Bethlehem and Chimham were eager to please the exiles. The citizens of the towns sat at their visitors' feet to hear stories of the Babylonian war. They brought food from their stores, and sacrificed lambs and calves for the large banquets.

Jeremiah stayed with Bedan's family. Worries faded, and Jeremiah enjoyed the singing and the dancing as much as anyone did—for a period of ten days.

But Johanan's question nagged at Jeremiah. He knew Johanan wanted to lead the people to safety in Egypt. But Jeremiah felt the Lord wanted them to return to Jerusalem. He wondered if his desire was selfish. He hadn't been able to take his eyes off his great-granddaughters. They were Hamutal's copies. Tamar looked exactly like Hamah, and Scota could have been a twin except for her flaming red hair.

Did he want to return to Jerusalem because he was anxious for his granddaughters to rule? If so, he was no better than Johanan. He remembered his father's words—that every man's joy was in his posterity. But there were other reasons to go back to Jerusalem. He was nervous about the artifacts hidden in the heavy barrels. They ought to be returned to their proper home.

Was Johanan really interested in what the Lord had to say? Jeremiah continued to ask the Lord for help until, on the tenth day, Jeremiah felt that he was ready to give the Lord's answer.

He hadn't counted on the crowd that gathered. Some huddled together on the ground. Jeremiah's voice was level and strong. *Thus says the Lord, the God of Israel . . . be not afraid of the king of Babylon . . . for I am with you to save you, and to deliver you from his hand. And I will show mercies unto you, that he may have mercy upon you, and cause you to return to your own land.*

There was a hush in the crowd. Jeremiah was not sure if leaders of the army accepted his words. He watched Johanan. The prince stood frozen, without moving a muscle, as though still waiting for what he wanted to hear.

Jeremiah continued speaking. *But if you say, "We will not dwell in this land . . . but we will go into the land of Egypt . . ." then it shall come to pass, that the sword, which you feared shall overtake you there in the land of Egypt, and the famine, whereof you were afraid, shall follow close after you there in Egypt; and there you shall die. . . . You shall be an execration, and an astonishment, and a curse, and a reproach; and you shall see this place no more.*

When he finished telling the people everything the Lord had told him to say, Azariah and Johanan and the others began to move among themselves, whispering and talking with each other.

Finally, Johanan said, *Jeremiah, you speak falsely: The Lord our God has not sent you to say, Go not into Egypt to sojourn there.*

Azariah interrupted Johanan. He stood in front of the others, his eyes flickering nervously. Then he began his accusation. "Baruch, son of Neriah, has stirred you up against us so that the Babylonians will gain power over us and can either kill us or take us away to Babylonia."

Jeremiah glanced toward Baruch, who was recording the speeches. Baruch's face registered despair. Of course! It was now obvious that Johanan's humility had been only an act. He'd approached a prophet to get confirmation for his own plan.

The crowd of onlookers seemed uncomfortable with the dissension. But they had nothing to say. They were in the hands of their protectors—Johanan's militia.

Sick at heart, Jeremiah turned away from the officers. He looked out at the hills and the skyline of the village of Bethlehem. He wanted to tell the people, "This is your home."

He continued to walk in the meadow away from the camp. For a long time he stood away from the crowd, pondering what had happened. From the beginning the leaders hadn't really wanted to hear the Lord's voice. Jeremiah would have no choice but to go with them to Egypt.

In the next two days Johanan and his militia rounded up all of the Judeans to begin the long journey to Tahpanhes. The trek was not a formidable one. But for Jeremiah it was a betrayal. He felt very old.

"Grandfather," his granddaughters asked. "Where are we going?"

He patted their slender hands resting on his arm. "We mustn't worry," he said. "The Lord will take care of us."

But the journey nearly broke him. It was a long, hot walk. And when they finally reached Tahpanhes, the citizens there made it plain that they didn't appreciate the Judeans straggling through their streets like beggars. The travelers' supplies from Bethlehem and Chimham were gone. Though the transients had money, it was sparse and foreign. The money exchangers charged them exorbitant fees.

When Johanan and his army finally allowed the group to scatter in Tahpanhes, Jeremiah was anxious to get away from them. The prospects looked dim. Baruch and Bedan seemed downhearted as well, struggling with the weary mules and safeguarding the treasures on the carts.

After much searching, they found an empty stable at the home of one of the Israelites who had come long ago and purchased property in Egypt. Baruch hid the barrels in a stand of flowering bushes by the door.

The proprietor mentioned that he had some old turnips still in his garden plot, and they were welcome to all they needed. Nanah was thrilled with the offer and, with the help of the children, moved about quickly in the dirt, gathering up the turnips along with some old sticks of wood so she could make a fire. Pahar sat in front of the stable, nursing his feet and watching Nanah put the sticks in a circle of stones. Princess Scota ran to a neighbor to get a bit of a flame. When the old turnips were boiled, they tasted fresh and delicious.

As Jeremiah rested, he listened to the Lord's instructions.

Take great stones in your hand, and hide them in the clay in the brick kiln, which is at the entry of Pharaoh's house in Tahpanhes, in the sight of the men of Judah; And say unto them . . . Behold, I will send and take Nebuchadnezzar the king of Babylon, my servant, and will set his throne upon these stones that I have hid.

The Lord was promising that Nebuchadnezzar would not stop with the conquest of Israel, but would follow all of them to *smite the land of Egypt.* The Lord's message was that Babylon would *kindle a fire in the houses of the gods of Egypt.* He promised that Egypt would not escape the same judgment Israel suffered. *No city shall escape: the valley also shall perish, and the plain shall be destroyed, as the Lord has spoken.*

Just before dawn, as weary as he still felt, Jeremiah woke to go to the center of the city to do the Lord's bidding. On the edge of a vacant lot he found rocks that were so heavy he was almost unable to carry them. He managed to bring seven large ones which he placed just inside the short walls of the open brick kiln by the Pharaoh's compound. Above him, the pillars of the entrance to the building seemed threatening.

Had there ever been anything more powerful than the architecture of the Egyptians? He managed to dig away the mortar in a space near the opening in the wall and place the stones where tiles had broken up.

In a moment of reflection he remembered his father had pointed out how seedlings broke up the tiles in Jerusalem's courtyard. The power of life was great. He would build a monument to it like the stone pillar Jacob built so long ago. He stood for a long time in the spot, looking up to the facade of the mighty building adorned with carefully carved columns.

By the time he finished the task, there were government employees coming to begin their workday. He was surprised to find among them Israelites who spoke the Hebrew language. They stared at him. Some came up to him to ask what he was doing. But when he told them that in the manner of Jacob's pillar of stones in

Bethel, he was building a pile of stones over which Nebuchadnezzar would be made king, they backed away from him.

He was in the square for several hours when a man in a large cart drawn by four handsome horses stopped in the road, got out of his vehicle and walked across the square. He was dressed in a spotless white, woolen cloak decorated with a large purple hem. His hair was cut short, but he wore a full beard streaked with gray. His face, wizened by many wrinkles in sun-hardened, leathery skin, was full of questions. His deep eyes, set back under heavy brows, were the color of cerulean blue. The color reminded Jeremiah of his mother's eyes.

"Are you . . ." the stranger began. "Are you by any chance one of the Israelites who have come to the city recently?"

"Yes," he said.

"They told me . . ." He hesitated. "Someone said that the man Jeremiah had come with the army of Johanan. Can you tell me where I might find this man Jeremiah?"

"I am he, that Jeremiah who has arrived in the city."

The man inspected him for a moment. "I am Gulan Horsha. I'm glad to see you." He nodded and smiled. "I have special sources that bring me news. And when I found out you were coming, I wanted to talk to you." There was a moment of quiet. Finally Horsha said, "Will you come in my cart with me?"

Puzzled and weary, Jeremiah hesitated. But when the man turned to walk across the square to the cart, he found himself following. At the cart, Jeremiah stopped, wondering whether or not he should converse with this person, who—although his name was Egyptian—spoke in Hebrew.

"Some of the government people told me why you were building the pillar in the square," Horsha said, standing by the cart. "We've heard of your pleas to cooperate with Nebuchadnezzar."

Jeremiah was surprised that news of his speeches had reached as far as Tahpanhes. This might be the beginning of an attempt to quiet him, to take him off the square. He wondered who the "government people" were and what they'd said to this wealthy citizen. But Jeremiah was strangely drawn to the man's face. There was honesty in his eyes. He looked like someone he'd known in Jerusalem, but he couldn't pin it down.

"It's important," the man continued, "for the Israelites to listen to a prophet. Will you come with me to my house and talk to my people?"

When the man pulled down the step to the vehicle, Jeremiah climbed in.

The people in the streets parted to let the horses draw the cart across the pavement. The rhythmic clatter of their hooves calmed Jeremiah. He wanted to nod off to sleep, but the man beside him wouldn't stop talking about Egypt, about the threat of Nebuchadnezzar, and about their wealth that had made so many of them shiftless and careless instead of being watchful and alert.

When they came to his house, Jeremiah wondered about this man's obvious wealth. Sitting back from the street behind a high wall and an iron gate, was a palatial building surrounded by a white stone courtyard.

The man took Jeremiah's arm and led him up the carefully laid white tiles to the front door. Two high, wooden slabs made an impressive doorway set back on a porch with three curved stairs. The doors were carved with hunting scenes: romping deer and a bear with an arrow in its throat. The handles of the doors looked as though they were hammered out of pure gold.

Jeremiah gazed at the door for a full moment before the stranger opened it and beckoned him to enter. The room was huge—much like the house of Captain Laban in Jerusalem—a vast hollow space lined with giant arches. In the center was a lush garden. On both sides, hallways led into rooms.

Gulan Horsha waited for a moment as though he'd observed the awe of new visitors many times. "Will you come with me?" he asked.

Jeremiah followed him to a large room with windows draped in light silk that rippled in the soft breeze. Shelves all about the room were stacked with documents. Other tomes stood on tables similar to those he'd used in Lehi's library.

The man closed the door to the room and moved behind the largest table, glancing at the shelves filled with manuscripts.

"Are these your histories?" Jeremiah asked.

"Yes," he said, and touched some of the rolls of papyri. His touch was light, performed with the tips of his long fingers. "There are some documents here written in Hebrew. We procured these with much trouble."

The light from the window shone in Jeremiah's eyes.

"You don't recognize me, do you?" his host finally said.

The bright sunlight from the window behind the man's head blurred his face in a shadow.

"It's not hard to understand why you don't recognize me. For I've changed in these twenty-three years. And you've changed."

Jeremiah leaned forward. Was he supposed to know this man? He thought it was his age that now often played tricks on him. He was three quarters of a century old. He and Baruch often joked about the hundreds of years some overzealous scribes added as a way of honoring their leaders.

He wished it could have been a fact. Proud record keepers had added hundreds of years to their beloved Methusalah. Baruch and Jeremiah had wondered if they should change the glyphs in transcription, but Baruch said they wouldn't know what numbers to put in place of them. Besides, there were many other errors in the old writings: names, places, chronologies.

"It doesn't make any difference," Baruch had said. "The main message always comes through—to accept God and his commandments."

Jeremiah rose from his chair and walked around the table. As he walked toward the window, the man turned and faced him. There were tears in his eyes.

Clearing his throat, Horsha stretched out his hand and took Jeremiah by the shoulder. "Jeremiah," he said. "You are my grandfather."

"You . . . you are . . ."

"I'm your grandson Jehoahaz. Remember, Necco brought me to Egypt."

Jeremiah looked into the man's face. Jehoahaz, his first grandchild, Jehoahaz. His hands began to shake.

"Oh, no, it can't be true! Heaven be praised," Jeremiah breathed. "King Jehoahaz, my daughter Hamutal's firstborn son?"

As he moved forward, he felt a flood of light behind his eyes. Close to Jehoahaz, he reached out and took him in his arms. When he let go, he held the man at arm's distance and studied him. "Of course. You are the same boy who rode the horses around the ring with the young King Zedekiah, your little brother."

Jehoahaz laughed through his tears and wiped his eyes with the tips of his fingers. "I prayed someone would come this way. I have sent pleas to the officials that I might hear from my mother Hamutal. But she is safe in Libnah with her grandmother Abigail, who is still alive as far as I know. The Assyrians block my messages."

Jeremiah studied Jehoahaz's countenance—the brow, the high cheekbones, the lips so like his Hamutal, and the beautiful mother, Hamah.

"When the trouble with Assyria happened," Jehoahaz continued, "they sent Zedekiah's son, Mulek, here because the enemy was going to kill him. I sent him by boat to the islands beyond the sea. I pray daily that he will be safe, though I haven't heard. To my sorrow I did hear that Nebuchadnezzar killed my brother Zedekiah and his wife and sons." Jehoahaz paused. "And only recently have I heard the news that you were in prison. I sent missives, but they were returned. And I dare not use my Hebrew name."

"Jehoahaz, my grandson, king of Judah," Jeremiah said, lowering himself into a chair. His filthy clothing wrapped around his legs and caught on the chair legs. He pulled it loose.

Jehoahaz also sat down, laid his hands on the arms of his chair and gazed at Jeremiah. "And so now, my dear grandfather, you are here." He paused. "The Judean visitors passed rumors that you were coming. I've been undecided as to whether or not I should approach you. There are keen conflicts among those in your group."

"Yes."

For a moment Jehoahaz looked out the window on the city square. "You were placing some stones where you said Nebuchadnezzar would build his throne."

"Yes."

"You needn't answer, Grandfather, if you think it's unwise. But by any chance were any of those stones you set in the kiln the sacred stones from the temple of Solomon? There are rumors that you have them."

"Dear grandson," Jeremiah began. "No. I would not put these sacred stones in such danger. But I'm amused there are rumors that this is the case. Actually . . ."

For a moment he felt uncertain, because he was about to tell his Egyptian grandson that the stones were safely hidden in the bushes by the stable. But he couldn't say it. He did not know enough about Jehoahaz or his involvements. But when he looked into Jehoahaz's eyes, he felt he'd already said too much. The man had guessed the rumors were true.

For a few moments there was a heavy silence. Jehoahaz's look told everything. He knew a great deal, though Jeremiah had not revealed a lot.

Suddenly the expression on Jehoahaz's face changed to one of compassion and concern. "Well, never mind about that," he said. "But there is something else. My intelligence has told me that my brother's daughters, Scota and Tamar, are with you?"

Jeremiah froze, unable to take his eyes from his grandson's face.

"My sources are telling me that there are not only Nebuchadnezzar's Babylonian troops on our doorstep to destroy us, but the clashing factions of Judah are both anxious to get hold of the princesses and the stones. And they vow they will not stop until they destroy you."

Jeremiah felt his face tighten.

"You are in great danger, Grandfather."

For a moment the tension resonated in the last light of the sun that came through the high windows of the room. In the silence, Jeremiah filled his heart with prayer.

"I may be able to help you and your party." Jehoahaz leaned back in the great chair.

"Yes?"

"The girls are royalty," Jehoahaz said quietly.

"Yes," Jeremiah replied.

"There is no Judah to accept them and enthrone them now." He paused, tapping his fingers on the surface of the polished wood arm of the chair. Before he went on, he cleared his throat. "And if you want to assure the safety of the treasures . . ."

Jeremiah stayed seated on the edge of his chair.

"You're probably weary of travel. But I have colleagues who will take the princesses and your sacred treasure in Phoenician ships to follow Mulek across the Middle Sea. There are Milesian princes of the ancient tribe of Dan who will be anxious to wed the girls. And the stones will be out of reach there."

Jeremiah didn't answer. His fingers tightened.

"I have men who will help them move in the dead of night."

Jeremiah gazed at the silk curtain that moved gently in the window. The light dazzled his eyes. "Yes," he said softly, though he still felt hesitant. He'd just barely become acquainted with his two little granddaughters, and sorrow weighed heavily in his chest at the possibility of parting from them. Every beat of his heart spoke against sending them away.

"I have contacts," the Egyptian executive said. "And it's important to go immediately. And, Grandfather, if you could gather your bones about you, it would be best if you would go with them."

Jeremiah studied the man's face. He'd barely been able to make the journey to Tahpanhes. His legs felt so weary he wasn't sure he could stand on them, much less journey on them to another land. Yet what his grandson said made sense.

"If your own people do not destroy you, Nebuchadnezzar will," Jehoahaz said, noticing the hesitation in his grandfather's eyes. "You and your party must go now, and you needn't be afraid. In two months I will be taking the same journey to join my family."

Jeremiah looked up. "Then I have more great-grandchildren?"

"I have two boys and a girl," Jehoahaz continued. "I married an Egyptian princess. They've already departed. They've made a home with the Milesians. I have civic responsibilities to take care of for another two months, and I will follow you."

Jeremiah nodded, though questions still coursed through him. He often wondered if Lehi had been able to escape the terror of their world. He never dreamed he would seek the same solution.

Finally Jehoahaz stood. Slowly, he reached across to Jeremiah to help him to his feet. "Go with my servants in the cart and fetch your people, Grandfather. All of them may stay here in this house. It will be safe until we can secure passage."

Chapter Forty-three

Hope

Scota and Tamar loved the palatial house and the servants. Bedan and his family were able to lease a house near the city center, where Bedan found employment as a builder.

For several weeks Gulan's guests settled into their spacious bedrooms. They enjoyed freshly laundered sheets and towels, baths in a set of descending pools, and bounteous banquet tables laden with fruit. There were plates of salmon, and lamb cooked to such tenderness it fell apart at a touch. The servants burned the guest's old clothes and brought them rich brocade robes, silken shirts, and woolen capes.

Jeremiah and Baruch laid their manuscripts on the library table and continued to copy and work as they'd always done. Baruch, still a master calligrapher, continued to draw the letters with his brush on the papyrus. Jeremiah spoke to him often—sometimes from lying on a divan to protect the body that had been ravaged by prison and chains at the palace wall. Sometimes for days he could not see well. And finally, day after day, he began to feel the weight in his bones confine him to his bed.

During the preparations for their escape, Jeremiah experienced his greatest joy with his great-granddaughters. They talked to him about their activities and how Uncle Jehoahaz was procuring ships to take them on a safe journey. They often stroked their old grandfather's hands. They came with the servants to change his linens, and they read some of Jeremiah's poems that Baruch copied for them.

It is of the Lord's mercies that we are not consumed,
The Lord is good unto them that wait for Him,
To the soul that seeks Him.

"Are we traveling across the water?" Tamar wanted to know.

"Yes," Jeremiah said slowly from his pillow. He barely saw the heads of the girls against the light streaming into his bedroom window. Their little bodies looked like two columns topped by the chiseled sculpture of marble figurines. Only if Jeremiah squinted could he make out their eyes, their noses, their pretty pink mouths. "Yes, it is what the Lord wants for you."

"Are you coming, Grandfather?" Scota wanted to know.

"Of course, I'm coming. But I need to get well first."

"Are Nanah and Pahar coming?"

"Yes," Jeremiah said weakly. A darkness came into his mind. Something hard seemed to weigh down on him, and the pain in his body sharpened.

"And Baruch, too?

"Yes, we couldn't do without Baruch," Jeremiah said. "He has all of the books that have the names of your ancestors in them."

"Why is that so important?" Tamar asked.

"It's important that people in families remember their ancestors. But you must remember especially, because you're the daughters of kings." Jeremiah turned his face upward and looked at the ceiling of the room. Canvas squares draped loosely from corner to corner swung slightly in the hot air. The servants wet the fabric with cold water to keep down the heat in the room.

Jeremiah often looked at the squares and mistook them for the billowing sails of the ships that would transport them across the Middle Sea. He knew he would go to any lengths to save the royal line of David.

"Long, long ago one of your grandfathers named David was promised that his children and their children would always be kings. The promise was from the Lord. When I found you, I knew why the Lord did not let you die like your brothers. The most important thing you can do in your life is to follow what is written in the pages of those records."

They stayed silent. They'd heard this from him many times, but they listened eagerly again and again.

"Tell us where we're going, Grandfather."

"People from the tribe of Dan live across the water," Jeremiah said. "There's a family Jehoahaz knows. The ancestor's name is Milesius. He has many sons. And they need princesses to marry them."

For a moment the girls pondered this statement. Scota stood beside the head of the bed and rubbed a knob of brass clean of some residue until it shone with the image of her face. Tamar leaned on the edge of the bed with her elbows, and her feet were dancing.

It was Tamar who finally spoke up. “Will we be happy?”

Jeremiah smiled. “Ah, yes,” he said. He had not been sure these last few weeks if his smiles actually came to his face. They were in his spirit, but the spirit no longer seemed to transfer his commands to his body. “You will be just as happy as you make up your mind to be.”

With the pain in his bones, he wondered if he ought not to stay in Egypt. He felt his tally had almost been completed. Everything that had ever happened to him seemed to be for some purpose. He felt like his life’s work pleased the Lord. But he knew he couldn’t choose the time of life’s end.

Often the girls stayed as late as they could with their grandfather, until Pahar called them to take scraps of food to the donkeys in the corral and help Nanah with the supper. When they heard his voice, first Scota and then Tamar leaned over Jeremiah’s old head. Both of them planted kisses on the paper-thin skin of his cheeks. Tamar planted another one on his nose.

Chapter Forty-Four

Sailing

As the days passed, Jeremiah's memories loomed with more clarity than ever. He thought he saw Hamah walking toward him in a dream.

The news out on the streets was troubling. When Johanan's people heard rumors that Scota and Tamar might leave, they were furious. There were rumors that Johanan would stop at nothing to retrieve them—even kidnapping.

Jehoahaz had taken Jeremiah's hands in his and said, "You're going away none too soon."

When the report came that the ships were almost ready, a special boat was prepared to take them to the seagoing schooner—a vessel fortified with heavy arsenals.

Jeremiah looked up at the small window that admitted a stream of brilliant light. It cut across the room and into the eyes of the two great-granddaughters who stood at his feet.

"Grandfather," Tamar said close to his ear. "Don't you feel well?"

"I'm an old grandfather," Jeremiah said. He smelled the perfume of a fragrant lotion Nanah had given her.

"Don't you want to come?"

"Sweet child," Jeremiah began.

"I'm not a child anymore, Grandpa," Tamar said. The little wind of her whisper touched his ear. He closed his eyes and concentrated on the sweetness of it. Her lips were so close they might have planted a kiss in his hair.

"My legs don't work yet," Jeremiah said. As he said it, the darkness he'd experienced lately began to crowd down around him. "You must go and do everything Baruch and Nanah and Pahar tell you to do. Be obedient like good and faithful servants. I will be with you."

When the day came that they were to leave, Baruch came into the room and sat by Jeremiah's bed. He talked about the rumors in town, and about the different parties who were searching for the hidden barrels. Even he, Baruch, was not exactly sure where the treasures were, as Pahar at one time had instructed the guards to move them from the bushes by the stable to Jehoahaz's barn, and cover them with hay.

The household was worried about transporting the heavy barrels of stones and artifacts that weighed as much or more than a man. The large cart must make a journey of an unprotected mile to the heavily armed ship on the river. The appearance of too many guards along the route would spark questions.

Feeling helpless when it came to the details, Jeremiah could only encourage Baruch. "God will open the way," he said. "Baruch, if I'm unable to go, will you take care of the girls?"

Baruch pressed Jeremiah's hand. "Jeremiah, I've been praying for you. You must go. Of course I'll always be beside you to take care of whatever I can. But you must come with us."

Jeremiah stayed silent for a long time. "I feel so weak."

As Baruch held the gnarled hand, he rubbed it gently. "You must also pray."

Jeremiah nodded and smiled. "Of course you're right. You're right. But in the meantime, just in case . . . will you write one last word for me?"

"Of course," Baruch said quickly. As he took a stylus from his bosom and laid out some papyrus, the rustle almost hurt Jeremiah's ears.

"I have spent my life praying for Jerusalem," he said. "But were my prayers answered?

> *For this our heart is faint; for these things our eyes are dim.*
> *Because of the mountain of Zion, which is desolate, the foxes walk upon it.*
> *Why do you forget us forever, and forsake us?*
> *Restore us to yourself, O Lord, that we may return;*
> *renew our days as of old.*

"Prepare well for the journey, Baruch. I will pray. And if I'm still on this earth and able, I promise I shall come with you," said Jeremiah. "I think it best you still encourage the girls that I'm coming."

"What if we put you on a cot?" Baruch said. "Please don't give up now, Jeremiah." He stayed by the bed until the sun went down. Jeremiah dozed, knowing his friend was still there. If he woke, sometimes he saw Baruch in the chair, sleeping soundly. He was half-awake when a great commotion arose in the yard.

A piercing cry awoke both of them. Jeremiah jerked suddenly. The sweat stood in beads on his brow. Outside the door of the bedroom appeared several armed guards, their metal swords clanking. With them was little Tamar in tears.

"Grandfather!" she screamed, running to his bed. "They've killed Pahar!" She covered her face with her hands and sobbed.

"What?" he asked. The lamps in the hands of the guards struck his eyes. He squinted. "What?"

"When I saw the bad men come, I hid in the bushes by the barn. But I watched. They wanted the artifacts. They thought Pahar was you! They yelled, 'Come on, Jeremiah, tell us where they are,' and they pressed a knife against Pahar's neck until he hurt so much he could only squeak. He said the stones were in the barn, and they tossed everything in the barn up and down. They found only one barrel. Nanah says that the barrel with Jacob's pillow broke several days ago, and that Pahar showed her where he put the stone outside to look like other stones."

Jehoahaz entered the room after the armed guards, his cloak rustling behind him. "We must go now," he said to Jeremiah. "They're looking for you."

The room was spinning, not only with light and talk, but with a wash of something otherworldly that Jeremiah couldn't help but notice.

"At this moment my men are burying Pahar in my family's plot," Jehoahaz said. "But we have another coffin to place on the cart. You must lie in it, Jeremiah. And we will place the precious stone of Jacob at your feet. It is the only way we can safely take both of you to the ship. They believe it was you, Jeremiah, who was killed. You must lie still. Keep the faith. God will bear you up."

Jeremiah could not see the faces gathered around, but he felt their hands as they lifted him into the extra long coffin and tucked him in. He felt Jacob's cold stone at his feet. If the coffin were placed upright, he would be standing on Jacob's stone.

He gasped at the wave of motion as the six guards lifted his casket and swung him through the doors and to the cart. When they lifted him up into the cart, he could hear the children and Nanah talking and weeping at the loss of Pahar. There were the voices of servants waiting to go with them. As he listened, he understood that there were other families meeting them at the dock to take the long journey.

The ruts in the road bounced his painful joints and shook him until his blood flowed quickly in his veins. He lifted his head and thought, I must remember this death is not real. God lives. No death is lasting.

The servants and Nanah and the girls sat about the coffin and whispered to him through the cracks. "We're almost there, Grand-father. Hang on just a little longer."

When the cart stopped at the boat dock, he heard a loud voice. "We must open it. The inspectors insist."

When the cover opened a few inches, Jeremiah lay still. A man with a lantern came to the edge of the box and peered inside. The lamplight beamed across Jeremiah's closed eyes. The prophet flinched, but held himself rigid.

"It's the old man Jeremiah, all right," the inspector shouted. "He's dead. They're taking him to be buried."

At the foot of the box he could still feel the stone. His feet had warmed it.

For another few minutes he felt the motion of rocking as he tried to breathe in the dark space. Then he felt them lower the coffin to a hard surface. For another few moments he heard voices murmuring, blending with the sound of water lapping against the sides of the ship alongside the quay.

Shortly, when the lid came open, Jeremiah peered out. A little face with large brown eyes was looking in. Two little hands grasped the edge of his box. The face belonged to Tamar. Her dark curls danced around her brown eyes and against her white cheeks.

"You can get up now, Grandfather," she said.

When they completely lifted the lid, she extended her hand. There was only a brief second in which he tried to gather his senses and absorb everything that had just happened to all of them. The ship was rocking slightly with a calm and soothing motion.

He didn't hesitate to reach for Tamar's tiny fingers. Although he hadn't been able to speak much in the past month, words came easily to him now. "Are we ready for a new adventure, my Tamara?"

"Yes, yes, Grandpa! We are going far away to marry some princes!"

With her little hand she couldn't lift him, so a guard stepped in to help. Jeremiah pressed his feet against the stone, and pushed. The guard put his strong hands under Jeremiah's armpits and drew him up on his feet to the floor of the coffin.

He got his sea legs under him and looked around. Baruch was there. Nanah was there with the two princesses, Tamar and Scota. Beyond the sails of the ship, he saw the sky, the rim of land sparkling with the light of oil lamps, and he heard the water lapping beneath his feet.

Again Tamar reached for his hand. "That's right, Grandfather. You are going on an adventure with us. Climb out of the box and come and see this boat. There are lambs in the hold!"

With her fingers curled in his, he stepped over the edge.

Glossary

The word "name" in the entry indicates that it is fiction. All others are actual.

Abigail: name for Jeremiah's mother-in-law
Abraham: patriarch of the Old Testament
Ahab: husband of Queen Jezebel
Ahaziah: grandson of Ahab and Jezebel
Ahikam: son of Shaphan, father of Gedeliah
Ammon: district southeast of Israel
Amon: son of Manasseh, father of Josiah
Anathoth: two miles northeast of Jerusalem
Asherah: pagan goddess
Assyrians: enemies north of Israel
Athaliah: Jezebel's wicked daughter, mother of Joash
Azaiah: Josiah's servant who captured Mattaniah/Zedekiah
Azariah: Johanan's officer

Baalis: King of Ammon, Ishmael's father-in-law
Baruch: Jeremiah's cousin and scribe
Bedan: name for Baruch's cousin in Mizpah
Ben Aman: name for the young man on the road to Mizpah
Beriah: name for Hilkiah's cousin/manager of the palace
Bethany: name for the vocalist wife of Beriah
Burka: cloth that covers the head and body

Calli: nickname used for Tamar, daughter of Zedekiah
Chaldeans: Babylonian people
Chimham: Johanan's camp near Bethlehem
Chilian: Hamah's brother at Libnah
Coniah/Jehoiachin: Josiah's first grandson who ruled three months
Covenant Box: stored with the Ark of the Covenant in the temple

Daniel: prophet who survived the lions' den
David: King of Israel who slew Goliath
Dinah: name for Bedan's daughter at Mizpah
Dolazah: Shaphan's daughter who married Zedekiah

Ebed-melech: Shali's giant Nubian slave
Edom: protectorate south of Israel
Egyptians: taxed Jerusalem, pursued Assyrians
Eliakim/Jehoiakim: King Josiah and Zebudah's first son

Elishama: court wrestler with cauliflower ears
Elnathan: his daughter Nehushta married Eliakim/Jehoiakim
El-Wad: a section of Jerusalem
Esau: Jacob's brother who sold his birthright for pottage
Ezekiel: poet-prophet

Gedaliah: red-headed grandson of Shaphan, governor of Mizpah
Gemariah: grandson of Shaphan who served King Jehoiakim
Gentiles: all who are not Jewish
Giddel: name for Lehi's slave who inherited Lehi's house
Glima: one Hebrew spelling of a woman's veil
Gulan Horsha: name for Jehoahaz in Egypt

Hamah: name for Jeremiah's wife, mother of Hamutal
Hamutal: Jeremiah's only child, second wife of King Josiah
Hananiah: Shelemaiah's false-prophet father
Hanameel: Shallum and Huldah's son who owned their field
Ha-Yehudim: a road in Jerusalem
Hezekiah: Manasseh's righteous father who built the aqueduct
Hinnom Valley: gully south of Jerusalem
Holy of Holies: the sacred temple room of the Ark and "pillow stone"
Horsha: (Gulan Horsha), name for Jehoahaz in Egypt
Huldah: Jeremiah's prophetess aunt who kept temple wardrobe

Irijah: Shelemaiah's son who hated Jeremiah
Ishmael: (early) helped Jeremiah on the road, took his daughters with Lehi
Ishmael: (later) opposed Johanan, then murdered Gedaliah's assembly

Jacob: ancient father of the twelve tribes
Jedidah: King Josiah's mother, married King Amon
Jeduthun: prophet in Zedekiah's court
Jehoahaz: first son of Josiah and Hamutal
Jehoiachin: Nebuchadnezzar's kingly title for Coniah, Josiah's grandson
Jehoiakim: Nebuchadnezzar's kingly title for Eliakim, first son of Josiah
Jehucal: Shelemaiah's son
Jehudi: a councilman who helped destroy Baruch's document
Jeremiah: the prophet
Jericho: city conquered by Joshua
Jeroboam: ruled the north when Solomon died
Jerusalem: the major city of the Judeans
Jezebel: wicked queen
Joash: Ahab and Jezebel's son saved from murder
Johanan: jealous second son of Josiah and Zebudah
Josiah: good king, son of Amon, grandson of Manasseh

Kamut: name for the evil father of Pazael
Kulna: one Hebrew spelling for the clasp on a woman's veil

Laban: captain in the Jewish army
Lag ba'Omer: one Hebrew spelling for the closing of Passover
Laman: Lehi's oldest son
Latham: name for a wealthy cousin of Jeremiah's mother
Lehi: wealthy metallugist who chose to leave Jerusalem
Lemuel: Lehi's second son
Levites: presided over the ordinances of the Church
Libnah: Hamah's birthplace

Manasseh: permissive king of Jerusalem for forty years
Marika: name for Jeremiah's mother
Mattaniah/Zedekiah: Josiah's second son, born of Hamutal
Mekhonit: one Hebrew spelling for a type of carriage
Melech: name for the man who confronted Jeremiah on the road to Mizpah
Menorah: six candlesticks flanking both sides of the temple shewbread
Milesius: the patriarch of a line of kings in Spain
Mishneh District: west of the temple in north Jerusalem
Mizpah: where Nebuchadnezzar installed the Jews, made Gedaliah governor

Neriah: Baruch's government-official father
Nabapolassar: Assyrian ambassador
Nahum: prophet
Nanah: name for the woman who took care of Scota and Tamar
Necco: emperor of Egypt on the warpath through Jerusalem
Nebuchadnezzar: Babylonian conqueror who devastated Jerusalem
Nebuzar-adan: Babylonian commander who let Jeremiah return to the Jews
Nehemiah: a poet-prophet who taught in the street with Jeremiah
Nephi: Lehi's third son
No'ahk bgadim: one Hebrew spelling for a certain type of dress

Ostracon: shards of pottery used like scratch paper
Omin: name for one of the henchmen who put Jeremiah in the pit

Pahar: name for Nanah's husband who cared for Scota and Tamar
Pashur: Jerusalem's governor who put Jeremiah in chains, then released him
Passover: the spring celebration that honors Israel's escape from death in Egypt
Pazael: name for the wicked son of Kamut
Pedaiah: Chief Magistrate married to Shali and father of Zebudah, first wife of Josiah
Pesach: Jewish Passover
Pharoah: Egyptian ruler

Reba: Name of first wife to Laban
Rechabites: People who refused to drink strong drink
Rehoboam: ruled the south when Solomon died
Riblah: where Nebuchadnezzar killed Zedekiah and his sons
Rumah: north city, home of Assyrian sympathizer Shali

Sam: Lehi's fourth son

Sariah: Lehi's wife, mother of Laman, Lemuel, Nephi, Sam
Scota: next to youngest daughter of Zedekiah
S'firah: thirty-three days of gifts to the priests
Shali: name for the wife of Chief Magistrate Pedaiah, Josiah's mother-in-law
Shallum: Prophetess Huldah's husband, Hanameel's father, Jeremiah's uncle
Shaphan: honorable farmer, secretary of the court, father-in-law of Zedekiah
Shelamin: celebration dinner
Shelemaiah: jealous enemy to Jeremiah
Solomon: King David's son who built the temple

Tahpanhes: destination city in Egypt for escaped Jews
Tamar: youngest daughter of Zedekiah who became queen in Ireland
Tse'ifim: one Hebrew spelling for a light robe

Urijah: brave prophet-groom of Sariah's sister
Uzziah: Manasseh's great-grandfather who killed his own children

Yoanna: name for Hamah's friend murdered by the guards

Zebudah: Pedaiah and Shali's daughter, Josiah's first wife
Zedekiah: Babylonian king's designation for Josiah's son Mattaniah
Zephaniah: read the letter from Babylon that encouraged Jeremiah's death
Zoram: Laban's servant who left Jerusalem with Lehi

Bibliography

Aleuinus, Flaccus Albinus. *The Book of Jasher.* Bristol, England: Philip Rose, 1929.

Anderson, James H. *God's Covenant Race.* Salt Lake City: Deseret News Press, 1937.

Brown, Kerry Ross and Lisa Lee. *The Ark of the Covenant.* Springville, Utah: Cedar Fort, Incorporated, 2000.

Charriere, Doris. *Tamar, the Tender Twig.* Oregon City, Oregon: Chalet Publishing Company, 1997.

Church Educational System. *Old Testament: Genesis—2 Samuel. Religion 301 Student Manual.* Salt Lake City, Utah: The Church of Jesus Christ of Latter-day Saints, 1981.

Church Educational System. *Old Testament: 1 Kings to Malachi. Religion 302 Student Manual.* Salt Lake City, Utah: The Church of Jesus Christ of Latter-day Saints, 1982.

Crowther, Duane S. *How to Understand the Book of Jeremiah.* Bountiful, Utah: Horizon Publishers, 1998.

Davies, Norman. *The Isles.* London: Macmillan, 1999.

Delaney, Frank. *Ireland.* New York: HarperCollins Publishers, 2005.

Diamant, Anita. *The Red Tent.* New York: Picador USA, 1997.

Good News Bible. New York: American Bible Society, 1978.

Hanks, Patrick, and Flavia Hodges. *A Dictionary of First Names.* New York: Oxford University Press, 1990.

Hansen, Vaughn E., Ph.D. *Whence Came They? Israel, Britain and the Restoration.* Springville, Utah: Cedar Fort, Incorporated, 1993.

Holy Bible, the King James LDS Version. Salt Lake City: Deseret Book, 1983.

Journal of Book of Mormon Studies, a Publication of the Foundation for Ancient Research and Mormon Studies at Brigham Young University, "Lehi and Jeremiah." Volume 8, Number 2, Provo, Utah: FARMS, Brigham Young University, 1999.

Lansky, Bruce. *Baby Names Around the World.* New York: Simon and Schuster, Meadowbrook Press, 1999.

Neusner, Jacob, and Alan J. Avery-Peck. *The Routledge Dictionary of Judaism.* New York: Routledge, 2004.

O'Hart, John. *Irish Pedigrees—the Origin of the Irish Nation, Volume Three.* The Long Riders' Guild Press, 1998.

Price, Lynn F. *Every Person in the Old Testament.* Bountiful, Utah: Horizon Publishers, 2002.

Raphael, Chaim. *Festival Days: A History of Jewish Celebrations.* New York: Grove Weidenfeld, 1990.

Rutherford, Edward. *The Princes of Ireland.* The Dublin Saga. New York: Ballantine Books, 2005.

Strong, James, LL.D. S.T.D. *The New Strong's Exhaustive Concordance of the*

Bible. Nashville, Tennessee: Thomas Nelson Publishers, 1984.

Wistenetski, Klara Ilana. *Hebrew Phrase Book.* Victoria, Australia: Lonely Planet Publications, 1999.

Woolley, Richard G. *Pillar of Fire.* American Fork: Covenant Communications, 1997.

______, *Power of Deliverance.* American Fork: Covenant Communications, 20000.

______, *Place of Refuge.* American Fork: Covenant Communications, 2003.

Acknowledgments

What is so extraordinary about this story is that we know most of it actually happened. What a miracle it is, that we can read what people wrote twenty-five hundred years ago!

We would not have this incredible record if people like Jeremiah and his scribe Baruch had not devoted their lives to transcribing, translating, and compiling the various histories of the rise and fall of governments, the cruelty of kings, wars and rumors of war, and the quest for righteousness and peace. Their records show, most of all, how prosperity breeds overindulgence and wickedness in every civilization.

Though strewn with contradictions and errors, Kings and Chronicles seem to bear out Jeremiah's account. But of course, a novel is allowed to explore between the lines. As a righteous Jewish man, Jeremiah was probably married. I have chosen to equate him with the Jeremiah recorded as an inhabitant of Libnah, the father of Hamutal. Jeremiah conducted himself like royalty. And like other religious leaders, he would have kept his family out of the limelight to keep them safe. And in his documentation, he may have kept his relationships to the kings quiet for political reasons.

Though half of my research claims he died in Egypt, there is no record of his death. However, Irish legends assert that he brought his great-granddaughters across the sea (explored in books by Doris Chariere and James H. Anderson: *God's Covenant Race,* Salt Lake City: Deseret News Press, 1937, and other records). We do know that the northern inhabitants who sheltered many of the ten tribes were notably receptive to Moses's teachings.

I am so grateful for the many writers and scribes who have illuminated this exciting story of Jeremiah's contribution to our history—to my scholarly friend, now deceased, Daniel Ludlow, for his careful first reading and his unforgettable encouragement, to my neighbors and friends Keith and Connie Clayton and Margaret Pope and Bill Pope. (Bill has since passed away, and we will miss him!)

Kristine Princevalle and Amie McCracken were invaluable first editors, while Elizabeth Petty Bentley furnished the much-needed polish. *Brigham Young Magazine*'s astute literary critic, Richard Cracroft, gave excellent suggestions and generously wrote the introduction. Thanks also go to readers Clare Johnson and her husband, author Douglas Johnson, for their response to the story and to Douglas for his outstanding cover design, to Andrew Hall for very helpful criticism, Douglas Alder, Marilyn Arnold, Steven and Mary Walker, Veda Hale, Sheila Olsen, Darla Isaacson, Angela Hallstrom, Jack Harrell, Harlow Clark, my sister Elaine Flake, my husband Bill, my daughter Simeen Brown, my granddaughter Elisa Parmley for an excellent YouTube video, and the many others who have offered their endorsements and kind assurance. I also wish to thank Parables for their careful consideration and attention to detail in the production of this book. It has been a labor of intense revelation, excitement, and satisfaction.

marilynbrown@dishmail.net or www.marilynbrownauthor.com

Marilyn McMeen Brown is the author of more than a dozen novels, most of which illuminate actual events and historical characters. Having won several state literary awards, and established the *Marilyn Brown Novel Award* out of the Utah Valley University (marilynbrownauthor.com or UVU.edu/english), she has also collaborated with others on two histories of Provo, Utah, and other nonfiction works. She has also published books of poetry and two stage musicals. Her goal has been to record her little-known regional history in an exciting, literary, yet accurate way. She and her husband Bill (six children, twenty-two grandchildren) live in the Utah mountains.

CPSIA information can be obtained
at www.ICGtesting.com
Printed in the USA
FFOW03n0930250614
6011FF